TRACE ELEMENTS

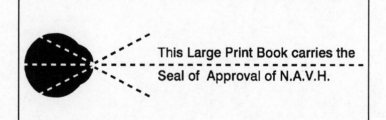

TRACE ELEMENTS

DONNA LEON

THORNDIKE PRESS
A part of Gale, a Cengage Company

LIBRARY OF CONGRESS CIP DATA ON FILE.
CATALOGUING IN PUBLICATION FOR THIS BOOK
IS AVAILABLE FROM THE LIBRARY OF CONGRESS

ISBN-13: 978-1-4328-7711-8 (hardcover alk. paper)

Published in 2020 by arrangement with Grove/Atlantic, Inc.

Printed in Mexico
Print Number: 01   Print Year: 2020

For Ana de Vedia

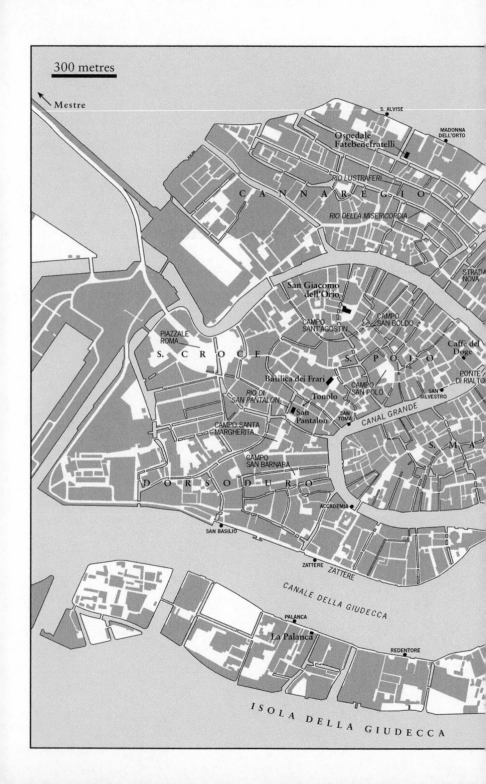

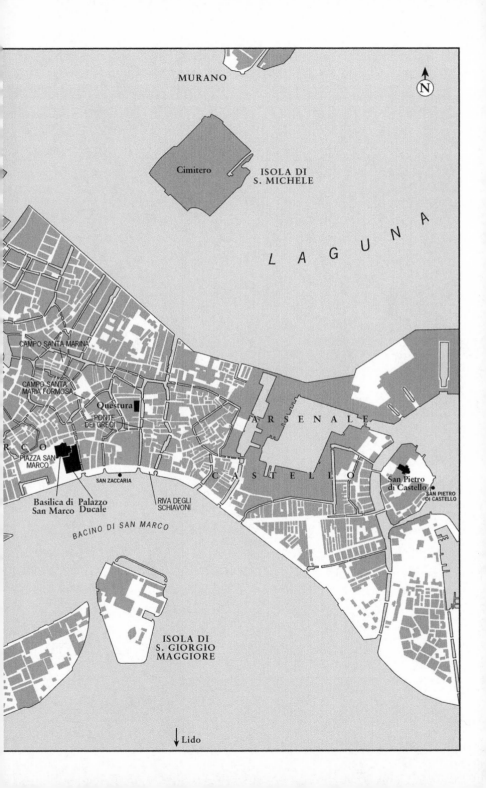

They loathed to drink of the river.
He turned their waters into blood.
Handel, *Israel in Egypt*
Part the First

1

A man and a woman deep in conversation approached the steps of Ponte dei Lustraferi, both looking hot and uncomfortable on this late July afternoon. The broad *riva* gave no quarter to anyone walking along it; the white surface of the stone worked in consort with the sun, flashing back into their faces the same sunlight that hammered down on their backs.

The man had refused to wear his jacket; instead, he carried it over his shoulder, one finger latched in the loop at the collar. The woman, blonde hair pulled back in a ponytail to keep it off her back, wore beige linen trousers and a white linen shirt with long sleeves against the sun. They stopped in their tracks at the foot of the bridge, staring at the enormous boat moored in the Rio della Misericordia, blocking other boats from entering Rio dei Lustraferi, which ran perpendicularly to the right. A wall of interlocking corrugated metal panels stretched from side to side of the smaller canal, creating a dam beyond which the water level had shrunk by half.

The disappearing water had exposed slopes of mud and nasty-looking black matter on both sides of a wide channel of oily black liquid that extended down the centre of the blocked canal. At the far end, perhaps fifty metres away, another wall of metal panels had been pounded into the mud, sealing off the canal. A boat with a yellow-bodied crane on a platform at the centre floated behind the far barrier, in front of it a hulk into which the crane emptied the sludge it dredged from the canal. A sudden gust of wind coming from the *laguna* dragged the smell of the mud ahead of it without disturbing the surface of the viscous fluid. A diesel motor on the boat whined as it sucked the remaining water through an enormous plastic hose draped over the metal panels and spewed it into the canal on the other side of the barrier.

'*Oddio,*' said Commissario Claudia Griffoni. 'I've never seen this before.'

Guido Brunetti, her friend and colleague, stood motionless, his right foot poised above the first step of the bridge, transfixed, like stout Cortez staring at the Pacific. With wild surmise, he exclaimed, 'I haven't seen this for years.'

Griffoni laughed and waved at the sight before them. 'I had no idea how it was done.' She walked to the top of the bridge to get a better look at the metal barrier.

Brunetti followed and stood beside her. 'Where'd they find the money for this?' he asked, as though speaking to himself. That morning's *Gazzettino* had printed a long article about the infrastructure projects diminished or cancelled for lack of funding. It listed the usual victims: the old, the young, residents who wanted to live in peace and quiet, students, teachers, even the firemen. Recalling it, Brunetti wondered how the mayor of the city, *deus ex machina,* had found the necessary funds in the city budget to begin the cleaning of the canals.

'How kind of the mayor to toss the city some table scraps,' Griffoni observed.

Brunetti ran his eyes down the slopes of the canal, where the mud and detritus of decades had been exposed. The black slime began just below the high-water mark, growing thicker as it slithered into deeper water. Dark, rotten, its smell strongly unpleasant, slippery and slick, it resembled nothing so much as human waste; it filled Brunetti with disgust almost as strong as horror. 'How fit-

13

ting that it would come from him,' he said.

Despite the smell, they made no attempt to leave. Brunetti remembered how scenes like this had been a part of his youth, when cleaning had been done primarily by hand and with far greater frequency. He recalled the wooden walkways built on both sides of the canals and the cat-like ease of the workers moving about on them with their shovels and buckets.

Thunder pealed beyond them, and they raised their hands to protect their ears. It was the motor of the crane on the boat. A black metal jaw stood in the centre of the deck, neck bent, giant mouth closed and resting.

They saw, inside a glass booth towards the prow, a man in dark blue overalls, a cigarette hanging from one side of his mouth, both hands busy with the knobs and levers before him. Returned to childhood glee, Brunetti stood transfixed by the wonder of it and by the desire for a job like that, so very close to play, but with oh, such power. Griffoni seemed equally rapt, though Brunetti doubted she longed for the job. Besides, it was unlikely that the city would hire a Neapolitan, a far greater handicap than being a woman.

Without speaking, they walked to the

14

other side of the bridge and watched, silent, as the clenched steel teeth of the crane rose from the deck and angled out over the water. They opened, creating a hideous black maw of jagged teeth, then slowly sank to the surface of the water and disappeared below.

The man's hands moved, and the long steel arm shifted minimally to the right, paused and seemed to shake about under the water, then began to rise. As it broke the greasy surface, Brunetti saw pieces of plastic, rubber, and metal hanging from the teeth: it looked like a particularly large Rottweiler eating a bowl of spaghetti. The long arm lifted and held the jaws in the air while water cascaded back into the canal, then swung to the front of the boat, already heaped with mud-smeared rubbish. It stopped just above the pile of trash and sludge. Slowly the jaws pulled open, and the junk inside crashed and clanged down on to the pile. A few small motions of the worker's hands shook the last fragments free, and then the jaws swung back and sank again into the water.

They had not noticed a second worker standing on the *riva* with a shovel in his hands. As soon as the metal jaws moved away, he stepped on to a board running across the boat and smoothed out the pile of debris, shifting rotting plastic bags filled with bottles to the sides, shoving at a decomposing radio, the wheel of a bicycle, and some other objects too decayed to be identifiable.

They watched in companionable silence for a long time, neither wanting to start walking again, each convinced that only the other person could understand the joint pleasure to be had in watching the machine at work. Neither spoke, united in a strange intimacy.

After ten minutes, the crane operator got to his feet suddenly, climbed down the short ladder from his chair to the deck, and hurried to the side of the boat. He leaned over the water and stared down, then put his hands above his forehead to block the glare of the sun and moved slightly to the right, still looking intently into the water. He went back up to the control panel and touched something that made the hum of the motor diminish. He called to the man with the shovel, then summoned him with a wave. Brunetti and Griffoni watched the man with the shovel jump on to the traverse board, almost immediately to be joined by the crane operator, who directed his attention to the same place in the water. The sound

16

of the motor drowned out their voices; the urgency of what the first one said was evident in his gestures.

Brunetti was struck by how stiff the two men's stance and motions had become. The man running the machine had been entirely at ease, but when he returned to his seat, he seemed awkward, and Brunetti had the strong sense that he was reluctant to continue.

Let it not be what I think it might be, Brunetti said to himself, unwilling to say anything to Griffoni for fear that he would seem foolish or be proven foolish by whatever the jaws might pull out of the water. He glanced down at his hands, grasping at the metal handrail attached to the edge of the bridge, and saw that his knuckles were white. He looked to his right and saw that Griffoni's were, as well. He turned minimally to his friend and saw her rigid profile, the stiffness in the line of her jaw.

Brunetti looked back at the metal arm of the crane. At a certain point, the mechanic took his hands from the controls and jumped down again to the deck to peer over the side of the boat. He exchanged a look with his colleague, who had returned to stand on the *riva,* shrugged and walked back to his place at the controls.

The noise of the engine deepened, and both Griffoni and Brunetti shoved themselves away from the railing and stood straight, waiting for whatever was to rise from those waters. They turned at the same instant and exchanged a glance, then turned back to the canal.

They heard the change of gear and the grating of the chain inside its rigid protection. The arm rose from the water, and then the jaws at the end of the crane's arm slipped up into the light.

Brunetti braced himself to look straight at it, whatever it was. Griffoni was a statue beside him.

The metal head swung away from them for a moment, and as it turned back it revealed the soiled white body of a refrigerator emerging from the waters of the canal. It was small, would barely have reached Brunetti's waist had it been on the floor of a kitchen somewhere. As it was, the door that hung from one hinge gave it the look of something destroyed in battle.

Brunetti and Griffoni turned to look at one another again. It was she who smiled first, then Brunetti, who added a shrug. Not speaking, they turned away and started down the other side of the bridge.

2

They walked in easy silence for some time until Griffoni finally asked, 'What did you think it was going to be?'

Feeling not a little foolish, Brunetti said, 'I was afraid — from the way the men behaved — that it was going to be a body.'

She stopped; Brunetti took two steps before he noticed, paused and turned to look at her.

'Does that happen often?' she asked, giving heavy emphasis to the last word.

Brunetti didn't know whether to smile or not. 'No, thank heaven. It doesn't.'

Griffoni raised her chin and stared at nothing for a moment, then asked, 'That murdered woman they found at Lido, when was it, six, seven years ago?' Brunetti recalled it, and how it had shocked the city. 'What were they, Bangladeshi?' she asked.

'Indian,' he corrected her. 'But that was before you came here.'

She nodded. 'I read about it. *Il Mattino* went wild for it, like all the papers. There was a feeding frenzy about the whole thing, remember?'

Brunetti had been in Ljubljana at the time, persuading the authorities there to extradite an Italian who had fled the country after murdering his employer. By the time Brunetti returned to Venice, the case had been solved and the murderers arrested.

'They found her in a canal on Lido, didn't they?' Griffoni asked. Then she added, 'There was something about a suitcase.' She shook her head when memory refused to function.

Brunetti tried to recall the lurid details of the case. 'They brought her here in a suitcase, well, her body — they'd killed her in Milano — and took her out to the Lido and dumped her into a canal.'

'It was an argument about money, wasn't it?' she asked.

'Isn't it always?'

'I forget the rest,' Griffoni said. 'Something about a taxi.'

Brunetti stopped and plucked at his shirt to pull it away from his body. The heat had done nothing but increase over the last week, as had the humidity, although there was no talk of rain. The boats were crowded, breezes had died, tempers were short.

Brunetti gave a brief snort; he didn't know if it was disgust or disbelief. 'As I remember, they missed the last train to Milano, so they took a taxi from Piazzale Roma, paid I think it was five hundred Euros for it. They still had the empty suitcase with them. When the taxi driver read about the body the next day and thought about how nervous they had been, he called the Questura.' He brushed his palms together and said, 'It was over within a day.'

'I never read anything more about it,' Griffoni said. 'Did you?'

'No. They killed her in Milano, so that's where the trial would have been held,' Brunetti said and glanced at his watch. It was almost three, the time of their appointment at the Ospedale Fatebenefratelli to interview a patient in the hospice who had asked to speak to the police.

They knew her name and age: Benedetta Toso, 38, Venetian and resident in Santa Croce. They knew no more than that about her, although her presence as a patient in the hospice had persuaded them not to delay in going to see her. Brunetti had been contacted by Cecilia Donato, the doctor in charge of Signora Toso's treatment, who had once worked with his brother, Sergio, an

X-ray technician at the Ospedale Civile, and remembered that he had a brother who was a commissario.

She had called the Questura the day before and asked to speak to Brunetti. When she explained that she was chief doctor at the hospice at Ospedale Fatebenefratelli, the man answering the call had told her he would have to see if Commissario Brunetti was there; when she added that she was a friend of Brunetti's brother, her call was transferred immediately.

The doctor would tell him no more than that Signora Toso was a patient under her care who, when asked if she would like to speak to a priest, had answered that she would like to speak to a policeman, preferably a female policeman.

And thus it was Griffoni who was chosen; Brunetti had come along to speak to Dottoressa Donato, hoping to capitalize on any trust she might have in his brother. He and Griffoni had discussed tactics, and she had suggested that he accompany her when she spoke to the patient, but show his submission to her.

They arrived at five minutes to three and went directly to the elevator. Brunetti had visited more than one friend who had passed through the hospice here on the way out of life, just as he had visited friends in the Ospedale Civile who found themselves at the same point. Should it be his fate to have to decide, he would want to come here.

They got out on the second floor, and Brunetti turned automatically to the left, down toward the nurses' station. His experiences in hospitals, visiting patients, had usually been exercises in patience: waiting until the staff allowed visitors on to the wards; finding an empty chair in a room with usually two, and often four, patients; listening to the clang of meals being delivered to the wards and then to the rooms.

Here, however, the hallway was silent; the nurse at the desk was a young man with long fair hair pulled back in a braid. He wore jeans and a white T-shirt under a white lab jacket and smiled in welcome as they approached. He had a tag on his jacket with only 'Domingo' written on it. 'Are you the police?' he asked in lightly accented Italian, sounding pleased at their arrival.

Griffoni, ostensibly in charge, confirmed this. 'Yes. Commissario Claudia Griffoni and' — this with a wave towards Brunetti — 'my colleague, Guido Brunetti.'

'Welcome,' the young man said with a smile. 'Dottoressa Donato asked me to take you to her when you arrived.' He got up

23

and came around the counter, revealing a pair of white Converse sneakers. He reached out to shake their hands. 'I'm glad you came. Signora Toso wants very badly to talk to you.'

Before they could ask about this, he turned and started down the hall. Brunetti noticed that the walls were decorated with black-and-white photos of beaches: straight or curved, surfless calm or raging waves, giant rocks or none. The only common element was the absence of human beings or human rubbish: no cans, plastic, chairs, boats; only space and water.

The young man stopped at the third door on the left, which stood open. From the doorway, he said, 'Cecilia, the police are here for you.'

A voice said something Brunetti could not hear, and Domingo stepped away from the door and waved them to go in. Brunetti followed Griffoni into the room.

An enormously fat white-haired woman was struggling to push herself up from her chair as they came in and succeeded only when they were almost at her desk. She braced herself against the top of the desk with her left hand and extended her right to Griffoni and then to Brunetti.

The woman had a nametag similar to the

young man's, though hers bore her title and name: Dottoressa Cecilia Donato. She smiled and waved them to the chairs in front of her desk, then braced both hands on the arms of her own chair and lowered herself slowly into it.

Her face was pear-like, as was her body: thin on the top and ballooning out at the middle. Her forehead and eyes were those of a far smaller person, but below them, her cheeks widened and seemed to come to rest on the straight column of her neck, almost as wide as her jaws. Below her shoulders, her figure swelled out, then disappeared behind her desk.

Reluctant to be perceived as staring at her body, Brunetti turned his eyes to her hands. They were slim, smooth-skinned. A thin indentation separated them from her chubby wrists, as though pieces of string had been tied tight around them, the better to illustrate the separate parts of her body. She wore a gold wedding ring on her left hand.

'Thank you both for coming, and please do sit down,' Dottoressa Donato said in a contralto voice that resonated for an extra beat after she stopped speaking. She glanced down to examine some papers on her desk, exposing the thinning hair on the crown of

25

her head, then looked up and said, speaking to Brunetti, 'I explained Signora Toso's request on the phone, Commissario, and can tell you no more than that.'

Brunetti nodded, thought for a moment and asked, 'Does that mean you do know more, Dottoressa?'

She hesitated to consider this. She would be a bad liar, Brunetti thought. Then she finally said, 'I don't think it matters what or how much I know about Signora Toso. She's my patient, so anything she's told me is private.' When Brunetti did not respond, she added, 'I'm sure you're aware of that, Commissario.'

'Of course, Dottoressa. I'm merely curious to know if there's anyone else who knows what she wants to tell the police.'

'For what reason?'

'To verify what she says. Should that become necessary,' Brunetti answered.

'And why would it?'

Brunetti spread his hands wide. 'Because she's here.'

Dottoressa Donato looked at Griffoni, as though interested in any contribution she might make, but Griffoni shook her head, so the doctor returned her attention to Brunetti, and said, 'I understand.'

'That way, there would be confirmation,'

Brunetti began, 'of whatever she says.'

The doctor put her elbows on her desk, placed her palms together, and rested her chin against the tops of her fingers. 'Why would that be necessary?'

Brunetti crossed his legs to suggest ease and said, 'If I might be frank, Dottoressa, this is a dying woman who wants to speak to a policeman. So it's . . . possible that whatever she says will concern a crime.' He paused to give the doctor the chance to reply.

When she did not, he continued, 'If you've been told what she tells us, Dottoressa, your confirmation would give greater credence to what she . . .' His voice trailed off: he was unable to decide what tense was appropriate.

'Chooses to say,' the doctor supplied, and Brunetti nodded his thanks.

The woman shifted in her chair, and Brunetti could not stop himself from thinking about the effort she must have to put into moving that mass. He glanced aside at Griffoni but said nothing.

When Dottoressa Donato was settled into a new position farther forward in her chair, she continued. 'This is a hospice, Commissario. My patients don't go home again.' She tightened her lips and gave him a level

27

gaze. 'It might be that, as her doctor, I can't repeat what she's told me even after she's gone.'

Brunetti leaned forward in his chair long enough to pull his shirt away from his back. 'It might be more helpful if we could speak to Signora Toso,' he said.

Before he could get to his feet, Griffoni asked, 'Do you have any idea how much longer Signora Toso might live, Dottoressa?'

The fat woman looked at Griffoni and gave a small smile, as though to show her relief that someone, finally, had displayed concern — or at least interest — in her patient. It was some time before she spoke. 'A few weeks. At best. Perhaps much less. It's in her bones now, and because of that, she needs sedation.'

'Where did it start?' Griffoni asked.

'Her breast,' Dottoressa Donato answered. 'Five years ago.'

Griffoni failed to stifle her deep sigh. 'Ah, poor woman.'

The doctor's face softened at this and she said, 'She was at CRO in Aviano for a time, began her treatment there some years ago. They thought they'd stopped it. She had radiation and chemo and was clear for a while, and then early this year she found a lump under her left arm.'

28

Brunetti was a stone. The women were intent on one another. 'By that time, it had already passed to her bones. They tried again at Aviano, but nothing worked. And then, a bit more than three weeks ago, she came here.'

Griffoni folded her hands and leaned forward, elbows on her knees. She stared at her shoes and moved her upper body forward and back a few times, just the faintest motion.

'She has children?' she said by way of question.

'Yes, two daughters. Livia's twelve and Daria's fourteen.'

'Their father?' Griffoni asked, one woman to another.

'Her husband died about a week after she got here.' The calm of the doctor's voice was in sharp contrast to her face.

'*Oddio,*' Griffoni whispered. 'What happened?'

The doctor seemed reluctant to add to the misery of the conversation but finally said, 'He was killed in an accident.'

'How?'

'His motorcycle went off the road when he was coming home from work. The police said it was possible he lost control, even that *un pirata della strada* sideswiped him.'

'And the driver?' Brunetti asked. 'Was he found?'

She looked at him with an expression that suggested he should know better than to ask such a question. 'When have you ever known a driver to stop after hitting someone?'

'Witnesses?' he asked.

She shook her head. 'You'll have to ask the police about that,' she said with no audible irony. 'As I understand things, no one ever came forward. I imagine they checked the scene and the motorcycle, but I've heard nothing about that.'

Silence fell after this exchange, not to be broken until Griffoni said, 'And Signora Toso?' Suddenly she lost control and asked, 'How can she bear it?'

Again, the doctor shifted her weight around in her chair in search of a more comfortable distribution of her bulk. This time it took her longer to find it, and when she did, she shook her head. 'She has no choice.'

'I don't understand,' Griffoni said, sounding honestly confused.

'She has the girls. They need her to be strong.'

After pausing for a moment to see if either of them had something to say, the doctor went on. 'Maria Grazia, her sister, came the day after it happened. And told her.' Suddenly, she placed her palms flat on the desk in front of her and studied them. She used her thumb to turn the wedding ring around, watching it move.

'I was on duty, and I heard her scream.' She watched the ring as intently as if some other person were moving it, or it was turning by itself. Her eyes did not leave it as she said, 'I went to her room and found her screaming at Maria Grazia, 'I did it. I did it.' She sighed and shook her head.

'The girls didn't come for two days after it happened, then Maria Grazia brought them again.'

'How was that?' Griffoni asked.

The doctor looked across at Griffoni and then Brunetti and went on. 'After they left, Domingo and I went in to check on her. She'd pushed the covers down and was trying to get up.' She looked at her fingers again. 'He and I held her to keep her in the bed.'

She paused for a moment and then said, her surprise real, 'It was very easy. All those things you read in books about the superhuman power of the dying: it's not true. Domingo held her, and I went to get something to calm her. There was no strength

31

left in her by the time I got back, but I gave her the injection anyway, and she slept through the night.' She stopped speaking. Long experience told Brunetti that the story was near its end and that to ask anything might annoy her.

'I mentioned his death some days later, only once,' she said, her voice falling into a terminal cadence, 'and told Benedetta how sorry I was. She ignored me and turned her face away.' The doctor did much the same, looked away from them and again stopped speaking. She studied the tops of a thin row of pine trees that were visible from the window of her office.

Brunetti got to his feet. 'I think it's time we spoke with your patient, Dottoressa,' he said. 'If we may.'

3

Griffoni stood. Dottoressa Donato pushed herself, not without effort, from her chair and moved towards the door. She paused there to wait for them, then opened the door and started back towards the nursing station. They followed silently, neither glancing at the other, eyes on the slow-moving bulk ahead of them.

The nurse's desk was empty, the counter entirely free of papers or instruments. Dottoressa Donato passed it and turned into a corridor on the left. Here, the photos were in colour, same size, and all of single, lone trees. Brunetti recognized a birch, standing alone beside a river; a cherry in the centre of a field; a chestnut nestled up against a cliff; and an enormous maple perched on the top of a hill. In each case, the photo was a portrait that managed, in a way that Brunetti noticed but did not understand, to show the life the tree had had. The birch leaned towards and longed for the water; the cherry's leaves were almost grey with thirst, no water in sight; the chestnut appeared frightened; while the maple claimed command of everything around it and looked as though it would somehow defend that claim.

The doctor stopped outside a door, turned to them, and said, 'I'll tell her about Dottoressa Griffoni first. I imagine you've planned to have her do the questioning, while you,' she said, glancing at Brunetti with a neutral face, 'try to remain meek and invisible.'

Griffoni laughed. She put her hand over her mouth, but too late to stifle the sound. Abandoning caution, she turned to the other woman and said, 'I wish you were my doctor.'

Dottoressa Donato smiled and lowered her head at the compliment, then looked at Griffoni and said, 'But then you'd be a patient here. And I wouldn't wish that on you, my dear.' Warmed by truth and sympathy, her voice resonated deeply in the space around the three of them.

The doctor tapped on the door, waited a moment, then tapped again. There was a noise from inside. She opened the door and stepped in. She turned to Griffoni and

Brunetti, held up her right hand and patted at the air. Turning back, she went into the room and closed the door.

Neither of them moved, nor did they speak. Griffoni took a step backwards and leaned against the wall, crossed her ankles and folded her arms. She looked as though she were waiting for a bus or a vaporetto and had all the time in the world.

Brunetti stuffed his hands in his pockets and walked to the window. He saw the row of pine trees and bent closer to the glass; the earth under them was raked clean. Flowers grew in no particular order around the trunks. He realized that the patients could see flowers if they stood by the window. If, he hastened to tell himself, they could manage to get to a window.

An elderly man came down the corridor towards them, leading an even more elderly dog, a fuzzy beige mass that walked sedately at his side. 'Come on, Eglantine, only a little bit and we'll see your *mamma*.' At the word the dog looked up at the man. 'That's right, sweetheart. You know where she is.' Saying that, he reached down and released the dog. Tossing away the years, the dog scampered down the hall, yipping in excitement, and disappeared into the last room on the right. Her entrance was answered by human

35

squeals, equal in delight. The old man wrapped up the lead and stuffed it in the pocket of his jacket. Woollen jacket, Brunetti noticed in amazement. The man excused himself for walking in front of them, went slowly down the hall and into the same room, where voices welcomed his arrival.

The door where Brunetti and Griffoni stood opened; Dottoressa Donato emerged and pulled the door almost closed behind her. 'She said she'd like to talk to you both.'

Griffoni pushed herself from the wall, asking, 'Would you prefer to be with us, Dottoressa?'

The older woman's face softened, but she said, 'No. I think it's better if there are only the two of you.' Seeing Griffoni's expression, the doctor explained, 'It takes her some time to understand what she's told. It would be better for her — and for you — to keep things quiet and calm and as simple as possible.' She saw the look Brunetti and Griffoni exchanged, and added, speaking very softly, 'She's still lucid; don't worry about that. She's not taking as much as she should to stop the pain.' When neither of them spoke, she continued, 'I think it's like having a television on loud all the time. She has to concentrate very hard to understand.' Again, she paused, then added, very quietly,

'It's bad, when it's in the bones.'

Saying nothing further, she turned back to the door and pushed it open. Silently, Griffoni and Brunetti passed in front of her, and the doctor closed the door from the outside.

A bed projected from the wall at the right of the door. Although a hand-knitted red blanket lay across it, there was no disguising the fact that this was a hospital bed: metal railings on both sides, lowered now; an outlet and mask for oxygen in the wall behind it. Two plastic bags containing liquid, one transparent and one orange, hung from a metal stand on the far side of the bed. The liquids dripped into plastic tubes that ran down and disappeared under the covers.

The head of the woman who lay there was covered with greying stubble that accentuated the hollows above her ears. She appeared to have been tossed or dropped on to the pillows that propped up her back and head, leaving her body tilted to the right. She nodded towards them but did not smile. Griffoni approached the bed and stopped beside the single chair next to it. The woman nodded again, and Griffoni sat. Brunetti walked to a second red chair that stood in front of the window but found the seat so hot that he sat upright, reluctant to press his back against the plastic panel that had been in the sun all morning.

No one spoke for at least a minute, then Griffoni started. 'Signora Toso, we came because of Dottoressa Donato's call. She said you wanted to see the police.'

The woman looked at Griffoni, then Brunetti, and then back at Griffoni. She nodded. She could have been thirty, or she could just as easily have been fifty. The flesh had fled her face, leaving behind the bones and the skin. The perfection of both still showed amidst the ruins of her beauty. The darkest of brown eyes looked at them as if from caverns. Grey circles surrounded them, reminding Brunetti of the eyes of lemurs he had seen in a television documentary years ago. Her nose, although still straight and fine, had been honed into a beak, its surface scabby and dry. Only her mouth retained its old beauty: lush, red, full, and now rigid in the grip of some spasm Brunetti did not want to consider.

Griffoni did not speak, and Brunetti did not move. He noticed two small lumps under the red blanket, a bit below where her waist must be. Not wanting to be seen staring at her face, he stared at the lumps while he waited for one of the women to speak. Could there be some medical apparatus hidden there? Some means of injecting and removing fluids — what a horrible word — from her body? The size of apples, they lacked that fruit's roundness and were covered with what looked like large bumps, on one of them lined up in a row, on the other fewer and larger. The silence remained in the room, as did his eyes on the lumps.

One moved. It stopped before Brunetti was sure of what he had seen, but he was certain it had moved. And then the other. The bumps seemed to undulate and then grew still again. Then, alarmingly, one began to move towards the other, scuttling across her body and yanking a noise from the horrified Brunetti. It was only then, as one lump was covered and absorbed by the other, that he realized they were her hands. He closed his eyes. When he opened them, one of her hands was on top of the covers.

'Signora?' he heard, and Griffoni's voice drew him back to normality. 'Signora?' she repeated.

'*Sì?*' the woman in the bed whispered with an almost imperceptible nod.

'We've come to hear what you want to tell us.'

Brunetti looked at Signora Toso, whose eyes were closed. Her chest rose once, twice, and then she opened her eyes. 'The money,' she finally said.

'What about the money?' Griffoni asked calmly, as though they were two old friends meeting for a coffee and a chat about their children.

'He said yes,' she gasped. Then, perhaps seeing their confusion, 'He took it.'

'When was that, Benedetta?' Griffoni asked.

Signora Toso shook her head minimally. 'I don't remember,' she began and then took two deep breaths before adding, 'time.'

'I see,' Griffoni said, leaning forward. 'It must be hard. To remember.'

Signora Toso looked at the other woman. Her lips moved; Brunetti had no idea if she was trying to smile or to speak. Finally she managed to say, 'Birthday.'

'I see,' Griffoni said amiably, then asked, as if from mere politeness, 'Yours?'

Signora Toso nodded again, though with less energy. Brunetti watched her hands contracting and expanding.

'What was it for, Benedetta?' Griffoni asked.

'Clinic.' The sound of the word was followed by an intake of breath that forced Brunetti to clench his teeth.

Griffoni looked around the room. 'This

clinic, do you mean?'

'No. Before.'

'Before you came here?'

Signora Toso's hands relaxed. *'Sì. Sì.'*

'That's good, that he found the money,' Griffoni said and placed her hand lightly on Signora Toso's, as if to enforce her approval.

Signora Toso stared at her but said nothing. Her breathing grew heavy, painful to hear, and then slowed and grew normal again. Brunetti saw her hand turn upwards and reach for Griffoni's.

'Did he tell you where he got it?' Griffoni asked with real interest and not a little admiration.

'Work.'

'What work did he do?' she asked. Somehow, Brunetti realized, Griffoni had become this woman's oldest, closest friend and now spoke with the liberty earned by secrets exchanged, promises made and kept all through their lives.

Again, that minimal shake of the head.

'Wouldn't he tell you?' When Signora Toso didn't answer, Griffoni went on instantly, 'My husband's like that, too. You know how men are: they never trust us about money.' It was only now that Brunetti noticed the pure Veneto cadence in Griffoni's voice, the scarcity of 'l's', and that she'd tossed the 'r'

41

out of the word *marito*. How did she do it?

'Bad,' Signora Toso whispered so softly that Brunetti wasn't sure he'd heard her correctly.

'Bad not to tell you?' Griffoni asked.

'Bad money.' Saying that, Signora Toso's mouth fell open, her power of speech replaced by a rough snoring noise.

Still holding the other woman's hand, Griffoni leaned back in her chair, turned to Brunetti and raised her chin in silent interrogation. He patted the air with his palm and put his finger to his lips.

Brunetti realized only then how hot he was. He tried to lift his right leg, but it was glued to the chair by sweat. More sweat ran down his back, sucked out of him by the heat radiating from the plastic. He braced his palms on the sides of the seat and started to push himself to his feet, his trousers slobbering as they pulled free. He stood and pinched the cloth at the sides of both legs and pulled until he felt it loosen from the back of his thighs.

Signora Toso whipped her head to the left, perhaps in an attempt to escape from questions, or from pain. Brunetti sat down, fearing she would open her eyes and see him looming over the bed. What was 'bad money'? he wondered.

42

Someone opened the door without knocking, and Domingo came into the room. He smiled and nodded to both Griffoni and Brunetti, then walked over to the bed. He replaced the now-empty bottle of clear liquid with a full one. Seeing that Griffoni was holding Signora Toso's hand, he reached under the covers to find her other wrist and held it long enough to take her pulse. When he was finished, he left her hand on top of the covers, made a note on the chart at the foot of the bed, picked up the empty bottle, and left the room as silently as he had entered it.

Brunetti and Griffoni sat, both staring at the sleeping woman, waiting to see what would happen. Neither risked speaking. The door opened again; Domingo came in with two glasses of water on a tray. He offered one to Griffoni, who thanked him softly, then one to Brunetti, who did the same. Both of them drank quickly and set the glasses back on the tray. The young man took them silently and left the room.

When Brunetti glanced back at the woman on the bed, her eyes were open again and she was staring at him. He forced his face to soften and nodded in her direction. Because he was no more than an assistant, he turned his attention towards the person in charge, Griffoni. Signora Toso, he noted, did the same.

Quite as if there had been no intermission in their conversation, Griffoni asked, 'Why was it "bad money", Benedetta?' Listening to her mild voice, Brunetti gave thanks that it was Griffoni who was doing the questioning, not he, with his masculine impatience and unexamined assumption that his questions had to be answered.

Implicit in Griffoni's tone was the understanding that she was not a police officer gathering information but a friend trying to find a way to understand so as perhaps to be of help.

Signora Toso stopped moving her head from side to side and gave Griffoni a steady look. Brunetti watched her mouth contract, as if she were straining at a heavy burden. Her eyes closed with the effort, but when she opened them again, they seemed clearer and better focused.

'It was bad money. I told him no,' she said in a clear voice. It was her first fully lucid moment, and Brunetti had seen the struggle it took her to achieve it.

He hoped Griffoni would not give in to the impulse to ask questions, but she was already saying, 'Poor man. But he had to, didn't he?' When Signora Toso did not respond, Griffoni asked, 'You'd do it for him, wouldn't you?' Then, upping the ante, she added, 'Or for your girls.'

'But . . .'

Griffoni cut the other woman off sharply. 'If it gave you more time with the girls, then there's no "but", Benedetta.'

Brunetti glanced at his colleague and saw her leaning towards the dying woman, one hand embracing Signora Toso's, the other anchored to her chair. Her hair had come loose and fell close to the other woman. Signora Toso lifted her hand free of Griffoni's and placed her fingers around one of the strands. She had time only to smile as she rubbed it between thumb and fingers before her hand fell.

She looked at Griffoni, then at Brunetti, and back towards Griffoni. 'They killed him,' she said in a completely normal voice, as if she were commenting on the weather.

'Who?' Griffoni asked, unable to hide her surprise but not making it clear whether she was asking about the victim or one of the killers.

'Vittorio,' she said. Suddenly her eyes closed and her head fell to one side; then her entire body began to slide from the pillows towards Griffoni. She began to moan and pulled her arms tight to her chest.

45

Brunetti leaped to his feet and took two steps towards the bed. He grabbed the railing and yanked it up into place, then leaned over the bars and opened his hands to block the motion of the woman in the bed and stop her from crashing against the metal rails.

But Griffoni had been faster and had her hands braced against Signora Toso's shoulder and ribs. She pulled out one of the pillows and stuffed it between Signora Toso and the railing. The woman didn't move.

'I'll get someone,' Griffoni said, starting towards the door.

Brunetti remained beside the woman, ready to help her, if he only knew how. He looked away and then back at her. Emaciated, lined, devoured by the disease that was soon to take her, she looked older than he, although he knew she was not yet forty. He longed to provide some comfort, to offer her some solace for all she was about to leave. He wanted to promise that he would see that her children were kept safe, that Vittorio's killers would be found, that she would soon be at peace, but he wasn't certain about any of those things. All he knew was that soon she would die, but not before she had suffered even more.

She made another moaning noise and

opened her eyes. Brunetti met her glance and tried to smile, wanted to speak. Her eyes wandered and then closed, and she was asleep again, although it was restless sleep, filled with intermittent whimpers.

'I'll do what I can,' he said to the sleeping woman. Because she was asleep, he assumed she had not heard or understood. But he had promised, and that would have to suffice.

4

Dottoressa Donato hurried into the room, followed by Griffoni. The doctor went to the side of the bed and took Signora Toso's hand, speaking softly as one would to a troubled child. After a few moments, the moaning stopped and the woman seemed to grow calmer. Dottoressa Donato slipped her fingers down to the pulse and held them there for some time, then nodded and lowered the limp hand to the blanket.

Turning her attention to Brunetti, she asked, her voice tight with anger, 'What happened?'

From behind him, Griffoni said, 'We asked her why she wanted to speak to us. She said someone had received "bad money" to pay for a clinic, and then she said that "they" killed Vittorio.' She waited to see if Brunetti would add anything. When he did not, she said, 'She had to struggle to speak to us.'

The doctor looked back and forth between the two of them but asked only, 'Anything else?'

As Griffoni did not speak, Brunetti said, 'Only that. But we don't know what clinic or how much money or why the money was "bad", and we don't know who Vittorio is, or was.'

'That was her husband, Vittorio Fadalto,' Dottoressa Donato said in a level voice. 'I told you: he died recently. She came to us from a clinic on the mainland. I don't know anything about money.'

'How long was she there?' Brunetti asked.

'I have no idea, Signore,' she answered, then added, as if she'd heard the chill in her own voice, 'It would be in her file.' She made no offer to give them the information, and Brunetti had the sense not to ask.

'Thank you, Dottoressa,' he said. Fearful that they had made a mess of this first interview, he asked, choosing his words carefully to make clear that he saw where power resided, 'Will you permit us to speak to her again?'

Dottoressa Donato looked at Brunetti and then at Griffoni but took some time before she said, 'That depends on how she is. This excitement hasn't been good for her.' Perhaps reading their expressions as acknowl-

49

edgement of this, she said, 'I have your number. I'll call you.'

Brunetti could do no more than nod in acceptance and turn to Griffoni, who had nothing to say. She extended her hand to the doctor, thanked her for her help, then walked to the door and opened it.

Brunetti too shook hands with the doctor; he and Griffoni left the room and then the hospital. When they emerged on to the *riva*, the sun assailed them. Brunetti put his hand to his forehead and tried to screen the light. Griffoni took a pair of sunglasses from her bag and put them on but still stepped back inside the entrance to the building in search of shade.

'You're the native,' she said. 'What vaporetto can we take?' Before Brunetti could answer, she said, 'I can't walk. It will kill me.'

'And this from a Neapolitan,' Brunetti said, trying to strike the proper light tone.

Refusing to re-emerge into the sunlight, she spoke to him from the shadow with Sibylline solemnity. 'In Naples there are tall buildings and narrow, dark, humid streets. There are tunnel-like entrances to courtyards with running fountains.' A hand emerged from the shadowed entrance and pointed an accusing finger at the canal behind him. 'Naples does not have wide canals to reflect light, nor white buildings — not even buildings with clean façades. We have darkness and gloom; the sun shines on the sea, but that's safely removed from the city centre and is enough for us.'

Brunetti had spent much of his life with an intransigent woman, so he recognized one when he encountered her. He said nothing but pulled out his phone and dialled Foa's number.

The pilot answered on the second ring. '*Sì*, Commissario?'

'I have an emergency, Foa.'

'What is it, sir?' Foa asked with real concern.

'Dottoressa Griffoni refuses to walk back to the Questura.'

The pilot changed his tone and said with approval, 'Sensible woman. Where are you?'

'At the Fatebenefratelli.'

'Hummm,' the pilot began, and Brunetti could all but hear his brain calculating route and time. 'Twenty minutes. There's a bar if you turn right when you walk out the front door. I'll pick you up there.'

Brunetti put the phone in his pocket and said, 'He'll pick us up at the bar down the street in twenty minutes.'

'He's married, isn't he?' Griffoni asked.

'What?'

'Foa. He's married.'

'Yes. Two kids.'

'Pity,' Griffoni said, emerging from the shadow and turning to the right.

Brunetti caught up with her and said, 'Why?'

'Because if I'm going to be here a few years, I'd like to spend them with a man who has a boat and who will come and pick me up whenever I call him.'

'I called him,' Brunetti said.

'Does that mean you want to marry him, instead?'

Surely the heat had got to her. 'I'm already married.'

'Does she have a boat?'

'No, but her father does.'

'And a driver?'

'A pilot', Brunetti corrected automatically. 'He's the man who takes care of everything for my father-in-law.'

'What sort of things?'

'Broken windows, leaking pipes, *acqua alta,* electrical problems, locks, the roof, and the boat.'

'Is *he* married?'

'Yes. To the cook. And he's more than sixty.'

Without breaking step, Griffoni turned

into the open door of the bar. Brunetti followed her and found himself greeted by a loud, cheerful clinking noise, as though the owner had started to shake a tambourine at the sight of two potential customers. That, however, could not be, for the man standing behind the bar — presumably the owner — was braced, elbows locked, staring down at the open pages of a newspaper. He was tall, broad, and bald.

The noise came from the back of the bar, where three slot machines stood, blinking happily into the reduced light, one of them clanking out victory in a crash of coins spitting into the metal till. A very short man holding the sort of plastic bucket used by children to dig beach fortifications moved to the winning machine and scooped the coins into the bucket. He slapped his palm on the face of the machine and let out a joyous hoot. 'Who says you can't win?' he shouted, perhaps at the machine, perhaps at the other machines standing in the row.

He took two steps to the side and fed a coin into the last machine, then plucked out another to feed the middle one. He poked the button on that one, then leaned over the last machine and poked the red button there. Lights flashed, whizzes and soft bangs came from both machines, but then they stopped, and the silence expanded into the room.

Not bothering to look up from his newspaper, the barman said, 'Don't hit the machine, Toni. It's bad for it, and it's bad for your hand.'

'My hand's all right,' the man called Toni yelled back to him and returned to feeding the machines, this time all three of them.

The barman shrugged and folded the paper closed. He looked up and asked, *'Sì, signori?'*

'A coffee, please,' Brunetti said.

'Acqua naturale,' Griffoni told him.

The barman turned away, shifting the paper to the side and leaving it on the counter for them to read if they chose. Brunetti ignored the offer, fearing that the heat in combination with the *Gazzettino* might be damaging to his health.

The familiar noise of the coffee machine — click, click, tap, thud, squeak, hiss — calmed him, as did the anticipation of the liquid that would show him what hot really felt like. Two lighter clicks and the cup appeared in front of him, and then a full glass of water, condensation beaded on the outside, slid towards Griffoni. He used what little energy remained to him to thank the barman, who moved to the other end of the

54

bar and busied himself there.

Brunetti turned to his colleague and asked, 'What do you think?' wondering if the mental distortion brought on by the heat had ended and she could think again. He poured sugar into the coffee and swirled it round without bothering to use the spoon. He sipped at it and relaxed into its bittersweet heat.

'First we have to find out more about how her husband died,' she said, then picked up the glass and drank half of it. 'Then we have to follow the money and see how the other clinic was paid.'

'And then?' Brunetti asked, happy at the jolt the coffee had given him and beginning to believe they would both return to their former state as sentient beings.

She finished the water and pushed the glass back on the counter, pointing to it and smiling to the barman, who came back and refilled it quickly. 'You can't drink enough in this heat,' he said, speaking Veneziano with what Brunetti thought was a Burano accent. 'Sweats right out of you,' he continued. He took a glass from the shelves behind him, filled it, and slid it across the counter towards Brunetti. 'Drink it,' he said, somewhere between a suggestion and a command, and Brunetti did as he was told.

'You people visiting at the Fatebenefratelli?' he asked, still speaking Veneziano but now in a tone sober enough to suit the question.

Brunetti nodded and thanked him for the water. With no introduction to the change of subject, the barman said, 'I never liked *terroni*,' using the pejorative term for southerners as though it were a word as neutral as '*pane*'.

He took Brunetti's cup and saucer and set them into a sink filled with cups and glasses. 'But then I went down there on vacation. My wife wanted to visit the Basilica of San Nicola in Bari, so we went last year.'

Brunetti nodded, and the blonde-haired Griffoni did what she could not to look like the *terrona* she was.

'And you know what?' the barman asked rhetorically; Brunetti shifted his feet about and ended up with the toe of one tapping against the side of Griffoni's left foot.

In her best and clearest Italian, sounding as though Dante himself had taught her elocution, Griffoni said, her voice eager with curiosity, 'Something wonderful, I hope.'

The barman gave her a quick glance, but she charmed it away with a smile that added a few degrees to the temperature of the room. 'That's right,' he said. 'It *was* wonderful. Everyone we met was helpful, friendly, honest.' He gave a rueful smile and added, 'It's what we used to be like up here in the North, maybe until twenty years ago. And then we all became *gran signori,* and now no one much cares about anyone else any more. But not down there; they still do.'

Brunetti and Griffoni competed with one another to seem more interested in what the barman had to say. Griffoni finished her water and set the glass on the counter, and the barman went on. 'And they'd never let us pay for water. After walking around, seeing things, being tourists, we couldn't drink another coffee, so we'd go into a bar and ask for mineral water. But they never let us pay. I'd offer, but they all said, *"L'acqua non si paga."* ' He raised his hands in surprise or praise. 'Think about that. Here, people get charged two Euros for a glass of water. And down there they won't let you pay.' Then he added, as if to forestall their question, 'And they don't try to give you tap water.'

He pulled a cloth from the sink, wrung it out, and wiped at the counter.

Brunetti pulled out some coins and the barman said, 'One Euro ten for the coffee,' and then added with a broad smile, *'L'acqua non si paga.'*

They both smiled as at Christmas, thanked him, and went to the door to wait for Foa. The barman, apparently having said what he needed to say, returned to his newspaper.

They stood side by side, waiting for the sound of the boat, saying nothing. Brunetti thought of how common the expression *'terrone'* still was, how casually people tossed it around without giving a thought to how offensive it was. How many times had Griffoni — blonde and blue-eyed, speaking Italian better than he did — heard it used? How many times had she heard, 'Did I ever tell you the one about the Neapolitan who . . . ?'? And how many times had he assumed that a person from the South was to be viewed through a different optic than someone from the North?

A noise from the right announced Foa's approach, but neither of them was willing to move out into the sun until the boat was in front of them. A minute passed, the motor grew louder, and the white prow slid up to and stopped at the bottom of the steps leading down to the water.

They emerged together, saw the word POLIZIA painted on the side, and waved to Foa: jacket abandoned, in short sleeves, white captain's hat, and sunglasses with lenses the size of saucers to protect his eyes from the reflection from the water. The pilot saluted them and then smiled and made a joke of revving the engine.

Brunetti stepped down into the boat and held out a hand to help Griffoni. Both thanked Foa and opted to sit inside the cabin; it was at least out of the sun. As they pulled away from the *riva,* Brunetti saw the barman at the door of the café, staring after them, the newspaper held protectively above his eyes against the sun.

The windows were open. Brunetti latched back both sides of the doors at the front and the back of the cabin, telling himself this was bound to help. When they were seated opposite each other, he asked, 'Well?'

Raising her voice over the hum of the motor, Griffoni said, 'We've got the combination of money that someone called "bad" and a death that might not have been an accident. I don't like it when those two words are used in the same sentence.' She slid back on the leather seat and moved her head closer to the breeze from the window. She put her arms behind her and lifted her hair away from the back of her head. It seemed not to help, so she let it fall back again and moved forward on the leather seat. The linen had failed to do its job against the heat and was irredeemably wrinkled.

'She was in another clinic, where payment was necessary, but moved to the hospice, presumably when whatever the clinic was doing failed to work,' she added, then paused to wait for what Brunetti might have to contribute.

'Or the money ran out,' he suggested.

Griffoni nodded and, after a moment's thought, said, 'It should be easy enough to find the report on a Vittorio Fadalto who died roughly two weeks ago.'

Realizing the direction of their minds, Brunetti said, 'We're dealing with an accident report, nothing else. There's been no murder in the Veneto in months.'

'In Naples, we'd declare a holiday at that news,' Griffoni said. She propped her elbows on her knees and sank her head into her hands, and Brunetti wondered if it was this Neapolitan reality that was causing her reaction or merely the heat.

Finally she said, her distress audible, 'The heat feels so different here.'

'The last few summers haven't been as bad as this,' Brunetti said by way of agreement. 'Go to the mountains for your vacation, why don't you?'

Head still lowered, she answered, 'I'm going home.'

'Naples.'

'Yes.'

'When?'

'I'd go now if Foa would take me that far,' she said, then straightened up, smiling. 'So what do we do?'

'Let's find the accident report.'

Griffoni looked out the window of the boat. 'You think the doctor will let us see her again?'

Brunetti considered her question for some time and finally said, 'If she thinks it will help her patient to talk to us, probably.'

'It didn't look like it was doing her much good today,' Griffoni said.

'Maybe dying people have different needs,' Brunetti surprised himself by saying.

Griffoni nodded, then turned aside and stuck her arms out of the window of the boat. The breeze apparently failed to help, so she pulled them back inside and said, 'It's worth a look.' He thought she was finished, but then she added, 'Besides, it will distract us from the heat.'

'As if anything could,' was the best Brunetti could offer by way of response.

5

After about five minutes, Brunetti suddenly realized that the motor was louder than it should have been here in the canals. He looked away from Griffoni to check where they were: Foa, knowing that Griffoni adored the sight of the *palazzi* lining the Grand Canal, always tried to use at least part of that route.

Brunetti saw the cemetery ahead on their left and went up to the deck to ask the pilot what had happened. They were just overtaking a number 5.2 vaporetto that was pulling into the Madonna dell'Orto stop. Foa kept the boat at an even speed while passing, then accelerated when the stop was behind them.

'We in a hurry?' Brunetti asked.

'No, sir.'

'But we're going back this way,' he said, waving an arm at the cemetery.

'I know, sir,' Foa said, then continued, 'I'd

like to take the Commissario up the Grand Canal. But I can't.' In response to Brunetti's expression, the pilot explained. 'A friend called me while I was coming to get you and told me that two tourists dived off the Rialto, and traffic is stopped. Nothing's moving either way.'

'Can't they find them?'

'They found them, sir, but they won't get on to the boats, keep swimming away.'

'*Oddio,*' Brunetti muttered. 'Just what we need. More idiots.'

'It was no better this morning, sir,' Foa said, sounding weary. 'It's Tuesday, so I took Signorina Elettra to the market to get flowers. I've never seen so many boats in the Canal. So many tourists means so much stuff has to be brought in. Or taken out. It's all done in the morning, so it's chaos. It took us almost half an hour to get to Rialto.'

'Half an hour?' asked an astonished Brunetti. It would be faster to walk, he knew: he did it every day.

'Yes, sir. There were at least thirty taxis, all filled with Chinese tourists; they rode beside one another and wouldn't move into single file so I could get past them.'

'You could have used the siren,' Brunetti suggested reasonably. Then, before Foa could object, he added, 'It's police business,

63

after all. Well, sort of.'

'We had a call from the mayor's office, sir. Last week,' Foa said uneasily.

'Saying what?'

'That we can use the siren only in cases of great emergency or when we're responding to a call where there's a danger of violence.' He removed both hands from the wheel to raise them in a gesture of incomprehension.

Puzzled, Brunetti asked, 'Was there any explanation?'

'No, sir: after the call, they sent a directive. They don't have to give reasons. So I called a friend in the mayor's office to ask.'

'And learned?'

'The sirens frighten the tourists if they're riding in taxis. Apparently, if it's the police, they're afraid there will be violence, maybe a crash. And most Chinese don't know how to swim.'

Knowing he shouldn't ask, Brunetti did. 'And ambulances?'

'He said the Chinese aren't afraid of them, the way they are of the police.'

Brunetti turned to the right and watched the hospital as it rode off into the distance.

Foa suddenly spun the wheel and swept to the left to draw up close behind two boys in a boat with a very large motor that was slapping down repeatedly from the effect of the tremendous surges of power the driver was giving it. He got within three metres of them and flicked the siren into life long enough for one sharp shriek, startling Brunetti and bringing Griffoni to the door of the cabin.

The boy at the motor turned and saw them. The prow thudded down on the water and remained there; the speed evaporated. Foa pulled up beside the boys and yanked the bull horn from a shelf behind the tiller. He switched it on and, into the silence of the two idling engines, shouted across at them, speaking in rough dialect. 'I've got your number, *ragazzi,* and I'm putting it on the list. Do that again, and you lose your licence. Do it twice, and you lose your boat. Then, ominously, *'Ti ga capio?'*

'*Sì,* Signore,' the boy called back, barely daring to look at the two men on deck.

Foa suddenly picked up speed and whipped past them. 'Good work, Foa,' Brunetti said and started down the steps to the cabin.

Griffoni had returned to her seat by the time he came in. 'No treat for you today, Claudia. Foa said there's too much traffic on the Grand Canal.'

Her smile froze for a moment, then removed itself. 'Traffic,' she said, as though

65

repeating a new word aloud so as to remember it more easily.

'Taxis filled with tourists, to be more exact,' Brunetti explained.

She folded her hands in her lap and sat without saying anything until they arrived at the Questura, when they both came out of the cabin, back into the power of the sun. Brunetti stepped up to the dock and turned to extend his hand to Griffoni. Before taking it, she turned to thank Foa for the ride, then joined Brunetti on the pavement, saying, 'I'll check for her husband's name in the accident reports for the whole province.'

Brunetti opened the door for her and held it while she entered the Questura. In the high entrance hall, the temperature was almost as bad as it was outside, the humidity certainly worse. The new city administration had cut back on spending for public services, and the allowance for electricity was not sufficient to provide air conditioning to the entire *palazzo*.

He followed her inside, saying, 'I'll try to find out where she was before she went to the hospice.'

Griffoni nodded and turned away. He saw her pause at the bottom of the stairs. Like a diver on the high board, she raised her head and stretched it back, arching her neck taut,

66

then quickly looked beneath her and launched herself upwards.

Brunetti waited a moment and, sparing himself the preparatory pause, went upstairs towards the office of his superior, Vice-Questore Giuseppe Patta. He lacked the energy to do anything but tap lightly on the door of Patta's secretary and open it without waiting to be told to do so.

The room was so cool that Brunetti paused on the threshold and waited to determine if this was a heat-induced hallucination. 'Please close the door, Commissario,' said the familiar voice of Signorina Elettra Zorzi, the Vice-Questore's secretary and *éminence grise* of the Questura.

'Of course,' he said. 'Sorry.' He closed the door quietly and came to stand near her desk.

'It's one of the Vice-Questore's chief concerns at the moment,' she said, smiling at him.

'To keep people out?'

'To keep the cool air in,' she answered. The state of her own unwrinkled linen jacket was evidence that the Vice-Questore's wishes, as so often happened in the Questura, had been granted.

'Foa told me he was going over to get you

67

and Commissario Griffoni at the Fatebenefratelli,' she said. 'I hope it was nothing unpleasant.'

'Why do you call her "Commissario Griffoni"?' Brunetti asked, surprising her with the question.

'It's to show professional courtesy, sir. While I'm inside this building, everyone is to be addressed by his or her rank.'

'Did you pick that up from a ministerial directive about appropriate behaviour among colleagues?'

'That wasn't necessary, Signore,' she said demurely. 'I learned it from my late grandmother, who always maintained that a person must be, first before all things, polite.'

'But you and Commissario Griffoni seem to be friends.'

'Oh, we are, sir,' she said, and left the matter there. With a change of gears Foa would no doubt have admired, she asked, 'Is there any way I can help you?'

He approached her desk, saying, 'We learned from the doctor at the hospice that the husband of the woman we went to see — Vittorio Fadalto — was killed recently in a motorcycle accident. Commissario Griffoni is looking into that and will get a copy of the accident report: it must have been somewhere in the Veneto.'

She nodded, as if to acknowledge how easy such a thing would be, and he went on, 'I'll try to find out the name of the clinic where she was before she went to the hospice, and perhaps then you could find out why she was transferred.'

'Was the other clinic private?' Signorina Elettra asked.

'I think so.'

'Then it's likely she left because of money,' she observed. 'Think about it, Commissario.' She pushed back in her chair. 'A person goes to the hospice only when they accept the fact that there's no hope, and they're going to die. And they can be accepted by the hospice only if that's true.'

Brunetti had seen Signora Toso and felt sure this was the case.

'So to move from one place to another in that state — so close to death — is an enormous decision. Physically. Mentally.' She closed her eyes and said, 'Think of the pain.'

'Her daughters are in the city,' Brunetti said.

'Where was the clinic?'

'On the mainland, but I don't know where,' Brunetti said, regretting that he had not asked Dottoressa Donato because he was uncertain the doctor would give him further information about Signora Toso.

'How does she look?' Signorina Elettra asked, surprising him with the question.

'She looks like she's dying.' He realized how sharp his voice sounded and tried to temper it with a different tone. 'I just saw her, and it's terrible.'

'Then it would have been easier if she had stayed where she was,' Signorina Elettra said. 'If there was no more money, however, she'd have to leave.'

She pulled her lips together and tilted her head to one side, looking away from him.

Brunetti finally accepted the appalling thought: a dying woman put out on the street because she couldn't pay for the hospital. Where were they, for God's sake, America?

Brunetti had a friend, a lawyer, who volunteered every week at the Ospedale Civile to push the coffee cart through the geriatric oncological ward, distributing free coffee and biscuits to the patients there. His office was in Milano, but he never missed a Friday in Venice with his patients. He had once described to Brunetti their excitement and delight, many of them the last survivors of their families and friends, when they were offered coffee and spoken to as guests in the ward, not as old people crowded into a room while waiting for death to take them.

His thoughts turned to an opera Paola had taken him to see in Paris, one where the villain, hoping to terrify the heroine into accepting his offer of marriage, gave her the choice of how she would die if she refused him: '*O la coppa, o la spada*': either the poisoned cup or the sword. Italy was being offered the same choice, though without the beauty of the music and the scene to soften the brutality of the situation: use funds apportioned to hospitals to offer the poor a decent death or spend them building hospitals that were never used and let them die in misery.

Shaking himself free of these thoughts, he said, 'I'll go up and call the hospice now.'

'If you find out the name of the clinic, sir, send it to me, and I'll have a look.'

Tempted, Brunetti asked, 'Should it be necessary, could you find out who was paying her bills?'

She looked at him in surprise, but then her expression changed to that of a leopard seal just noticing a baby penguin paddling in the water above it. 'I suspect I could.'

6

The phone on Signorina Elettra's desk rang;
she checked the incoming number and let it
ring four times before picking it up. *'Sì,
Vice-Questore?'* she said in her formal voice,
the one a person would use if spam came
by phone.

'Ah, how fortunate,' she answered. 'He's
just come in. Shall I send him to you?'
There was a long pause before she said,
'Certainly,' and replaced the phone.

Looking up at Brunetti, she said, 'How
very strange.'

'What?'

'He was in a very good humour when he
came in, but now he's . . .' She left the
sentence unfinished for a moment, and then
said, 'furious.'

'Any idea why?' Brunetti asked.

'None,' she said. 'You'd better go in.'

Brunetti thanked her and started for the
door. From behind him, he heard Signorina

Elettra say, 'If you aren't out in fifteen minutes, I'll call the police.'

'So kind,' Brunetti said and entered Patta's office without knocking.

The Vice-Questore's office, Brunetti noted immediately, was even cooler than Signorina Elettra's. In contrast to the outside temperature, the room might have been called chilly. Because he was not wearing a tie, he felt the cold on his throat; then it passed to the small of his back, still soaked with sweat.

Patta stood, posed in handsome profile, by the window. As was usually the case at this time of year, there was little evidence on his face that he had spent time in the sun; he reserved that for the winter, when it would be seen as something that had had to be paid for, not distributed free to just anyone by a profligate summer.

He must have moved there after hanging up his phone, or else he had used his *telefonino* to call the next room. Seeing that phone on the desk, Brunetti concluded that Patta had finished the call and hastened to the window so as to be found standing there when Brunetti came in. And that was meant to indicate either that the Vice-Questore was unburdened with work at the moment or that he was so overwhelmed by an excess of it as to be driven to seek respite by looking out the window, perhaps to clear his head after hours of concentration.

He glanced at Brunetti and indicated one of the two chairs in front of his desk. As Patta returned to his place, Brunetti chose the chair on the right and thus closer to the microphone he was convinced Signorina Elettra had had installed somewhere in Patta's desk.

'How can I be of service, sir?' he asked, hoping that Signorina Elettra — if she was listening — would recognize it as one of her favourite phrases.

'It's about these two girls, the pick-pockets,' Patta said as he took his seat. It was evident from his entire manner that the Vice-Questore was trying to restrain his anger, something at which he did not excel.

'The Gyps— Rom?' Brunetti inquired.

'Yes,' Patta said brusquely, probably stopping himself from demanding if Brunetti knew of another kind of pickpocket.

'What about them, sir?'

'They've reached the foreign press,' Patta said and named a German newspaper. 'There was a reference to them yesterday.'

He picked up a pencil and tapped the eraser against his desk, then tossed it down as if angry with it for making so much noise.

74

Oddio, Brunetti thought. This means trouble.

'The article says that one of the girls has been arrested twenty-seven times,' Patta said, voice filled with indignation. Then, unbanking the fires of his anger, he said, 'It makes us look like fools.' At the last word, he thumped his palm down on the desk and left it there. Leaning across, he demanded, 'And where did they get that number?'

It came to Brunetti to ask himself why Patta was so enraged about this. After all, the Vice-Questore had sat quietly through the first twenty-six arrests. The two possible explanations that came to him were that Patta had been asked to explain the situation by someone in a higher position who had seen the article: the Questore, the Prefect, even the Governor of the province. Or, possibly worse, some personage had been a victim of the thieves.

He remained silent and gave evidence of great concern with what he was being told.

Patta closed his eyes for a moment and took a breath, released it, and said, as if in answer to Brunetti's speculation, 'An important person was the victim of an attempted robbery yesterday. On the Number One vaporetto.'

He paused to glare at Brunetti and then

continued. 'We can't have this,' he said, raising his voice. This time he brought a fist down, though lightly, as if he wanted a hand gesture to show his frustration while leaving his voice to take care of his anger. 'These things cannot be in the international press,' he said loudly.

The identity of the important victim would explain Patta's anger, Brunetti realized, although surely the names of the victims of crimes, even attempted crimes, were protected by law.

'This is a very delicate situation,' he said in a solemn voice, although he thought it would have been worse had it been an old woman whose entire pension was in her bag.

'It's not only delicate,' Patta began, giving a sarcastic sound to his repetition of Brunetti's word. 'It's also potentially disastrous.'

He took a few deep breaths and gave Brunetti a long look, then said, 'She noticed the girl and what she was about to do, so she grabbed her arm and started to scream.' So it was a woman, Brunetti thought. He was about to say, 'Good for her,' but paused to let Patta finish his story.

Patta placed both hands, palm down, in front of him and continued. 'When the sailor didn't come out of the cabin, she screamed louder, and when he finally got to her, she screamed at him that he'd lose his job if he didn't do something.'

He ran a hand through his hair, failing as ever to displace a single strand. Then he surprised Brunetti by asking if he were familiar with a certain weekly magazine, known to favour the current junta.

'Of course, sir,' Brunetti said and, in thanks for not having interrupted Patta's story, stopped himself from saying that he often saw it at the barber's. 'Why do you ask?'

'The cover story for the next issue is Venice.'

Oh my God, spare us from yet another article about the pearl of the Adriatic. It would do nothing but encourage more people to come and view the pearl. He put an interested expression on his face but said nothing.

'It mentions that the city is virtually free of crime,' Patta said in a solemn voice. 'So the incident on the vaporetto cannot become public information, Brunetti. Cannot.'

'If it hasn't appeared by now, Dottore, it's not likely to, is it?' Brunetti offered by way of reassurance and then added, uncertain of how familiar Patta was with the law, 'Besides, they can't name the person involved.'

'Do you think that would stop the journalists here?' Patta demanded in a loud voice. 'They'd love nothing more than to report this story — there were witnesses. Think how they'd enjoy describing the way she behaved, what she said. And they'd be sure to make it clear who she was.'

For a second, Brunetti didn't understand which woman Patta was talking about, the thief or the victim. 'Do you really think this is so important, Dottore?'

Patta did not answer. Instead, he said, 'I'm going to have them removed.'

'I beg your pardon?' Brunetti asked, thinking of the journalists.

'I said I want these girls removed until a few days have passed,' Patta said. 'And I need a magistrate who can organize it.'

'Passed until what, Signore?'

'Don't be an idiot, Brunetti. Until after the magazine's been published. And read. And forgotten. People remember things for a day or two, no more. That's all the time we need. While they're reading this article, there should be no stories in the newspapers about pickpocketing or street crime. None.'

'But who knows about this?' Brunetti asked, keeping himself from asking who the 'we' were who needed time to be allowed to pass. That would no doubt be revealed. 'I told you this: she was on the vaporetto.'

'And so?' Brunetti asked.

'She felt the Gypsy put her hand in her bag, so she grabbed her and shouted for the *marinaio* to come and help her.' Calming himself, Patta said, 'It's what anyone would do.'

'Certainly, Dottore,' Brunetti said, making no mention of the woman's threat that the sailor would lose his job.

Patta suddenly gave an exhausted sigh and said, 'It was the mayor's wife, Brunetti.'

The Number One vaporetto, filled with Venetians, Brunetti thought, and her husband wanted no one to talk about it or tell the press.

'If this goes public, it will cause me nothing but trouble, Brunetti. I'm in the middle of buying an apartment, and if this gets out of hand, the mayor might force them to transfer me somewhere else. It has to be contained.' The anger was gone from Patta's voice, replaced, Brunetti suspected, by fear or something approaching it. He lowered his head and studied his shoes, trying to think of what to say, but he could not free himself from thinking about the revelation that Patta was buying an apartment. That bespoke an intention or desire to remain in the city, perhaps even a certainty that he would.

The Vice-Questore went on holding his position for year after year, something almost unheard of in the police corps. It was a fact that left a whiff of something behind it, like a strong cheese, perhaps Gorgonzola. Most officials were moved from city to city at the whim of the bureaucracy, with no regard paid to children's schooling, proximity of family — least of all to personal preference. Yet here was Patta, becalmed in the *laguna di Venezia,* well into his second decade, boys educated here, sent to university here, ever in search of work here, while whatever mechanism had first sent him here had failed to transfer him to some other city or back to Palermo, the magic city upon which the Vice-Questore could never heap sufficient praise.

Suddenly Brunetti was overcome by the chill in the room and raised his hand to feel just how cold his throat was. Brunetti came of poor people, patient people who had accepted the climate of the place where they were born and lived their lives in obedience to it. Summers could be spent going to the Alberoni, where there were dunes to play in, clean sea water, breakwaters to play on, and the chance to roam free over the beach with friends, catch crabs in the rocks, or dig for clams when the tide went out. At home, you left all the windows open, hid under the sheets to escape the mosquitoes, and waited for the first rains of August to unburden life of the devastating heat.

Air conditioning was in the hotels where you sneaked in to use the toilet, the ones that had the private cabañas where you excavated under the wide-planked floors in search of coins dropped into the sand. It was not in the vaporetto, though certainly in the taxis and private boats that followed the same routes to the Lido. Even now, Brunetti didn't have it in the apartment, where they fought the heat by leaving all the windows open and the mosquitoes by leaving VAPE burning all night.

Thinking about it, he began to feel the full force of the air conditioning. He pushed himself against the back of the chair and pulled his jacket closed in front. He wished he had a scarf to wrap around his neck.

'What are you thinking, Brunetti?' Patta asked in a surprisingly polite voice.

'They've been arrested in Treviso, as well, haven't they, Dottore?' Brunetti asked.

Patta gave him a long look before answering. 'Yes.'

'If there are many arrests, then perhaps Treviso might want to question them.'

Patta turned his glance away from Brunetti

and looked out of the window of his office. Seeing him so distracted, Brunetti realized how seldom, over the years, he had seen him do that; it was almost as if the view didn't interest him. Brunetti sat quietly, telling himself to think of the heat outside and enjoy the cold.

He looked across at his superior and saw how much Patta wanted these girls to disappear. Patta turned back, his face less tense. Their eyes met in a glance suggestive of understanding. 'Interesting idea, Brunetti,' Patta said slowly. 'Let me consider this.' Then, in a more active voice, he added, 'I'll let you get back to work.'

'Thank you, Dottore,' Brunetti said and got to his feet. Experience, wisdom, and survival stopped him from saying anything else, and he left the office, zero at the bone.

He walked over to Signorina Elettra, who removed a single white earbud from her left ear and left it dangling over her keyboard.

'As soon as you give me the name of the clinic, sir, I'll have a look.'

'Ah, yes,' Brunetti said, having been distracted by his conversation with Patta. 'I'll call now and find out where she was.'

She slipped the earbud and its cord under a pile of papers on her desk and switched on her computer.

■ ■ ■

He sat at his desk and put all thought of the pickpockets out of his mind. 'First things first,' he muttered in English, then smiled, remembering how he'd picked up the phrase from Paola, who always finished it with a line from Dickens, something about wicked King Richard and the 'babes in the Tower'. Brunetti had no idea what it referred to, but he loved the frightening menace of it.

Before he made the call, he considered — as he did each time he was forced to think about how it might be interpreted — *'La Legge sulla Privacy'*. Why did a European regulation enforced in the Republic of Italy have to use a foreign word in its title? He was of the opinion that the word was foreign because the concept was, as well. Governmental decisions made behind closed doors appeared in the next day's papers, were posted online even sooner; photos of actors of a variety of sexes engaged in various intimate acts were available online; the real sexual orientation of any one of a number of prelates and government ministers was common knowledge, though never proclaimed. In these circumstances, what did 'privacy' mean?

He reined in speculation and forced himself to consider practicality. The hospice had the right, as part of its obligation to protect the patient's *privacy,* to refuse to divulge any information about that person. Thus, if he phoned the hospice and explained who he was and what he wanted, there was every chance that his request would be refused until it was authorized by some higher authority, and that meant Signorina Elettra would have to spend time penetrating their system to find the name of the clinic Signora Toso had been transferred from.

He found the number of the hospice online and called. When a man answered the phone, Brunetti began to speak in his strongest Veneziano. 'Ciao, this is Piero. I'm a friend of Domingo's and I have to talk to him.' Before the man could ask anything, Brunetti went on. 'I'm his next-door neighbour, and the cops want me to move his boat.' He sounded entirely exasperated, as if he were barely holding his anger in check.

'They say Domingo's parking space belongs to someone else. So could I talk to him?' He put his hand partially over the mouthpiece and said, letting go of some of his frustration, 'Just wait a minute, would you, officer? I have the key, so all he has to do is tell me I can move it.' He muttered a few obscenities and went back to the speaker. 'Could you get him?'

Without question, the man said, 'He just walked past. I'll go get him. Can he call you back?'

'These policemen won't like that. All I have to do is move the damn boat.'

'Sure, sure,' the man said. Brunetti heard footsteps, a voice calling, 'Domingo,' and then, '*Sì*, who is it?'

'Hello, Domingo, it's Commissario Brunetti,' he said in his normal voice, striving for calm. 'Sorry to disturb you, but I want to ask you something.'

There was a long pause, but then the young man said, 'Sure, what is it?'

'Could you tell me where Signora Toso was before she came to the hospice?'

'That's all?'

'Yes.'

'The guy who gave me the phone sounded like the house was on fire.'

Brunetti laughed easily, one man to another. 'No, only that.'

'The place she was in is called Istituto Rovere. It's in Noale.' Then Domingo added, 'It offers a lot more than we do.'

'For example?' asked an interested Brunetti.

'Rehab, a covered pool, rooms for relatives to stay in.'

'Do they let people's dogs come to visit?'

After a moment, Domingo said, 'No, I don't think they do.'

'Then she's better off with you, I'd say.'

Domingo's confusion was audible. 'But she doesn't have a dog.'

'That doesn't matter,' Brunetti said, thanked him again, and hung up the office phone.

7

Brunetti returned to Signorina Eletttra's office and this time waited for an answer after knocking on the door. 'Avanti,' she called, and he went in.

She was motionless in front of the computer, apparently rapt in contemplation of the screen. So as not to disturb her, he went and stood at her window, gazing across the *campo,* and rolled himself back and forth on the balls of his feet, as though waiting for the next vaporetto.

The only sound in the room was the creaking of his shoes. Outside, people who looked to be on the brink of melting walked slowly across the bridge that led to the deconsecrated church, where there was nothing to see but the façade and that not very interesting. Some didn't bother to cross the bridge, but stood and looked at it, then trudged down towards the Greek church and took that bridge to cross the canal.

Some went into the church; others disappeared into the narrow *calle* that led on from the bridge.

Why would people come to the city in July and August? he asked himself. Every Venetian who could, left; those who had to stay in the city did not venture out during the hours of peak sunlight but did their errands in the early morning and returned inside for the rest of the day, with or without air conditioning, usually without; or they placed their hopes in the plastic exhaust pipe of a little Pinguino cooler to expel hot air through a specially cut hole in a window.

Comfort was excluded for the old and for those who could not afford to pay for either the Pinguino or, in some cases, the electricity necessary to run it. Brunetti refused air conditioning because he had been raised to suffer the heat. To suffer many things, in fact. It was too late now to install it anyway; not with a daughter whose environmental principles abhorred its use.

It came to him to wonder how this room managed to be cool: not as cool as the office of the Vice-Questore, of course, but still cool. He stepped back and studied the windows, but he saw no sign of exit tubes, nor was there an air conditioning unit outside on the balcony. He looked up and turned to check the entire ceiling, and there, just above the door to the Vice-Questore's office, he saw the horizontal slash of a cooling duct. He walked over and stood beneath it, and indeed he felt the cool air flowing into the room.

Turning towards Signorina Elettra and seeing that the spell had been broken, Brunetti asked, waving his hand in the draught, 'When was this done?'

'I called the technicians last month, when you and the Vice-Questore were both on vacation.'

'Without telling him?'

She put her elbow on the desk and propped her chin in her palm. 'He would have been troubled if I'd told him I was having it done.'

'Troubled why?' Brunetti asked. 'Because no one else in the building has it?'

Surprise flashed across her face and then a look of distress, as if she were disappointed by his question. 'No. Hardly. Because he lacked the courage to call and have it done and find a way to pay for it.'

'And you found a way?'

'Of course,' she said and continued, even before he could ask, 'The man in charge of the procurement office in Mestre has been buying all of our computers from his cousin's shop for years. I called him and told him to expect a bill for an overhaul of the heating system.'

'In July?'

She smiled. 'He asked the same question. I told him there's no better time to work on the heating ducts than when the system's off.' She waited to see if Brunetti had digested this, and when he nodded, she continued. 'When the workmen came, I told them to extend it to this room, as well.'

'I can't believe this,' Brunetti said.

'As you choose, Commissario,' she answered and smiled. 'Was there something you'd like me to do?'

'Yes, there is,' he said, happy to move to a new subject. 'The name of the clinic is Istituto Rovere.'

'Somewhere on the mainland?'

'Noale.'

'Do you want to know about the clinic or simply about the money?'

'Only the money for now, Signorina,' he answered.

'Fine. I'll get to it as soon as I can. I have a few things to do for Dottor Patta.'

Surprised at the possibility that Patta might still be in his office, Brunetti asked, eyes moving towards the door, and concentrating upon removing all surprise from his

90

voice, 'Is he still here?'

'No, Commissario. He went home an hour ago.'

Brunetti looked at his watch and said, 'Ah, what a very good idea.'

The reality turned out to be as pleasant as the idea. Because Raffi was staying on Mazzorbo at the summer home of a classmate, whose father was teaching them how to sail, Brunetti had dinner on the terrace with Chiara and Paola. Victims of the heat, they could face no more than an enormous insalata caprese with mozzarella a friend of Paola's had brought back from Naples the day before.

Because Paola knew they would need bread to mop up the olive oil, she had sent Chiara to the farmers' market at Santa Marta the previous day to bring back both tomatoes and an enormous round loaf, Paola being of the opinion that the market had the only edible bread in the city, as well as tomatoes that tasted like tomatoes.

As his first bite of mozzarella began to dissolve on his tongue, Brunetti set his fork down and declared, 'We're moving to Naples.' Accustomed to her father's verbal excesses, Chiara looked up, but before she could tell him what a wonderful idea that was, he said, 'You'll make new friends, Chiara; I'll buy you a motor scooter, and you won't have to wear a helmet.'

'If you can get me a position as full professor at the university, I'll come, too,' Paola said after tasting the cheese.

Brunetti selected a few slices of tomato, set them on his plate, and added a few leaves of basil: that done, he quickly speared basil, mozzarella, and then a slice of tomato. 'The strange thing,' he began, his patriotic green, white, and red forkful halfway to his mouth, 'is that I suspect, if I were to ask him to do it, Giulio could find a way to get you the position.'

'I think I'd rather come by it honestly,' Paola sniffed.

After finishing the mouthful, Brunetti said, 'Then I'm afraid there's no chance you'd ever get it.'

'My degree is from Oxford, you might recall,' she said with exaggerated condescension.

'It's more a question of where your friends are from, my dear,' Brunetti replied and tore a slice of bread in half to soak up the olive oil on his plate. 'Giulio's family was in Naples before the Bourbons arrived,' he added, raising the bread to his mouth. 'And they're still in power.' That said, he placed the bread in his mouth and smiled across at her.

Chiara, suddenly interested in the conversation, abandoned her salad to ask, 'Is it really like that, Papà?'

Brunetti, caught off guard in making what he meant to be a joke, set his fork down and took a sip of Pinot Bianco to give himself time to figure out what to answer.

'I really don't know, Angel,' he said. 'I've heard stories that tell me it is, and stories that tell me it isn't.'

'And stories — from me — that tell you the situation's not much different here,' Paola broke in to say.

Chiara's head moved back and forth from one to the other.

'But which is it?' she asked, looking at her father but certainly including her mother in her question.

Brunetti decided to wait before taking a second helping and used his time in spooning up olive oil from the serving platter and drizzling it on the other half-piece of bread. 'I'd say,' he began, turning his fork over and punching holes in the bread, the better to allow the oil to sink in, 'it's parts of all three. Anyone looking for a job in a university in the city where they grew up probably has family and friends — and friends of the family — who already teach there or have positions of power there or in the city administration, or know people who do, so they have that advantage.'

'From the way you talk, it sounds like more than that,' Chiara said.

'Part of that is your father's low opinion of southerners,' Paola said. Brunetti's hand, halfway to his mouth with the piece of bread and oil, stopped in mid-air. 'Though, strangely enough,' Paola continued as she cut herself another slice of bread, 'I've never known him — not in all these years — to act because of this feeling. Only talk.'

'Well, that's at least something,' said an offended Brunetti.

Paola turned her head with such deliberate slowness that she resembled nothing so much as a lighthouse. 'Are you going to say it's not true, Guido?' she inquired.

'It's true, I think, that I've never said anything bad about any southerner I know,' Brunetti said, then quickly added, 'Because he's a southerner, that is.'

'Except for Zio Giulio,' Chiara said, naming an old friend with whom her father had been at school. As if encouraged by her parents' frequent reference to him, she set down her fork and asked, 'Is he in the Mafia?'

94

After reflecting for a moment, Brunetti admitted, 'His father was.'

'You're a policeman,' she said instantly. 'Does that mean Raffi and I are doomed to the same job?'

Brunetti didn't like the verb in her question but was determined to give no sign of this. He was about to answer when she asked another question. 'Was he ever in prison, his father?' She was rapt with wonder at the very possibility.

'For a time, years ago. That's when his family sent Giulio to live with a cousin here so he could go to school: and we became friends.'

'Even though his father was in the Mafia?'

Brunetti's father, although he had been a manual worker at the port, loading and unloading ships, was a man of rigorous honesty. He was a labourer, but he read Marx and Thomas Aquinas. He sometimes drank too much, but he could quote enormous passages of Foscolo and Leopardi. He failed miserably in every attempt he ever made to support his wife and two sons, but he never stole so much as a piece of bread, and he always paid for the cigarettes that added to his early death.

Thinking of his father, Brunetti said, 'Angel, I'm not sure that we become our parents. And I don't know that loyalty to the Mafia is a hereditary trait.' He didn't know it, but he believed it; this was, however, an idea he could spare his daughter. He sopped up more olive oil and set the piece of bread to the side of his plate.

Pushing himself back in his chair, he paused to see if Chiara was following and went on when she nodded. 'I read an article once, years ago — I forget where — that said we're all born with a kind of thermostat in our bodies. If we're born in a hot place, then our thermostat is set to hot, and for the rest of our lives, we never really adjust to a different temperature. We'll feel comfortable where it's hot and hate having to be in a cold place.'

He looked across at her, but she had no questions. He went on. 'Same if we're born in a cold place. That sets the thermostat, and we don't like hot weather, even if we move to somewhere hot and live there for a long time.'

'So?' she asked when she realized he had finished.

'So that's what the Mafia is like. If you're born where it is, your thermostat adapts to it. Not everyone's, but lots of people's.'

'So it's a kind of moral thermostat?' Chiara asked.

He glanced at Paola, afraid that she would think this sort of reasoning might corrupt their child, but she looked across the table at him quite calmly.

'You make it sound like it's in the air, and you can catch it that way,' Chiara said.

'It's definitely in the air,' Brunetti agreed. 'But not everyone catches it.'

'Did Zio Giulio?' Chiara insisted.

How to tell her about Giulio and his connections, his law practice and the clients he defended, the things he could make happen with a phone call? It took Brunetti a long time to decide. Finally, he said, 'I don't know, Chiara.'

'May I make another comparison?' Paola broke in to ask.

They both turned to her, almost as though they'd forgotten, in her silence, that she was there.

Brunetti looked at Chiara and waved a hand in her direction. This was her conversation, so she got to decide who could or could not join it.

'Between what, Mamma?'

'Disease. If you have flu, you have a fever, but if you have a fever, it doesn't mean you have flu.'

'And all of this means?' Chiara asked.

Brunetti suspected she knew but would still

97

prefer to have it spelled out to her.

'That although Zio Giulio might have symptoms . . .' Paola began, but before she could finish, Chiara demanded, 'Like what?'

'Knowing in advance who will win elections or get a government contract; being named to the boards of companies; buying a number of properties at extraordinarily low prices.' Paola stopped with these, although Brunetti had certainly told her, over the years, of further examples of the extraordinary luck Giulio had in his financial affairs.

To make the comparison clear, she continued, 'Although these are symptoms, they don't prove that he has the flu.'

Chiara, who had met and quite liked Giulio's daughter, a year younger than she, said, 'And Raffaela? What does this mean for her?'

'It means, in the main,' Brunetti broke in to explain, 'that she has a very privileged life and goes to an English school in Switzerland.'

'And will probably go on to law school and go to work in her father's practice,' Paola added.

'But that's not fair,' Chiara said without thinking.

Silence fell while Paola poured them all

more mineral water. Then she asked her daughter, 'Why?'

'Because it isn't,' Chiara answered without hesitation although equally without explanation.

'Not fair to whom?' Paola asked.

'To everyone,' Chiara answered. 'She gets brought up in that system and knows from the beginning that she's going to be a winner. Whether she works or not, she's going to be successful and have whatever she wants.'

Brunetti looked at his daughter, proud beyond his ability to express it that she still didn't understand that the same privileged foundation was hers. Her grandfather's name and wealth would puff strong breezes into the sails of whatever boat she chose, leaving others becalmed in the absence of sufficient wind or slowed by weaker currents.

Paola got to her feet, perhaps because she saw the reef towards which this conversation was heading. 'This is all very interesting,' she said in a way that made clear that she did not think it was, 'but I have a committee meeting tomorrow and have to prepare for it.' She stacked their dishes, grabbed up the knives and forks, took them to the other side of the kitchen and placed them in the sink. Chiara carried over the glasses and set them on the counter, then went back to her room. Brunetti brought the platter, hating to see the olive oil still on it going to waste.

'What committee?' he asked. Paola rarely attended committee meetings, and never had he known her to prepare for one.

She turned to him with the smile she reserved for exemplary examples of human misbehaviour. 'We are deciding among three candidates for a position teaching Contemporary Colonial Literature.'

'Do you know anything about *that*?' Brunetti asked, never quite sure what she got up to, back there in her study, reading.

'No, but I've read a lot about Kabuki theatre.'

'I beg your pardon?'

'It's closer to what will happen tomorrow,' Paola explained. 'All the characters speak in an extremely stylized way, it opens slowly, lasts five acts, sometimes there is a battle, and the ending is satisfying to most of the characters in the play as well as to the audience.'

'A committee meeting?'

'We on the committee are stylized characters, and we will speak the standard text. There will be turbulent drama and a battle a bit after the middle of the play, but I could tell you now who will win, and that the victory will be satisfactory to us all.'

Brunetti saw from the look on her face just how proud she was of her comparison and observed, 'As the Americans would say, "The fix is in"?'

'Clever you,' she said and patted his cheek.

While she washed the dishes and Brunetti made a great business of drying some of them, he told her about his visit to the woman in the hospice, failing to sound as dispassionate as he wanted to. When they were both finished, she nodded but said nothing, and he went back to the bedroom to retrieve his copy of *Lysistrata,* which he'd decided to read as temporary relief from the Greek tragedies he'd spent his time on during the last months. How pleasant he hoped to find it, to be in the company of a man with a sense of humour.

8

It would not be correct, nor would it be fair, to say that Commissario Brunetti dawdled on his way back to the Questura the following morning. He'd had an appointment with his dentist, which he'd entered on the Questura's weekly schedule as 'Witness questioning'. Well, Dottor Ruffini had been his dentist for twenty years; thus he'd surely been a witness to the condition of his patient's teeth, about which Brunetti did occasionally question him.

When Brunetti left the dentist's office at 10:30, the thought of the crowding he was sure to encounter on the vaporetto eliminated the idea of his going to the boat stop at San Silvestro. Instead, he stopped at Caffè del Doge, one of the few places that still served excellent coffee, then stood at the door of the café for a moment before committing himself again to the heat and to the unavoidable crowds at Rialto.

Crowding there was, the kind seen in war movies as the inhabitants of a walled town flee through the gates: men, women, children, all shattered by defeat and surrender and capable only of forward motion. They plodded, they did not walk; many carried their children on, or over, their shoulders as they streamed ahead. Occasionally, they shoved to the side of the mass and paused for long enough to take a sip of water, but they all quickly slipped into a new place in line for the onward trek towards some unknown and unfathomable place of rest.

Since they knew no destination other than that taken by the person in front, they needed no guards, no dogs snapping at their ankles. The sun beat down on their already-burnt faces, sweat blotted their backs and shoulders, exhaustion closed in on them from behind. Yet on and on they trod: miserable, lost; they barely glanced at the milestones they were told lined the sides of their march; heat, dehydration, hunger numbed them to everything they saw. Only forward motion gave them peace. Soon, soon, there would be water or food or a place to rest, but until then they had only the mindless, step-by-step advance towards something they did not want to see and even less wanted to understand.

Brunetti did not break free until he was entering Campo Santa Marina, where the obstruction lessened and he could walk without dodging. By now, however, he'd removed his jacket and carried it over his shoulder, damp and heavy with sweat. So far this summer, four old people had died in their homes, discovered after a day, or days, by neighbours or family.

He stopped for a glass of water, for which he was asked to pay one Euro. Obviously, Campo Santa Maria Formosa had not heard that *'l'acqua non si paga'*.

By the time he reached the Questura, he was ready for a shower or a nap. He went up to Signorina Elettra's office, only to find it empty, so he tapped on Patta's door. The familiar voice told him to come in.

When he entered, he found Patta behind his desk; sitting before him was a robust man who appeared to have collapsed in his chair but who managed to turn at the sound of Brunetti's entrance. Seeing them — Patta looking up in surprise and the other man's face lit up with a stronger emotion — Brunetti switched on the radar that assessed posture and expression to tell him how things stood in the scene he observed.

Patta was evidently well pleased with himself: Brunetti had long familiarity with the look that had slipped back on to the Vice-Questore's face to replace his surprise and so recognized it instantly. Patta was incapable of disguising his bright-eyed glee each time he succeeded in imposing his will on someone: in this instance that someone was Magistrato Salvatore Pascalicchio, a much younger colleague, with whom Brunetti had worked during the time he was stationed in Naples. They had collaborated for years, and, after Brunetti's transfer to Venice, the success of Pascalicchio's investigations had led to his being transferred to Sassari, after which he and Brunetti had lost touch.

And here he was again, still youthful though more robust in form, looking at Brunetti with the expression of a person in deep water about to be pulled under by the weight of his boots. His dark brown eyes still put Brunetti in mind of a Labrador Retriever, and he still wore the kind of suit that exaggerated even the faintest wrinkle or fold. He wore his hair cut short now, as if he hoped to disguise how much it had thinned over the years.

When he saw Brunetti, the Magistrato put his hands on the arms of his chair, as if to push himself up to stand and shake hands. But then, without any need of a warning sign from Brunetti, Pascalicchio changed the movement to shift himself in the chair so that he could cross his legs the other way and returned his glance to Vice-Questore Patta.

'Ah, Commissario,' Patta began in his most amiable voice. He put his hands together, as though he were about to rub them in delight, then decided not to and let them fall back on his desk. 'Magistrato Pascalucchio and I were just discussing the young women who were arrested yesterday.'

Pascalicchio was not Pascalucchio, but to correct Patta was useless, Brunetti knew, and quite possibly a tactical error, so he did no more than nod.

Patta waved to the other chair in front of his desk and said, 'Sit down, Commissario, and we can discuss how to handle this matter.'

Brunetti did as requested, making a point of bending to shake the magistrate's hand as he passed his chair. 'Magistrato,' he said neutrally and offered the other man's hand a firm grip that he held for the fraction of a second meant to renew friendship and inspire solidarity.

Pascalicchio said only, 'Commissario,' thus confirming the cool formality of their meeting. But the smile he gave Brunetti, whose back momentarily blocked Patta from seeing his face, was as warm as Brunetti's grip.

When Brunetti was seated before him, Patta began, 'I'm glad you're both here, gentlemen.' His affability immediately put Brunetti on his guard. 'It's time we came up with a solution to the problem of these pickpocket girls.'

Brunetti was entirely at sea. He had no idea in which Tribunale Pascalicchio was working and why, if it was in one of the nearby cities, he had not contacted Brunetti. Until that was made clear, Brunetti would be well advised to say nothing.

As if aware of that, Pascalicchio cleared his throat and said, 'The fact that I'm working in Treviso, Vice-Questore, means that I might be able to be of some assistance.'

He paused and at once Patta leaped into the silence. 'Before you continue, Magistrato, I'd like you both to keep in mind that my intention is to see that the law is followed carefully, one might even say rigorously.' Without waiting to observe their response, he continued, addressing his words to some larger audience invisible to the two men sitting in front of him.

'I've looked at the long record of their arrests,' he told them, and Brunetti wondered how long that had taken Signorina

Elettra to prepare. 'And when I saw that both of them had been arrested for the first time in Treviso, I realized, and thus decided, that it is our colleagues there who should begin the necessary investigation of their stories, speak to or assign defence attorneys, set, as it were, the legal ball rolling in the direction — at long last — of justice.'

When the Vice-Questore paused to smile at both of them, Pascalicchio directed his attention towards Patta and said, 'Dottore, I could not agree more fully, more strongly.' The accent was there, Brunetti heard, with its different vowels and softer consonants.

'Excellent,' Patta said. 'My colleagues in Treviso have the legal right — and the responsibility, as well — to see that offenders of this sort — repeat offenders, habitual offenders — are treated with the rigour that will prevent them from any longer damaging the image of their city.' Well, thought Brunetti, at least he didn't say 'our city'.

Patta dropped his mask long enough to ask the Magistrate, 'You think you can do this, shift them to Treviso?'

Pascalicchio let his voice slow and deepen, as though he found himself looking for the proper way to speak his deepest thoughts. 'I believe it can be done, Vice-Questore.'

Brunetti saw Patta open his mouth to

speak, but Pascalicchio looked at his hands, folded neatly in his lap, and continued. 'I foresee no legal obstacle to our doing it.'

Oh, thought Brunetti, he's very good. This appears to be his first appearance in the Questura, and already he's using 'our', as though he were the augur of the Vice-Questore, linked to him by the casual use of the plural.

Brunetti nodded and put on his most sage look. Seeing it, Patta asked, 'What do you think, Commissario?'

Brunetti decided to take advantage of the benediction bestowed by Patta's use of his title and answered, 'I must defer to the legal expertise of the Magistrato, Dottore.'

'Well, that's decided, then,' Patta said. Looking at Pascalicchio, he said, 'I'll leave it to you to handle things.'

Ah, thought Brunetti, hearing Patta say, 'leave it to you', if ever a person had a slogan that could be carried in advance of him, as the flags bearing the words *Deus vult* led the Crusaders to their fate, this was Patta's. His attention drifted back to the conversation in time to see Patta lean forward to pull a pile of papers towards him, the burdened official who had the safety of the city in his care.

Brunetti and the Magistrato, taking their

cue, got to their feet, thanked Patta for his
time, and left his office.

9

Outside Patta's office, Brunetti saw that Signorina Elettra had still not returned. 'Can we talk in your office?' Pascalicchio suggested. Hearing him speak normally to a colleague and not in order to create an impression, Brunetti was struck, as he had been years ago, by the rich tone of his voice, deep and resonant, surprising in a man of so unprepossessing an appearance. Even though his accent remained and the vowels were no clearer, the warmth of the tone cancelled those things.

'Upstairs. Third floor,' Brunetti said, then added, 'It's nothing special, but it does give me a lot of exercise, going up and down the stairs.' No sooner had he said it than he realized there was precious little evidence that the Magistrate was much interested in exercise.

Smiling, Pascalicchio said, 'Truth to tell, I'd prefer it to be on the first floor.'

'I suppose it's the absence of elevators that upsets everything,' Brunetti said.

Pascalicchio stopped halfway up the first flight of steps. 'What? I'm sorry, but I don't understand.' He smiled for the first time, shedding a few years.

Brunetti started up again, but was careful to go slowly so that the other man could keep up with him easily. 'In most places,' he continued, 'the important person gets the highest office: the top floor, view of the city, rooftops. Well, at least in films.'

'But here?' Pascalicchio asked.

'Here the worker bees go to the highest place in the hive. No elevator. And the important people get to stay downstairs.'

'Of course,' Pascalicchio said, smiling in understanding and pausing at the landing to take a few deep breaths. 'One more?' he asked.

Brunetti nodded, touched his shoulder, and said, *Coraggio,* and they continued. When they reached the third floor, Brunetti turned towards his office but, hearing the sound of Pascalicchio's heavy breathing behind him, stopped at the third door along and opened it. The other man stopped beside him and looked into the room, only to turn his head to Brunetti in real surprise and ask, 'What's this?'

'Part of the archive,' Brunetti answered. 'These three rooms,' he began, pointing down the corridor to the next doors, 'hold the three decades before we turned everything over to the computers.'

The Magistrato stared in at the floor-to-ceiling shelves of manila folders 'It's incredible,' he whispered.

'What is?' Brunetti asked, honestly confused.

Sounding like a child on Christmas morning, Pascalicchio said, 'The way they're kept. It's just like this in Treviso. They're so neat. All the files are tied up carefully and shelved; they're more or less in chronological order; and the name of the person involved is on a tag on the upper right corner of the folder.'

Brunetti was about to ask how else files would be kept but stopped himself in time and asked, 'Is that surprising?'

Pascalicchio gave him a level glance and said, 'I've been in questuras and courthouses where the files are stacked up in piles along the walls of the corridors, spilling papers everywhere'. He raised an arm to indicate a place on the wall about the height of his hip. 'No order, neither alphabetical nor chronological. No hope of finding anything. Anyone who wants to can pick one up and take it out of the courthouse to read it, or destroy it. You do that . . .' he began, clasping his hands together in front of him, then yanking them apart and fluttering his fingers in the air to expose emptiness '. . . and all trace of the investigation disappears: all the witness statements, all the interviews with suspects, all the notes taken by the police. It all vanishes, and it's as if nothing had ever happened.'

Brunetti grimaced, then nodded, slow and resigned. He recalled, but did not mention, the state of the ground-floor storeroom the day after a particularly high *acqua alta* about ten years before: the legers and papers on the bottom two shelves had been turned to porridge, strips of plaster hung in shreds from the lower parts of the walls, electric sockets were useless for weeks afterwards, until the masons and electricians ripped them all out and rewired the entire floor. He remembered, as well, the ant-like lines of officers going up and down the stairs to the third floor, each of them delivering an armload of the surviving files, no doubt to be stored in the rooms behind these doors.

'It's at the end,' he said, turning away and moving off down the corridor. Inside, he saw, the windows were open, although that

114

made no difference against the heat, in full possession of the room.

The Magistrate went over to the window on the right and looked across the canal.

'The church is deconsecrated,' Brunetti said. 'It's rented out for shows now.'

Pascalicchio nodded and pointed to the building on the other bank of the canal, 'What's that? Looks abandoned.'

'I think it is,' Brunetti answered. 'They're probably waiting to turn that into a hotel.' He turned away from the window and went to sit behind his desk.

'Is that a bad thing?' the Magistrate asked as he took his place opposite him. 'At least that will save the building.'

Without thinking, Brunetti said, 'I'd rather see it rot and collapse.'

Pascalicchio failed to hide his surprise. 'I thought you Venetians loved the city.'

Brunetti, deciding he did not regret his remark and ignoring Pascalicchio's, said, 'If that would save it from being turned into another hotel, then let it rot.'

'Are you joking?'

'You've heard this a thousand times,' Brunetti said. 'You don't need to hear it again.'

'The tourists?'

Brunetti shrugged and said, 'Same old stuff.'

The other man leaned forward. 'I'm really curious. I don't understand the North.'

Brunetti laughed aloud. 'That's exactly what we say about you: we don't understand those southerners.'

Pascalicchio smiled and shrugged. 'Let's leave it for now and talk about these two women.' He straightened up in his chair, and Brunetti was reminded of the time — he must have been fourteen — when he had been sent to Friuli to visit his uncle Claudio, his mother's brother, who had decided to take him hunting. Brunetti had hated every minute of it: forcing his way through the thick brush, the harsh hand of his uncle squeezing his shoulder when he made too much noise, the cold, and the awareness that they were there to kill things.

His uncle's dog, Diana, an English Setter, slim and black and white, and much given to licking Brunetti's hand, slipped through the trees and underbrush soundlessly, out for a romp. At a certain moment — she was ahead of Brunetti — she stopped still, raised her nose and moved her head from side to side, and as he watched, she became a different dog: her body quivered with excitement, her right forefoot rose in the air, and she turned to stone.

Pascalicchio did not quiver, nor did he lift a paw, but his body was pulled tight, and his eyes were no longer the soft eyes of a southerner. Like Diana, for him the fun was over: he was a hunter now.

Curious, Brunetti replied neutrally, 'Yes, let's talk about them.' When Pascalicchio remained silent, Brunetti pushed back in his chair and folded his arms. 'How did he involve you in this?'

Pascalicchio shot him a sharp glance, then looked as quickly away. 'I've had nothing much to do since I got to Treviso, about a month ago,' he said with studied calm, 'so when Dottor Patta called me in and told me it was time, finally, to put an end to what he called "the scandalous situation of the pickpockets", I had no idea what was going on.'

'You didn't know about them?' Brunetti asked.

'I knew about them, yes, but I didn't understand why they were suddenly such a problem.'

Brunetti considered his options, wondering how much Pascalicchio could have learned about the situation in Venice in the time he had been in Treviso. It came to him to ask himself how different this Questura could be from any other in the country. There would be the same cast of characters, both on the side of the police and on that of the criminals. The police, regardless of rank, would always be looking for advancement. Their friendships would be formed or affected by that, trust and confidence serving as bargaining chips, information never to be given freely.

'The Vice-Questore wants them out of the way for a few days,' he said. 'As soon as the time's over, they'll be free to come back here and go back to work.'

'Picking pockets, presumably?' Pascalicchio said.

Brunetti nodded and gave the name of the magazine in which the article mentioning the absence of crime in Venice was to appear. He then proceeded to describe the incident involving the mayor's wife.

'So this article cannot appear at the same time as the newspapers are carrying a story about the pickpocketing of the mayor's wife,' he said. 'Or her behaviour.'

'However delicious that story might be,' Pascalicchio said, and Brunetti began to believe he'd made the right decision in trusting him.

'So I've been chosen to be Patta's willing helper,' Pascalicchio said, 'and request that

118

they be sent to Treviso for a few days to keep them out of the way. And out of the papers. And for them to be charged, and launch the mechanism of the law that is destined to go nowhere. And all this time and energy tossed away so that the mayor won't be embarrassed?'

'That's as clear an analysis of what's happened as anyone could hope to give,' Brunetti said. He looked at Pascalicchio, studying his face for signs of indignation, even anger, at this profligate waste of time and energy, to make no mention of personal insult to him.

The Magistrate looked across at him and smiled. 'It's things like this that make a man finally feel at home in a new job,' he said, then put his head back, and laughed until tears came to his eyes.

When Pascalicchio had recovered himself, Brunetti said, 'Before we do anything about the girls, we should have a look at their records. I'm certain Signorina Elettra could do that.'

'Elettra Zorzi?' Pascalicchio asked, as at the invocation of Pallas Athena. 'People at the Questura in Treviso speak of her.'

'How is that possible?' Brunetti asked.

'I've no idea. But it seems she's a legend, at least in the Questura.'

'Then why don't we go down and see what she might be able to find for us?' Brunetti said.

Pascalicchio smiled and got to his feet. 'I'd be delighted.' Then, with impish glee, 'Perhaps I can take back word of her true nature.'

Because hot air rushed up the stairwell towards the open windows on the top floor, there was a sense of greater coolness; they stood a moment at the top of the stairs, basking in the breeze. Pascalicchio did not move; Brunetti encouraged him by saying, 'She doesn't bite. It just takes time to get to know her.' Better that the Magistrate be warned, he realized, that her confidence was not lightly bestowed. Had he not spent years earning it?

As they started down the steps, Brunetti thought the other man fell behind. 'Salvatore,' he urged, using Pascalicchio's name for the first time. Then, in the spirit of camaraderie he felt with his younger colleague, he added, *'Forza! Avanti!'* He paused until Pascalicchio was beside him and patted the younger man on the shoulder, saying, 'We'll go and see her now.' Encouragement? Command?

He led the way down the corridor, then knocked at her door and heard the usual impersonal *'Si'* from within. He pushed open the door.

Signorina Elettra was standing by the windowsill, lifting flowers from a half-filled vase and placing them, one by one, on an open copy of *Il Gazzettino,* which he recognized from the masthead. She was dressed in honour of the particoloured dahlias: a cream-coloured shirt and a scarlet linen skirt. Her sandals were a yellow that at first shocked Brunetti, then delighted him.

He could almost hear the flowers panting as she pulled them from the vase, half the size of a fire hydrant. When they were all lying to the right of it, she picked it up — too quickly for either of them to offer help — and started towards the door. The Magistrate reached it first and pulled it open for her.

She smiled in thanks, said, *'Scusi,'* and passed in front of him.

Pascalicchio stood for a moment, then moved to stand in the open space, as if using his body to block the escape of cool air. The two men hovered, uncertain what to do.

A few minutes passed, the room grew warmer, then Signorina Elettra appeared at the end of the corridor, the vase held before her in two hands, filled now with fresh water. Pascalicchio walked towards her and took it from her, then stepped aside at the door to allow her to precede him into the room.

'You can bring it over here, Magistrato,' she said when she reached the windowsill. He walked over to her, removed a white linen handkerchief from his jacket pocket, pressed the vase against his chest and wiped the bottom, set it down, and then went back and closed the door very quietly.

When he returned, Signorina Elettra was busy putting the flowers back in the vase one by one, occasionally turning it to see how they looked, then shifting one or two flowers to fit them into whatever arrangement she had in mind.

Once they were all back in the vase, Pascalicchio walked over and removed the newspaper, folded it in half, and half again, and went back to her desk to slip the paper into the appropriate wastebasket. He returned to her and, unprompted, picked up the vase. 'Where would you like me to put this, Signorina?' he asked.

She moved to the next window and patted the place where her flowers usually stood, saying, 'Right here would be perfect.'

When he set it down and moved back to admire the flowers, she said, 'Thank you so much, Magistrato. The poor things were suffering from the heat. I hated to see them like that.' She smiled: Brunetti felt the temperature in the room rise again.

Pascalicchio folded his handkerchief and then refolded it another way. The triple points were gone, destroyed by unfolding and water and his amateur attempts to fold it back into its proper shape. When he'd turned it into a damp rectangle, he stuffed it back into his pocket, where it hung over the top as if the liquid in the vase had been gin and not water.

Brunetti thought it time to intervene. 'You know Magistrato Pascalicchio, then, Signorina?' he asked.

She smiled at him and then at Pascalicchio. 'Not formally, I'm afraid.' Then, turning to Pascalicchio, she extended her hand. 'I saw your photo in the *Gazzettino* when you arrived in Treviso, and when I read that you'd served in Naples, I checked the years and discovered that it was the same time as Commissario Brunetti.'

Well, well, well, Brunetti thought, but said, 'The Vice-Questore has asked the Magistrate to help with the case of the young Rom who have been sent to Treviso.'

The look she gave Pascalicchio was surprisingly serious, but she addressed Brunetti in her usual bantering tone. 'So kind of the Vice-Questore to lighten our load by sending them somewhere else.'

'Indeed,' Pascalicchio allowed himself to say.

'Ah,' she let escape her, looking at him and then away, then back to Brunetti. 'If there's any information that's needed, you have but to tell me what it is, and I'll have a look and see what I can find.' She walked back to her desk, pulled a notebook towards her and flipped it open, adding, 'I've already found their files in our records but haven't had time to read them.'

Hearing this, Pascalicchio turned to Brunetti, who said, 'I've seen only the report from Treviso, where they were first arrested: the record had their place and dates of birth. In Treviso, both of them.'

'Did you note the year we first arrested them, Commissario?' she asked, looking up from what she was writing.

'Four or five years ago, I'd guess. We've been arresting them with . . . some frequency since then.'

Signorina Elettra nodded and made a noise by way of comment. He watched her consider this information, and then asked, 'Do you know what citizenship they have?'

'No, there's no mention of it in the

records.'

In an ideal world — or a well-organized country — there would be an easily found record of their birth, the names and citizenship of their parents as well as their criminal records, if any. Brunetti thought of the rooms on his floor and wondered how long it would be before the files stacked there would be entered into the database. Since so many documents were missing or misfiled, there was no certainty about what absence of information meant.

Signorina Elettra looked across at him and said, 'I assume there must be records in the juvenile court.'

Brunetti shot a glance at Pascalicchio. He was, after all, a magistrate, with an equal obligation to see that the law not be broken or infringed upon.

'It would perhaps be helpful if you could give us some idea of their past behaviour, Signorina. But if they were arrested in some other city, the record might not have been transferred, and so you might not find it there,' Pascalicchio said, nodding towards her computer.

'How clever of you to think of that, Magistrato,' she said and, as if wanting to reward him for having ventured away from monosyllabic replies, brushed his face with a beamed smile. 'I'm sure there's some way I can overcome that obstacle and find you the necessary information.'

'What way might that be?' Pascalicchio asked, unable to disguise his curiosity.

Brunetti watched her expression and saw the precise moment when she decided to lie to Pascalicchio. She smiled and her body relaxed into complete calm, as in the company of a trusted and dear friend. 'I'd thought of consulting the list of children who have disappeared. If the reply says that these girls have been reported missing, I can then ask if they appear in any police record in the country.' Her face clouded and she spoke with poignant realization. 'But if that doesn't work, Magistrato, I'm not at all sure I'd be able to get the information about their early lives.' Her face was the very emblem of disappointment.

'If I were looking for the same information . . .' Pascalicchio began, then paused, as if modesty prevented his suggesting this idea to someone so renowned for finding information.

'What *would* you do, Magistrato?' she asked demurely.

'I'd hack into the central system of the Department of the Interior and go to the restricted section where the crimes committed by children are kept under cyber protection.'

Brunetti had his eyes on her and saw the flicker of surprise that flashed across her face, only to be replaced immediately by an ecstasy of near-celestial delight.

Pascalicchio, who was standing near the window, said aloud but to neither one of them directly, 'Is this the point where I should quietly leave the room and thus not be an accessory to further conversation?'

'Why, Magistrato Pascalicchio, how very polite of you to suggest that,' Signorina Elettra exclaimed, using the formal *'lei'*, but uttering it with the tone ordinarily used for *'tu'*. 'It's hardly necessary.'

She and the Magistrate exchanged smiles, and she said, 'Might I ask you for advice?'

Pascalicchio took a step backwards and leaned against the windowsill, bracing his hands on it. 'Of course, Signorina,' he said.

'I've noticed that they've recently added a new password and some deviations that make me uncertain I can still sneak in and fill my pockets without their noticing that I've been there.'

Pascalicchio's cheeks blossomed with delight. 'Ah, yes, they have done that. It's very irritating. I spent an evening working on it, even had to cancel a date to go to the cinema with friends.'

'And were you successful?' Signora Elettra inquired.

'If you open the site of the Department of the Interior and click on the section "Job Application",' he began, 'and then scroll down to the space where they ask you to give a phone number where you can be reached, and you put in their own central number, their entire databank is open to you, and you are free to do with it as you will.'

Like Nausicaa listening at her father's court to Ulysses' account of his travels, Signorina Elettra sat enthralled. 'Oh, how very clever,' she exclaimed when he finished. 'Do you think it was deliberate?'

Pascalicchio appeared genuinely surprised by her question and took some time considering it before he answered. 'Oh, if only that were so,' he replied and lowered his face to stare vacantly at the wall while he ran through the possibilities. After a long time, he looked back at her and said, 'I'm afraid it can't be. I spent a great deal of time in there, looking for tripwires that they might have set to detect anyone who came looking, but there weren't any.' He shook his head with every sign of real distress and said, 'I'm afraid it was simple incompetence.'

Signorina Elettra sighed. 'Oh, how very disappointing,' she said, as if to triumph over such paltry opposition was entirely without worth.

10

Because Signorina Elettra had accepted so
easily the idea that Magistrato Pascalicchio
understood, and did not question, her
methods, Brunetti decided to leave them to
continue their conversation, explaining that
he had to see someone that afternoon.
There was no reason to tell Pascalicchio
about Signora Toso or her story, so he
decided to wait until he could speak to
Signorina Elettra alone to ask her what she
had found. The habit of discretion was
welded into him, like the watertight com-
partments of a ship. Partitions had to exist,
else things might flow from one section to
another and contaminate or destroy.

He went up to Griffoni's office, but the
door was locked. Did southerners know
something everyone else didn't? He pulled
out his phone and dialled her number, but
the familiar voice told him she was busy and
the caller could leave a message. He said

only that he was going to the hospice and left it at that before hanging up.

Downstairs, he saw Foa in the glass-doored office with the guard on duty. The pilot was sitting upright in a straight-backed chair, legs stretched out in front of him, hands clasped tight on the arms of the chair, pushing himself up and down while the guard watched.

Brunetti opened the door to hear Foa saying, '. . . forty-seven, forty-eight, forty-nine, fifty,' at which he dropped back into the seat of the chair. He looked up and saw Brunetti. 'It's not as easy as it looks, Dottore,' he said, panting.

'Especially in this heat,' Brunetti agreed, almost faint at the idea of doing what he had just seen. 'I'd like to go back to the Fatebenefratelli,' he said.

Foa got to his feet, leaving his jacket on the back of the chair. 'Good,' the other officer — Brunetti thought his name was Giusti — said. 'If you kept that up much longer, I'd collapse.'

'You don't understand, Luca,' Foa said. 'I'm nothing but a taxi driver: I never move, just sit around all day, waiting for someone to ask for a ride. And then I stand at the wheel until we get to where we're going, then sit around again until it's time to leave.'

He started towards the door. 'You guys who get to walk around all day, you don't know how lucky you are.'

That said, he stood back and held the door for Brunetti, then followed him out. The pilot moved ahead and crossed the *riva,* jumped up on to the deck, leaving Brunetti to follow him, and stuck the key into the ignition.

As he emerged into the heat, hunger suddenly assaulted Brunetti and, stepping on to the boat, he said, 'Take me down to the bar, Foa. I have to eat something.' Foa took the boat under the bridge and pulled to the side, saying, 'I'll go out into the *bacino* and turn around while you eat, Signore.'

'No, no,' Brunetti said, 'I'll just be a minute.' True to his word, he was back quickly, a white paper bag in one hand, two bottles of mineral water in the other. He jumped on board, and Foa took the boat out into the *bacino* to turn around. When they were back in the canal, Brunetti, standing beside him, opened the bag and handed the pilot a *tramezzino,* then took one for himself. The two men ate in companionable silence as they rode towards the hospice. Brunetti thought of Foa's remark: he was a taxi driver. Did that mean he'd rather be on foot patrol, pushing his way through herds

132

of people and past windows filled with plastic gondolas? Brunetti had always considered himself deprived of deep understanding of people, of what they wanted or what they did, and here was proof: he understood nothing.

Foa pulled the boat up to the dock in front of the hospice and slid the motor into neutral. 'Thanks for the ride, Foa,' Brunetti said as he stepped up to the pavement.

'Thanks for lunch, sir,' Foa answered, and then asked, 'Should I wait?'

'No. I'll take the vaporetto back.'

Foa saluted, shifted a handle, did a quick three-point turn that was a feat of precision few could equal — as well as an illegal manoeuvre — and started back the way they had come. As Brunetti was passing into the hospice, his phone rang. He saw Griffoni's number and answered.

'Sì?' he said.

'I got your message. I'm on my way.'

'Where are you?'

'The boat's pulling into Sant'Alvise,' she told him.

'I just got here,' he said. 'I wanted to talk to Domingo again and see if there's anything he can tell me.'

'About what?' she asked.

'How she is. Who's been to see her. If

she's said anything to him.'

'Good. I'll come up.'

He grunted and broke the connection.

Brunetti took the elevator and went in search of Domingo. He found him at the nurse's desk, head bowed over a small pile of manila folders. 'Domingo . . .' he said as he approached.

The young man looked up, recognized Brunetti, and smiled. 'Ah, you've come back,' he said. 'I'm glad you did.'

'How is she?' Brunetti asked.

Domingo started to speak but stopped. When he resumed, his voice was softer and more hesitant. 'Not so good, Signore.' Then, after a long pause, he added, 'It helps her if her girls come, but they aren't coming today.'

'Who brings them?' Brunetti asked.

'Her sister. They're living with . . .' he began and quickly modified it to 'staying with her', almost as if he thought that changing the word might help to change the reality.

'How often do they come?' Brunetti asked.

'Their aunt tries to bring them every other day, but sometimes we have to call her and tell her not to come. That's what happened today,' Domingo said, obviously troubled to have to say it.

'Why?' Brunetti asked, sure that his own first visit was the cause and wanting to confirm his guilt. The young man raised both hands and let them drop to his sides in a gesture of helplessness. 'It wasn't your fault, Signore, if that's what you're thinking.'

'Are you sure?' Brunetti asked, remembering how he had held his hands against the woman's body to keep her from falling.

'Signora Toso was so weak this morning that the doctor said she thought it would be too much for her if the girls came, and she agreed. It always exhausts her to be with them. Because she has to pretend to be . . .' Leaving that unfinished, Domingo added, 'But she said she wanted to see your colleague again, and the doctor gave in and told her it would be all right.'

'The Dottoressa didn't call us,' Brunetti said.

'It's been very busy, Commissario: one of our patients left us this morning, and the Dottoressa has been occupied with that. She may have forgotten to call you.' He paused, as if to assess how much he could trust Brunetti with, and then went on, 'It's different here when we lose someone.'

For a moment Domingo seemed uncomfortable to find himself saying such things. 'You'd hope it would be easier, because we

135

all know what's coming.' He shook his head and plunged ahead. 'Maybe it's because of that.' He stopped again. Brunetti watched the younger man's face show what that loss meant to the people working there. He waited for Domingo to continue.

'Because we all know they're going to die, and they know it, too, things are closer between us. There's no need to pretend or to hope, or for them to try to pretend about anything to us. Or lie.'

He looked directly into Brunetti's eyes. 'Are you a spiritual man, Commissario?'

'You mean religious?'

'No. Spiritual.'

'I don't know,' Brunetti answered.

'I wasn't either, when I started working here. But if you work with death, you have to become spiritual, or you can't do it any more.' He made the helpless gesture with his hands again. 'I'm not explaining this well, I know. But when they get close to the end, you can sense their spirit, or you sense that it's there. They do, too. And it helps them. And us.'

'Why are you telling me this, Domingo?'

'So you won't feel bad about yesterday, that she was upset. It happens to many of them. When they get close to the end, there are things they have to say to people and things they need to do.' He nodded, as if agreeing with his own truth.

'I've seen it for years. Once they get rid of it, they're better and calmer. It's almost as if then they're free to stop fighting and let go.'

'Do you mean they can die?'

Domingo was silent for a long time before he said, 'That's what usually happens, but before that you can see how they've changed. They aren't angry any more, or frightened. It's as if they've decided to accept what has to happen.' He shrugged one shoulder. 'We all can see she needs to do something. And then . . .' His voice drifted away, but before either of them could say anything, the doors of the elevator hushed open, and Griffoni emerged.

'Ah, Dottoressa,' Domingo exclaimed, making no attempt to disguise his pleasure in seeing her. 'Signora Toso has been asking for you.'

Griffoni's face was red and covered with sweat; the humidity had turned her hair into a golden nimbus surrounding her head. She looked damp.

Brunetti watched her steady herself by taking a few deep breaths. 'I know,' she finally said. 'The Dottoressa called me while I was on the way here. She told me. So I hurried.' Brunetti was pleased to learn the doctor had called, since it somehow legitimized their visit.

Domingo smiled and turned to lead them towards Signora Toso's room. He said nothing as they walked, perhaps having talked himself out with Brunetti. Sensing that Griffoni was falling behind, Brunetti turned to see what was wrong. Although she was following them, her attention was on her *telefonino*, which she held in one hand while trying to finger something in.

'What are you doing?' he asked.

'I want to record our conversation. I didn't think of it yesterday.' She touched something else, studied the screen and said, 'Good,' then slipped the phone into the pocket of her skirt.

She put a hand on his arm to stop him and said, 'I found the accident report. Usual thing: scratches and dents on the left side of the motorcycle: traces of different-coloured paints. No witnesses to what happened. He was tossed free but landed in a ditch. The cause of death was drowning. Fadalto's body wasn't found until someone noticed the tail light sticking out of the water and climbed down the slope to see what it was.' Then, seeing that they had reached the door, she said, 'That's all the report said.'

When they caught up with him, Domingo knocked on the door and went in. Over the other man's shoulder, Brunetti saw Signora Toso where she had been the day before, but not as she had been.

As if in a fairy tale — one of the savage ones — she had grown older during a single night. Her short hair stuck to her head in patches, greasy with sweat. Her nose had thinned to hooked prominence, and the shadows under her eyes and the hollows in her cheeks had grown darker. And yet, and yet, it appeared that this devastation had calmed her. Her glance was clear, and even though her mouth was pulled tight as if to resist a surge of pain, she nodded at the sight of Griffoni and then, seeing Brunetti, at him, as well.

Domingo disappeared without a word, closing the door behind him.

'We've come back, Benedetta,' Griffoni said, sitting in the chair she had used the day before and leaning towards the bed. Not wasting time, she went on, 'You told us about Vittorio.' She placed her hand on the other woman's arm and said, 'But you fell asleep before you finished. That's why we've come back.'

The woman on the bed said, 'He's dead.'

Her eyes were still capable of tears, but

139

she ignored them and let them run down both sides of her face and into her hair.

'You said yesterday that they killed him, Benedetta,' Griffoni began. The nod was so minimal that it might not have been there. 'Do you know who it was?' This time, the nod didn't appear, and after a while she moved her head to one side but appeared to lack the energy to pull it to the other.

'How did Vittorio get the money, Benedetta?' Griffoni asked, sounding curious but not particularly interested, as if this were the sort of thing you talked about when you went to visit a friend in the hospital in order to pass the time.

Signora Toso took a deep breath, held it for a long time, and then freed it. She did this a few times, and Brunetti watched her chest rise and fall, amazed that she still had the energy to pull in sufficient air to make it move.

After a time, her breathing grew normal. She closed her eyes to rest a moment, then opened them and looked at Griffoni. 'Took the results.'

Hearing this, Brunetti thought of what he would ask next and whether Griffoni would think the same. Find out where they are, find out where they are. As she's mentioned them, they're important, and you don't have to ask what they are, just where we can find them.

'Do you have them, Benedetta?' she asked.

It took some time for Signora Toso to push the word out, but when it came it was 'No.'

'Can you tell me where they are?' Griffoni asked in the most conversational way, as if checking an irrelevant detail.

Brunetti watched as Signora Toso considered the question. She looked at the windows opposite her bed. The one on the left revealed a narrow slice of the *laguna*. He saw small waves twitching on the surface of the water but realized her position on the bed allowed her to see only the sky, where clouds tumbled over one another in the same breezes that played with the waves. Time held its breath. Far off, what appeared to be the upper part of the mast of a sailboat disappeared, swallowed by the sea as the boat sank beyond the horizon. He looked back at the dying woman and felt a chill at the thought that she was making the same passage. He hoped there was someone on the opposite shore who would see the top of the mast slowly growing taller as the boat grew closer. He thought of Domingo's question, thought of his evasive answer, and felt a fool.

He heard the sound of the handle of the

door behind him and the squeak of a hinge. Signora Toso looked towards the door for some time, then back at Griffoni and said in a clear voice, 'The girls. The girls.'

Brunetti turned, expecting to see her daughters and curious to learn why they had disobeyed their mother's request not to visit.

Instead, when the door opened, it revealed only Dottoressa Donato.

He looked nervously back at Signora Toso, hoping disappointment would not trouble her, but she seemed calm, even pleased, at the arrival of the doctor. The older woman nodded to the people near the bed and approached it, asking, 'How are you today, Benedetta?'

'Alive,' she answered instantly and gave a smile that made fun of the answer, the question, the situation, perhaps even the cosmos. It seemed fair to Brunetti that the dying take full liberty in how they chose to speak. 'And you?' she asked the doctor, using the familiar 'tu'.

'Fat,' she answered, a response which surprised Brunetti and Griffoni, but seemed to delight the woman in the bed, who gave a quick grunt of laughter. 'But happy,' the doctor continued, 'to see you looking better than you did yesterday.' That said, she

142

looked away from the patient she had lied to and at the two visitors. 'I'd like to examine my patient. If you'd wait outside . . .' However politely phrased, it was an order, and they obeyed.

In the corridor, Griffoni said, 'She must have forgotten.'

'Saying she didn't want the girls to come?' Brunetti asked.

Griffoni nodded. 'She must have thought they'd come anyway. And then they weren't there. Poor woman.'

Brunetti surprised even himself by blurting out, 'What are we doing here?'

Her confusion was audible. 'I don't understand, Guido. Don't you believe her . . . I don't want to call it a story, because it's not a story. It's her suspicion that something bad happened. She said he had "bad money" and that they killed him. Whoever "they" are.'

'What do you make of it all?' Brunetti asked. 'The money, that it was somehow "bad" money, and that Vittorio was killed?'

'She's a dying woman and these are her last days. She's filled with painkillers.'

'Don't you believe her?' he asked, but before Griffoni could answer, he went on. 'It's not that I don't. It's more that I don't know what it is she wants us to believe.'

143

'Meaning?' she asked.

'You asked where he got the money, and she said he "took the results",' Brunetti said. He searched for a way to make clear his thoughts. 'It's as if we'd come into a film halfway through. We're trying to reconstruct things from what we hear, but she isn't lucid all the time.' He paused, then added, 'Or doesn't seem entirely lucid.'

'So we should discount it all and go back to the Questura?' Griffoni asked. When he refused to answer, she put her hand on his arm and said, 'Guido, I didn't mean that. I just don't understand why, at this point, it all suddenly looks strange to you. Or untrue.'

Remembering where they were, Brunetti lowered his voice and moved a few steps away from the door. He regretted having been so abrupt with Griffoni, knew he should have been more discreet and suggested they step back and reassess what they had heard. He regretted his choice of words; he did not regret his doubts.

There was a loud noise from the room, perhaps a voice, perhaps something being dragged across the floor. This was followed immediately by an even louder, metallic clang. They looked at one another; Brunetti strode past her and opened the door.

He saw Dottoressa Donato leaning over her patient, mouth on mouth, one hand pressing the centre of Signora Toso's chest. He took three giant steps to the other side of the bed and placed both of his hands next to Dottoressa Donato's. She looked at him and nodded, moved her hand on top of his and pushed down, release, down, release, down, while she put her mouth back on her patient's.

Brunetti was aware of Griffoni beside him and back a step, perhaps waiting to take her turn if it became necessary. He continued, the pressure of his hands guided by the hand of the doctor, again and again, and then again. He did not take his eyes from his hands, refused to look towards the woman. Finally, after what seemed to him a long silence, the doctor withdrew her hand from his and stood upright.

'You can stop now, Commissario,' she said. 'She's gone.'

Brunetti lifted his hands and stood back from what was now a dead woman. He felt the sweat dripping into his collar, stuffed his hands in his pockets, and forced himself to look at her.

The doctor was right: Benedetta Toso was gone, but part of her had returned. Her mouth was relaxed again, and her nose was again in harmony with her other features. Peace had been restored to her face, as if, by dying, she had paid the price and been given back her normal appearance. Even as he thought these things, Brunetti was conscious that they were strange and probably untrue. But he had just felt her die under his hands, and he was shaken beyond bearing by the experience.

He thought of Paola. She would understand how terrible the experience had been. And how spiritual. As that word came into his mind, he could no longer remain silent and so asked the doctor, 'What happened?'

Dottoressa Donato was making no pretence of clinical dispassion: she was weeping openly, wiping her face with the crook of her arm. She took a few deep breaths and, with what Brunetti thought a major effort of the will, quieted her breathing. 'I think it was a heart attack. Or a stroke,' she said. 'It sometimes happens near the end.'

She leaned down over the bed and pulled the sheet up to cover her patient's face, but not before she had wiped her palm over Signora Toso's eyes to close them. Brunetti looked around and saw that the tall stand from which the bags of liquid had hung had fallen or been knocked over. Signora Toso's arm had been yanked free of the sheets, the plastic tubes pulled taut but trapped in her arm by the tape that held the needles in place. Without thinking, he bent and righted the rack, releasing the tension.

He glanced out the window. The sailboat had disappeared. He felt pressure on his arm and had no idea what it could be. He turned and saw Griffoni, saw her hand, pulling at him gently.

'Come with me, Guido. We should leave the doctor with her,' she said and gave him a gentle tug, starting to move towards the door.

Brunetti followed, wondering if they'd bother with an autopsy and, if so, why. To determine cause of death? Well, it would be one less for cancer, if nothing else. Heart attack. Stroke. He found himself wondering if she had smoked: if so, she could be yet another person who had died from smoking. And if she hadn't smoked? Then there would be yet another error in the records, and what did any of this matter?

His next clear moment was being in the corridor, looking out the window and down at the rioting colours of the garden. Griffoni stood to his left, talking in a soft voice to Domingo. Brunetti glanced at his watch, but he didn't understand what the hands meant. He looked out the window again, and the light showed him that little time could have passed since they entered the room.

Griffoni, perhaps responding to the ease that had seeped back into his body, said, 'Are you ready, Guido?'

'Yes,' he answered, though he had no idea what she meant. 'What shall we do?'

'Go home, I think,' she said.

Brunetti nodded. 'Good idea.'

11

Outside, Griffoni had the grace not to ask him if he wanted her to go along with him, nor to ask him if he felt all right. She said goodbye and that she'd see him the next morning, patted his arm and walked away, probably to the vaporetto stop at Sant'Alvise.

Brunetti turned left and right at the first bridge, hoping that this was the way home. The heat assaulted him. He stopped at the first bar he came to and drank two glasses of water, then left, conscious only of his duty to walk home.

As he approached Strada Nuova, he girded his spiritual loins and put his eyes into that special focus he used for walking through crowds: look ahead, don't ever focus on a face or person, merely calculate whether to slip past them on the right or the left. Do not see them; do not engage with them, do nothing other than flow through them and get home. Keep your arms at your sides, try to avoid contact.

As he walked, he felt his breathing change: he held each breath until he could hold it inside no longer, pushed it out through his mouth, replaced it with another. After what seemed a long time, he found himself at Rialto; he lowered his eyes and looked at his feet as he trudged up the steps of the bridge. At the top, encircled by the bodies of strangers, he shuffled across to the descending steps and stared at what was coming towards him. He realized he couldn't bear it, couldn't try to work his way through the upcoming mass. There was a jewellery shop on the left; he opened the door and slipped inside.

Careful to speak Veneziano, he said to the salesman, a tall man with a thin face, 'Can I stand in here for a few minutes? I don't feel well.'

The man, who was Brunetti's age, perhaps slightly older, answered in dialect. 'Come over here, Signore.' He wore thick glasses and had lost most of his hair, but he had a kindly smile and spoke softly, as though Brunetti's condition demanded that. He waved his hand to draw Brunetti closer and came out from behind the counter, carrying a cane-seated wooden chair. He set it in the tiny open space in front of the counter. 'Here, Signore, just sit down and rest for a while, and you'll feel better.'

Brunetti lowered himself into the chair and leaned against the back. The man said, 'Let me get you some water.' He disappeared through a curtain behind the counter and was quickly back with a glass of water. He handed it to Brunetti, saying, 'You can have more if you need it.'

He folded his hands together and waited while Brunetti drank the water. 'There, that's good. I hope you feel a little bit better.'

'I do, thank you,' Brunetti said, realizing it was true. Whether it was their shared solitude inside the shop or the simple act of kindness, he had no idea. But he did feel better.

He looked at the jewellery under the top of the glass cabinet. It was the usual machine-made gold-plated stuff that tourists liked. Souvenir of Venice: give it to your girlfriend; give it to your wife. He said, 'You shouldn't leave strangers out here when you go into the back room, Signore.' He pointed towards the curtain.

'Oh, that's all right,' the man said.

'Why do you say that?' Brunetti asked.

'Because I've seen you on the street for

151

years. Besides, there's a camera up there,' he said, pointing to the ceiling, where there indeed was a camera.

'Ah, I see,' Brunetti said, wiping the bottom of the glass with his hand before placing it on the counter. He stood and felt much more secure on his feet than he had when he came in. 'I'm all right now,' he said, then, 'Thank you for the water.'

'It's the best thing we have,' the man replied. 'Be careful when you leave. It's like stepping into the current of a river.' He shook his head, as if passing on bad news.

'Thank you. I will be,' Brunetti said, offering his hand.

The other man shook it, saying, 'It was a pleasure. It's seldom we get a chance to help people.' Brunetti waited for him to say something further, perhaps add a remark that would make it clear that he was speaking ironically. But he was speaking in earnest, and Brunetti found himself strangely moved by this simple act of kindness.

He thanked the man again and left the shop, reinserted himself into the flood of people descending the steps, and continued on for home. It was not long before he found himself in front of the door to his building, key in hand, filled with desperate relief at the thought that he could go inside, close the door, and be alone in the building, and then, after climbing four flights of stairs, be within the walls of his own home.

When he entered the kitchen, Paola turned and smiled at him. Her face changed when she saw him, and the knife she was using fell to the floor. 'What's wrong, Guido?' she asked, walking over to him and putting her hand to the side of his face.

'The woman in the hospice died,' he said, aware of the solace her hand provided.

'Ah,' Paola sighed. 'Poor thing. Poor girls.' She said nothing else, asked nothing.

'I was there,' he said.

'Ah,' she repeated. 'That's probably better for her, but not for you.'

'No. It was terrible.' He saw her face and decided that this was not the time to tell her more; he had no idea if that time would ever come. Probably not, but that didn't matter.

He looked at his watch and saw that it was after five.

'Why don't you go and read for a while, Guido. All I have to do is peel the scampi and boil them, and then we can go for a walk.' With this heat, they never ate before nine, when the terrace had cooled down sufficiently to allow them to sit there comfortably.

He nodded, fully in agreement with her suggestion, but said, 'I think I don't want to continue with *Lysistrata.*'

'Why?'

'Because I've realized that, however serious its intention is, it's really not very funny.'

Paola said, 'Then read something that's funny and not serious.'

'Like what?' he asked.

She picked up the knife, rinsed it quickly, and went back to peeling the shrimp. She stared at the pale pink crescents in the pot of cold water, and Brunetti wondered if she was asking them for suggestions.

'Your English is good enough. Why don't you read *The Importance of Being Earnest?*'

'I don't think I've ever read it.'

'All the more reason, then.'

'You sure?'

'It's not serious in any way, and I've always found it very funny.'

'But you love the English,' he said, suddenly wanting this conversation never to end, to stand and talk about books with the woman he loved and to know he had the good sense to see this moment as one of the great gifts life had given him.

'Take a chance, then. Start it and see what

you think.'

'And then we'll go for a walk?'

'I can think of no more joyful thing to do,' she said. Then, 'It's on the third shelf down, near the end on the right.'

Half an hour later, Paola came into the living room and found Brunetti standing at the window. A book lay on the table in front of the sofa, tellingly closed and not left face-down as he usually left the book he was reading.

'No luck?' she asked.

Brunetti turned at her question. 'Eh?' he asked.

'No luck with *Earnest*?'

He shook his head and tried to smile. 'I think I'll go back to Aeschylus.'

'Even if he's serious?'

'Yes.'

They went for a walk then, to San Giacomo dell'Orio, where they had ice cream, but not before each made the other promise not to tell the kids they'd eaten ice cream so close to dinner time, then wandered without purpose past Campo San Boldo and through Campo Sant' Agostin and towards Campo San Polo, and then home again. Before San Polo, they had passed few people on the street, but once they reached what was a major *calle,* that changed, as did their pleasure in the evening quiet.

Dinner was subdued: Brunetti found it impossible to pull himself free of the intrusion of the day's events and join in the conversation of the others, even to find sufficient interest to follow it.

There was what seemed an entire school of cold shrimp, a bowl of carrots and red peppers, and a surprise: Chiara had brought a kilo of ice cream home from the same gelateria where they had stopped for their cones. Both of them insisted they were so full from dinner that they could have only one ball of ice cream; well, perhaps two. That left the remainder for Raffi, returned from Mazzorbo, and Chiara who, in the face of the amount remaining, did not have to squabble over who got how much. To their parents' horror, they finished it all.

Brunetti woke often in the night and twice found his hands pressed against Paola's back. Luckily, she was an Olympic sleeper and did not stir, but both times he found it difficult to get back to sleep. Finally, before seven, he got up and went down to the kitchen and made himself a coffee. He took it to the door left open to the terrace and stepped outside, hoping to find a bit of lingering coolness there. Instead, the heat had sneaked back overnight, smack in the face of the optimism the evening's coolness had given. He decided to go back and take a shower.

The man who emerged from the door of their building half an hour later was freshly shaven and wore a grey linen suit he'd bought a month before and never worn. He went down to Caffè del Doge and had another coffee and one of their mini-brioches, then another brioche, this one with *crema pasticciera.*

But by the time he got to the bridge, he was regretting his choice of clothing. The trousers were wide in the leg, the jacket cut generously, but still, wearing the suit allowed no ease of motion and certainly failed to provide the coolness the salesman had guaranteed would come with linen of this quality.

He crossed the bridge and, passing the kiosk in Campo Santa Marina, where he usually bought his papers, thought of what would result if he stuck both papers under his arm while walking to the Questura. He did not want the fresh print rubbing against light grey linen; even less did he want to hold them in one hand, careful not to let them touch his body. Is this why men carry briefcases? he wondered.

As he continued, he tried to calculate the effect of not reading that day's papers. He would not know which recently declared government policies would that day be reversed, nor would he learn which businessmen and politicians had been arrested the day before. He would achieve no greater understanding of the pact believed to have been made years ago between the government and the Mafia and what new evidence regarding it the courts had decreed must be destroyed. Given this, Brunetti decided that he might make it through the day without reading the papers. Besides, his *telefonino* would tell him the weather report, and nothing else much mattered.

He got to the Questura at half past eight, went up to his office and hung his jacket in the large wooden wardrobe left there by the previous occupant of the office. He checked his desk and found a printed copy of the report filed by the Polizia Stradale of the accident in which Vittorio Fadalto had died. Griffoni's account, however short, had been accurate: no traces on the road of an attempt to brake, neither from a car nor from a motorcycle, scrapes of paint of different colours, no witness, victim drowned. The investigation was 'ongoing'. 'I wonder where?' Brunetti said aloud and switched on his computer to check his emails. Nothing.

He opened the window, put his hands on the sill and leaned out. As they had since he moved into this office, his windows faced east, and the sun was already high enough to sear into the room. He reached out and pulled the shutters almost closed, until only a sliver of light cut across the floor towards his desk. Ever optimistic, Brunetti believed that closing the shutters would help.

He went downstairs, hoping that Signorina Elettra had arrived. She had and was already at work. He noticed that she wore a sea-blue cotton dress with long sleeves. He was surprised by the sight of them until he again became aware of the change in temperature in the room.

'I saw Foa as I was coming in,' she said before he could speak. 'He told me about Signora Toso. I'm sorry.'

Brunetti forced out the words, embarrassed that they were so trite. 'At least it's over for her,' he said. 'She suffered.'

Signorina Elettra said nothing. Together, they let time pass until it was seemly to speak again, of other things.

'Thank you for the report on the accident.'

'Accident,' she repeated with deafening neutrality.

It was too early for him to be willing to rise to that, so he let it pass and merely asked, 'Have you had time to take a look for more about him?'

'I've got his school and health records, bank statements, access to his Facebook account — which he opened and used twice — and job assessments from his employer.'

'Who is?'

'A company called Spattuto Acqua.'

'Where are they?'

'Quarto d'Altino.'

'That's where the accident happened, isn't it?' Brunetti asked. She nodded. 'What sort of job did he have?'

'He was a water distribution technician.'

'I'm not sure that tells me very much,' Brunetti said amiably.

She smiled and said, 'Then it's like their website. The only thing I could understand is that the company's involved with the provision and distribution of water in the Veneto, but they didn't provide a clear idea of what that means.'

'They could be selling mineral water,' Brunetti suggested.

She smiled up at him. 'Exactly what I thought, Commissario, but it seems they deliver it through the pipes and taps.' She touched the screen and said, 'Their website talked about the need for the oversight and maintenance of the system of pipes and conduits to see that the water is moved in the safest and most efficient way, and thus its highly skilled and trained technicians . . .' She let the sentence run out, suggesting her opinion of this sort of bureaucratic language.

'So he kept the water flowing.'

'That's what I'd assume, Signore.'

Brunetti nodded. 'Anything else?'

'His bank records are interesting.' She spoke neutrally, almost as though this sad story — a mother who died before forty and left two orphans, a husband killed shortly before in a motorcycle accident — was not one she wanted to spend more time considering.

Nor, truth be told, did Brunetti, but then he remembered having promised the sleeping woman that he would do what he could. He assumed that promises made to dying people had more weight than those made to healthy people in the prime of life. If you promise food to a hungry person, it's more important that you give it to them than if you promise it to a fat person. He realized that the comparison would not stand up under the examination of logic, but he didn't care. It felt right, and that was enough for the moment.

He turned his attention back to Signorina Elettra and said, 'Could you send me the documents you haven't already sent, and I'll take a look?'

If she felt surprised, she gave no indication of it and said she'd send them all immediately.

The documents were waiting for him when he got back to his office and turned on the computer. Vittorio Fadalto had attended the same elementary and middle schools as Brunetti, although years after him, and had been a good student. He'd gone on to take a degree in chemistry at the University of Venice and had worked for the University of Bologna for eight years in a project dealing with the contamination of the soil, before taking the job in Quarto d'Altino. Venetian, he had returned to live in the city and commuted to work each day. He had married Benedetta Toso fifteen years earlier, and two daughters had since been born.

His work records were excellent at both places: the comments of his superiors were always filled with praise, and his salary increased from year to year. He was, in short, an exemplary worker.

Signorina Elettra had managed to provide

copies of both his bank records and the invoices from the private clinic where his wife had spent two months. His account at the beginning of his wife's illness held a little more than fifteen thousand Euros. On the first day of each of the two months his wife was there, six thousand Euros had been transferred from Fadalto's account to Istituto Rovere. In the last week of her stay at the private clinic, three cash deposits, each for one thousand Euros, had been made to his bank account on successive days. Brunetti assumed Fadalto had managed to borrow this money from friends or family, only to fail in the attempt to raise enough to pay for the entire month.

Brunetti studied the numbers and the dates and tried to make them tell a story. Stricken with cancer and aware that there was little or no hope of survival, Signora Toso had entered a private clinic and stayed there until the money ran out. Was it in the final days of her stay, money spent, account almost exhausted, that Vittorio Fadalto had turned to 'bad money' to keep her there? When he could no longer pay for Istituto Rovere, or when his wife had refused to accept 'bad money', Benedetta Toso had been moved to the Fatebenefratelli hospice, where, although there was no luxury, dogs

163

could come along to visit the humans who loved them and where the people who cared for her were a male nurse with a long braid and an acute sensitivity to suffering and a doctor who laughed and called herself 'fat' and who wept without restraint at her patient's death.

12

Out of nothing more than curiosity, Brunetti put in the name 'Spattuto Acqua, Veneto' and found their web page. After reading through the introduction, he understood that it was one of many private companies 'concerned with the safe delivery of drinking water to towns and cities in the province of Venezia as well as in other provinces'. He studied the accompanying map, which indicated their offices and purifying plants, their main conduits, and their projected plans for the renewal of pipes and infrastructure.

He went back to the list of articles and glanced through them. The first he opened was a newspaper article which mentioned that Spattuto had won, three years before, the contract for the supply of water and sanitation services of a large urban area in the Veneto. The decision to award this contract to a private company was being contested in the courts by an NGO called Acqua Santissima, basing its objection on the 2011 Referendum against the privatization of tap water. Other articles offered openings for employment opportunities at Spattuto as well as information about the company's campaign of sensitizing children in schools to the need to save water in the home. Brunetti watched a thirty-second video of a small girl asking her mother, who was washing the dishes, why she was letting the hot water run all the time and didn't just fill up the sink once and save water.

The little girl looked nothing like Chiara had at that age, but her earnestness and her desire to save water were identical to Chiara's, as was her question. At the time when Chiara had asked it, Brunetti had jokingly begun to call her 'The Water Police'. The passage of time and change in weather patterns had removed all humour from the name: he had stopped using it years ago.

Brunetti recalled the referenda, spread over two days, almost ten years ago, when he had joined 95 per cent of the population of the country in voting against the privatization of water. He remembered the second vote as having repealed a government regulation guaranteeing private companies the right to profit from the sale of water.

He looked away from the screen and stared at the wall. If both referenda had won — and almost everyone who voted had voted against the privatization of water — where did Spattuto Acqua come from, and how had they acquired the right to sell water? He followed this train of thought, considering that a company's business was making money. Presumably, then, they were making money by selling water. Where did that permission come from? And where did the money go?

Out of habit, he closed his server and turned off his computer before he went down to talk to Vianello.

The Ispettore glanced up when Brunetti came in and waved him over. When Brunetti was beside his desk, Vianello stood and said, 'I heard that the woman in the hospice died.'

'Griffoni tell you?'

'Yes,' Vianello said. 'She seemed quite shaken by it.' Having paid his respect to a person's death by getting to his feet, he sat back in his chair.

Brunetti took the one beside the desk and said, 'It's strange, you know? I've always heard that it's good for people not to die alone or in a hospital, with strangers around them, that it's better if it happens at home or there's at least someone with them that they love and who loves them.' He paused a moment and then spat out what had been haunting him. 'She died with the police around her, touching her.'

Because both of his parents had died when things were different from the way they were today, Brunetti and his brother had been with them when it happened. Brunetti knew the experience had enriched his life, although he would never be able to explain how.

Vianello's voice pulled him back from his last memories of his parents. 'Did it help her that you were there?'

Brunetti had to consider this for some time. 'Yes. Probably. She wasn't alone. And her doctor loved her.' He cleared his throat and said, 'It helped her . . .' He found himself reluctant to use the word 'die' and said, instead, 'leave.'

Vianello did not find it necessary to speak.

Eager to free them from the subject, Brunetti said, 'There's nothing keeping us busy here.' Vianello nodded, so Brunetti continued. 'I'd like to go up to Quarto d'Altino and find out more about Signora Toso's husband. Would you like to come along?'

The Ispettore nodded again.

Brunetti used Vianello's computer to find

168

the web page of Spattuto Acqua. Then he called and said who he was, and explained that he would like to speak to someone there about a recently deceased employee, Vittorio Fadalto. After being put on hold for some time, he was transferred to Antonio Riotto, Assistant Manager of Human Resources, who put on a heavy voice at the mention of Fadalto and said that, yes, someone would surely be free to speak to the Commissario, and yes, he could come up that afternoon if he preferred to do it in person. When Brunetti said that yes, he did prefer, Riotto agreed to his suggestion that he arrive after lunch, say, about three? Brunetti replaced the phone and turned to Vianello. 'Let's have lunch, and I'll tell you about it,' he said.

As it turned out, the offices of Spattuto Acqua were not in the centre of Quarto d'Altino but were to be found in one of many multi-storey buildings on the outskirts, along the road leading to Treviso.

As they headed north from the centre — it was more a town than a city — they passed the usual gas stations, automobile repair shops, discount furniture stores, Thai takeaway restaurants, nail salons, and office buildings, these last distinguished by cleaner façades and more orderly parking spaces in front. 'My God, when did this happen?' Vianello asked.

Having no ready answer to offer, the driver remained silent, leaving it to Brunetti to suggest one. 'It's part of the trade-off of living in the city,' he said. 'We get thirty million tourists, and they get this.' Before Vianello could answer, Brunetti added, 'Almost every highway in the province is more or less like this: empty wasteland, or fields, or ugly stores selling junk.'

The driver, who was part of the squad from Mestre and thus unfamiliar to Brunetti, coughed a few times and said, 'If I might make a minor correction, Commissario . . . ?'

'Certainly,' Brunetti said.

'It's not almost every highway, sir,' he said, keeping his eyes on the road ahead and not so much as glancing in the mirror. 'It's every highway.'

'Thank you, officer,' Brunetti said. 'It's always good to have expert testimony.'

After another ten minutes, during which Brunetti reflected upon the common factors that led to a description of something as 'ugly', they pulled into a large parking area on their right.

At the end of it stood a two-storey building with a glass façade. The name 'Spattuto' was spelled out in golden tiles above the entrance. The driver let them out in front and said he'd park the car in the shade. He wrote his number on a piece of paper and gave it to Brunetti, telling him he could call when they were finished and he'd come and get them.

Brunetti put the paper in the pocket of his jacket and started towards the front door, Vianello close behind him.

In the centre of a marble-floored atrium, a young woman sat behind a metal desk. She had blonde hair that appeared not to have been helped in that direction and pale blue eyes; she wore a white blouse and a dark blue jacket that gave a military impression, though her face expressed a very civilian response to the sight of a real uniform.

'Buon giorno, Signori,' she said, looking from one to the other and quickly back to Brunetti: she was not worried, but she was not completely comfortable.

Brunetti smiled and offered his most friendly 'Buon dì' in return. Stretching the truth, he added, 'We've come up from Venice at Signor Riotto's suggestion. He assured me that someone would speak to us.' Some of what he said was true, and most of it would probably dispel her original uneasiness.

'What time is your appointment, Signore?' she asked, bowing her head and tapping at her keyboard.

Brunetti looked at his watch and said, 'Three o'clock.'

Keeping her attention on the screen, she tapped in another command, then another. She looked up at Brunetti and asked, real concern audible in her voice, 'It wasn't an appointment for lunch, was it, Signore?'

'No, it wasn't. I told Signor Riotto I didn't know how long it would take us to get here, but it would surely be after lunch, probably about three. He assured me that someone here would speak with us.'

She looked again and ran a finger down the screen. 'Ah, yes, here it is: Signor Riotto's superior, Dottoressa Ricciardi, will speak to you.' Then, as if this needed explaining, she added, 'She's the Director of Human Resources.'

Brunetti nodded, as if to suggest this was exactly the answer he was expecting. The young woman got to her feet and surprised Brunetti by being taller than he was. He looked down and saw that she was wearing stylishly tight and equally tattered jeans and ten-centimetre heels, fashion statements that were at wild variance with his initial martial fantasies.

'If you'll follow me, gentlemen, I'll take you to her.'

It was not until the young woman had taken a few steps away from them that Brunetti trusted himself to look at Vianello, whose relaxed smile was still plastered on his face. He pushed his lips together and nodded a few times to show approval of Vianello's obvious harmlessness. Their guide continued down the corridor and stopped at a door on the left. She knocked and, at a sound from within, opened it and took a step into the room. 'Two gentlemen to see you, Dottoressa,' she said, moving aside to allow the two men to enter.

A woman who looked to be in her late thirties sat behind a desk that held a computer and a pile of folders. More of them, open, lay to the left of the computer. She gave the visitors a nod and a friendly smile and said, voice falling into the usual Veneto cadence, 'You must be the policemen from Venice Signor Riotto told me about. Please, please, come in,' she continued, gesturing towards the chairs in front of her desk.

She had green eyes and light brown curly hair cut very short in an almost boyish style. The boyishness, however, contrasted with the fullness of what Brunetti could see of her body and the beauty of her mouth.

'Yes, we are, Dottoressa,' Brunetti said, starting towards her. She got to her feet awkwardly and, listing a bit to one side, extended her hand towards them. He gave his name and leaned over the desk to shake her hand, followed by Vianello, who did the same. They took their places in the chairs in front of her desk and waited for her to speak.

'He told me you'd like to know something about Vittorio Fadalto,' she said, placing her palm on the top file and leaving it there.

'Yes,' Brunetti said.

'Because of his death?' she asked, making no attempt to disguise her curiosity.

'Yes,' Brunetti said again, offering no further explanation.

Her voice changed and she said, 'It must be terrible for his wife.'

Brunetti allowed some time to pass before he said, 'She died yesterday.'

She raised her right hand and pressed the palm against her mouth, as if to suppress any sound she might make. 'Oh, I'm so sorry.' She closed her eyes for a moment, but then they flew open and she asked, 'But what about the girls?'

Brunetti folded his hands together and put

them between his knees. 'They're with her sister now,' he said, glancing up at her. He knew it was no answer, but it was the only information he had.

Dottoressa Ricciardi shook her head from side to side three, four, five times: Brunetti began to wonder if she would be able to stop the motion. He pushed himself back in his chair.

The woman grew quiet and said, speaking clearly although still apparently not fully in control of herself, 'I knew she was sick, that she was in the hospice. And then he died in that stupid accident, and —'

' "Stupid", Dottoressa?' Vianello broke in to ask.

She looked at the Ispettore as though seeing him for the first time. 'Stupid because he should have taken the train to go home,' she answered shortly, as though she'd found his question impertinent.

'Instead of his motorcycle?' Brunetti asked.

She nodded, and again kept moving her head for longer than seemed necessary before finally saying, 'I checked his work report: he'd worked more than eleven hours that day. He'd lost weight during the last months and he was exhausted. Anyone could see it.' She gave Brunetti the chance to nod in understanding, which he hastened to do. 'He should have taken the train — they run every half-hour up until midnight — and not been out on these roads on a motorcycle, not after working so long.'

Brunetti thought that a man would use any means available to get to his dying wife as quickly as he could, and at the idea that Fadalto was still working, and working overtime, the question escaped his lips. 'Excuse me, Dottoressa, but why was he still working? Couldn't he have taken a leave of absence or a sabbatical?' He was about to say that any employer would be eager to keep such a good worker, but stopped himself in time from revealing that he knew anything about Fadalto.

She looked down, apparently not wanting to risk nodding her head again, then said, 'He'd used it all up.' She reached for the folder at the top of the pile of papers in front of her, opened it and turned a few pages, then turned it around, and passed it across to Brunetti. 'As you can see,' she began and picked up a pencil to point at the paper, 'he used up all possible time: vacation, compassionate leave, his own sick leave, even a special one-month sabbatical that can be given in extraordinary circumstances.' She tapped at the page, then slipped down to the bottom and tapped at something else. 'He was given that twice.'

Brunetti followed the pencil down the listed categories, read the number of days each of these absences had lasted, and realized how indulgent the company had been to Fadalto during the last years, ever since his wife's illness had begun.

'But, in these circumstances . . .' he began but let his voice trail off.

'If I might put it frankly,' she replied, seeming almost embarrassed at what she knew she had to say, 'he needed the money.' When neither spoke, she went on: 'He had a sick wife and two children to support, so he had to continue to work.' She lowered her eyes and looked at the report after saying that, as though to apologize for, or at least distance herself from, the reality of what the papers told her.

When she looked back at them, Vianello cleared his throat as a way of returning to the conversation, and asked, 'Could you give us an idea of what it is Signor Fadalto did, Dottoressa? I think I read — in one of the reports — that he was a water distribution technician.' He held up a hand, pulled a notebook out of the pocket of his jacket and flipped through it quickly, then flipped back to the early pages. 'Yes, yes,' he said, tapping at the page, a page that Brunetti saw was quite blank. 'Here it is: "water distribution technician".' Keeping the notebook open, he pulled out a pencil and glanced across at the woman. 'I have no idea what that means. What he does.' Then, embarrassed, 'Did.'

Dottoressa Ricciardi smiled at Vianello, an expert eager to display her knowledge to the less well informed. 'He did the fieldwork that kept the water clean and flowing. That is, he ensured that it was tested to be clean and safe and that the above-ground conduits it flowed through were free of obstacles or contamination of any sort.' She spoke slowly enough to allow Vianello to take notes, which he did.

When he finished and turned a page, she continued, pausing often to give him time to write. 'His other duties were to monitor membrane systems, control the chemical feed, check the equipment and isolate system malfunctions, read all types of meter, perform field checks, create and update daily logs . . .' Her voice ran down; Vianello wrote to the bottom of the page and flipped to another to finish writing. He glanced at her and nodded, and she started again.

'There are other things he had to do or

know how to do, but those are the ones that come to mind.' After she said that, her voice trailed away.

'May I ask why you're so familiar with what he did?' Brunetti said.

Her glance shot to him and she asked, roughly, 'Are you surprised that a woman would know all of this?'

Brunetti smiled and held up his hands, palms facing her, in a pacifying gesture. 'No, Dottoressa. I'm simply curious about why a person in a high administrative position and with what seems to be an encyclopaedic knowledge of the detailed inner workings of a company this size would be assigned to answer basic questions to the police.' He allowed that remark to linger in the air, and then added, 'Or would offer to do it.'

Her face froze and, although it seemed she wanted to shoot back a remark as provocative as Brunetti's, she proved incapable of doing so. Brunetti decided not to help her out of this but to wait and see what answer she came up with.

Keeping her eyes on the papers, she pulled back Fadalto's file and closed it. She returned it to the top of the pile and tapped its sides until it was in straight alignment with the ones below it. He could almost hear the noise of the gears in her brain straining to turn again as she thought of a way to respond to his comment.

He hadn't even asked a question, merely made an observation, but it seemed to have shut her down. Her irritation had been very close to the surface. He wondered if this was a habit she had, throwing her gender at anyone who questioned her or her authority.

She was still holding the stack of files, palms pressed against both sides, as if she believed only her help could keep them from collapsing to one side or the other. Her gaze was fixed on the cover of the file on top, the one with 'Fadalto, Vittorio' printed on a tab.

Brunetti said, 'Dottoressa, I'd like to ask you a few more questions.'

He waited; at least half a minute passed. Finally she looked across at him and said, quite as if she'd forgotten their last interchange, 'Please go ahead.'

'In the last month of his life, did you notice, or did anyone here notice, anything strange in Signor Fadalto's behaviour?'

'Strange?' she asked. 'Or strange for a man whose wife was dying?' She spoke so calmly and reasonably that Brunetti was unable to tell if it was sarcasm or an honest question.

He decided not to provoke her again and

answered, speaking softly, 'Strange in any way.'

'Could you give me an example?' she asked.

'Did he have trouble with any of his colleagues? Make errors in his work?' He was about to ask if Fadalto had seemed stressed, but that would give her the chance to remind him again that the man's wife had been dying. So he asked, instead, 'Did he seem unduly concerned with his work, or perhaps worried about it?'

She removed her hands from the files and placed them flat on her desk. 'Not that I was aware of. And not enough to cause any of his colleagues to mention anything to us.'

'Us?'

'Human Resources,' she said. 'It's the place where our workers can come to talk about problems they're having with their jobs or colleagues.'

'And do they?' Vianello asked, surprising them both.

She turned to the Ispettore and said, 'You might find it unusual, but many of them do.' When Vianello did not question her response, she added, 'It's taken some time for people to learn to trust that nothing they say to us will be reported to their colleagues. They seem to believe it now, and so we learn about many . . . shall we call them situations? . . . before they become problems.'

Hearing her, Brunetti considered what might happen if the Questura had such a system. He wondered if anyone there would trust the people assigned to listen to their complaints or comments and dismissed the idea as impossible. They were all convinced, Brunetti along with them, that the institution itself was not to be trusted: only colleagues whose behaviour had been observed and judged for years were worthy of trust and worth the risk of confidence.

'And is it you with whom they speak, Dottoressa?'

She nodded and removed her hands from the stack of files. One of them went automatically to grasp a pencil and brought it back to the other. 'Or with Signor Riotto, should they prefer that,' she said.

'Did anyone ever mention Signor Fadalto?' Vianello asked.

'In what context?' she asked in a level voice.

'As someone who might have become part of a potential problem,' Vianello answered.

She tilted her head and looked out of one of the windows of her office; it offered a view of fields of corn growing towards the horizon. After some reflection, she answered, 'Not that I can remember.'

'Does the company keep records of what people have spoken about?' Brunetti asked, and, before she could answer, clarified the question. 'That is, if a person's name comes up repeatedly as a potential source of difficulty, is there a system of intervention?' He felt quite proud of his use of the elaborate language in which business wrapped the realities of human behaviour.

Dottoressa Ricciardi smiled, either at his grasp of the language or his understanding of how delicate the process of reprimand had to be made to appear. 'We make brief summaries of our meetings with employees,' she said.

'And who, might I ask, has access to these summaries?' Brunetti asked. Out of the side of his eye, he noticed that Vianello had his notebook on one knee and was still taking notes.

She seemed surprised by his question. 'Signor Riotto and I, of course, and then, if either of us thinks the problem might become serious, we speak to the supervisor of the person concerned.'

Brunetti shifted around in his chair, then asked, 'Was any complaint ever made about Signor Fadalto?'

'Certainly not to me,' she said. 'And Signor Riotto would surely have told me if he had heard anything.'

'Were you particularly interested in Signor Fadalto,' Brunetti began and then finished the sentence with a perfectly proper, 'as an employee?'

She glanced at Vianello, at his notebook, and back at Brunetti, and finally said, 'Not particularly, no, Commissario. I wasn't. But he was a model worker and colleague, and so it would have been very unusual if anyone had made a complaint about his work or his behaviour.'

She went on. 'I knew about his wife's sickness. He spoke to me about it, and I helped him with the applications for the sabbatical and for extra leave.'

'Is it possible that other workers might have seen this as favouritism?'

She allowed a long time to pass before she spoke, sounding confused, as if Brunetti's failure to understand what she had just told him was evidence of some deep-seated inhumanity in him. 'I suppose some people could see it that way, if they chose to,' she began and left a long pause, keeping her eyes on Brunetti's, then continued, 'but no one said anything to me.'

Eyes still on Brunetti's, she went on, 'In

fact, at the time of his death, the Director was considering a request he'd made, that he be allowed to ask his colleagues if they would give up some days from their holidays to him.'

'Would it have been possible?' asked Brunetti, who thought it an interesting idea.

'The Director still had not made his decision when Signor Fadalto had his accident.'

'I see,' Brunetti said and deliberately did not ask what the response would have been.

She suddenly shifted the stack of files to her left, opening up the space between them. 'If I might add this, Commissario,' she said in a calm voice, speaking slowly and clearly. 'For the last few weeks, we've been trying to find someone to fill Signor Fadalto's position.' Seeing that she had captured Brunetti's full attention, she continued. 'So I've read through the list of his duties a number of times and, to date, have discussed them in detail with . . .' Reaching to the other side of her desk, she slid a thin folder towards her and opened it slowly. She extracted a small pile of papers, some single sheets and some more than one, held together with paper clips. Then, like a croupier asked to show her hand, she spread them out, slowly, in front of her, counting them slowly: 'One, two, three, four, five, six applicants.'

Both men looked at the papers fanned in front of her. 'These are their curricula. I discussed the duties of the position with all of them. At some length.' She looked at Brunetti and gave a smile that touched her lips but not her eyes. 'Perhaps that will explain why I'm familiar with Signor Fadalto's duties.'

Brunetti sat silent for some time, looking at the accusing papers. He uncrossed his legs and said, 'Would it be possible to speak to Signor Fadalto's superior, Dottoressa?' He did not allow her time to think before he added, 'So that we can have a judgement from — as it were — someone who had direct familiarity with him and the quality of his work.' Even to his own ears, his explanation sounded as false as it was, but he added nothing and sat, face open and friendly as he gazed at her.

She was a long time in deciding: neither Brunetti nor Vianello spoke or moved.

'Certainly,' she finally said. 'That would be the director of the lab.'

Remembering the list of Fadalto's responsibilities, Brunetti recalled that Dottoressa Ricciardi had made no mention of his having been involved with the laboratory or tests performed there. What had she said?

Fieldwork? That conjured up outdoor work and surely not a laboratory.

'Ah,' he said, 'that would certainly be a great help.' In response to her sudden glance, he smiled, and she lifted the phone.

13

A few minutes later, a man in a white lab jacket knocked and entered the office without waiting to be told to do so. He was tall, perhaps in his early sixties, shoulders stooped forward, a parody of the scientist who spent his life bent over his microscope. He added to that impression with a shock of unruly white hair and a pair of dark-framed glasses with lenses thick enough to distort his eyes faintly.

'What is it, if I might ask?' he said with barely concealed impatience. 'I'm in the middle of something.' His voice was pitched high with irritation, sounding like something that would emerge from one of the larger birds; a crane, perhaps.

'So am I,' Dottoressa Ricciardi said with false sweetness, waving towards the two men in front of her. 'These are two policemen from Venice who want to talk about Vittorio Fadalto and what sort of a worker he was.'

'Oh, the one who was killed?' the man inquired with little display of interest.

'In a motorcycle accident, in case you don't remember.'

'I remember that he died. How it happened isn't important.' Brunetti assumed this man might not have been among those who offered vacation days to his dead colleague.

The man stepped towards them and extended his hand first to Vianello, who was closer to him. 'Eugenio Veltrini,' he said. 'I'm the laboratory director.' He shook hands with Brunetti. 'What is it you want to know?'

Brunetti stood and took a step away from Dottoressa Ricciardi's desk and towards the door. 'Perhaps we could continue this conversation in your laboratory, Dottor Veltrini?'

'I'm not sure that's necessary,' the lab director said.

'My brother's a lab technician in Venice,' Brunetti said, enjoying the luxury of being able to tell the truth for a change, 'so I'm always curious to know how other places organize and run them.'

'What sort of laboratory?'

'He's in charge of Radiology at the Ospedale Civile.'

'Does he work with Lorenzini?' Veltrini asked and watched Brunetti's face while he answered.

'Until Marco retired, he did,' Brunetti answered, again telling the truth and hoping he'd won a prize.

'Come along, then, and I'll show you around,' Veltrini said in an entirely different voice.

Brunetti turned to the woman on the other side of the desk and said, 'Thank you, Dottoressa. You've been very generous with your time, and with the information you've given us.'

Veltrini led them down a corridor, walking quickly, as if pushed forward by the weight of his bent back. He turned to the right, to the left, and then stopped in front of a door. 'It's in here,' he said as he opened it and held it for them to enter ahead of him.

Because Brunetti had visited his brother Sergio at the hospital, he anticipated the rigorous order of the room, and the reality did not disappoint: glass-fronted cabinets covered the walls; two long counters held various instruments he could not identify. Two women in white jackets sat side by side at a steel-surfaced table; one was peering into a microscope and did not bother to look up to see who had come in. The other glanced from a steel rack that held a number of red-topped test tubes but, seeing Dottor Veltrini, turned back and pulled one of the tubes from the rack. Each of them had a computer on the table beside her: because they both had short dark hair and seemed about the same age, their bodies obscured by the white lab coats, one seemed a visual echo of the other.

Brunetti gave an easy smile and said, looking around the room, 'It's very much like my brother's, except that the machines are bigger.' Veltrini smiled in return and Brunetti asked, 'Could you tell us what it is you do here, Dottore?'

'We test the water in the system to see that there's nothing in it that shouldn't be.' Seeing that both Brunetti and Vianello were looking at the women, he raised a hand and made a waving gesture, as if he were conjuring them into being. Ignoring him, the woman working on the test tubes tapped something into her computer and replaced a tube in the rack. Brunetti had not ignored the watch Veltrini's gesture had revealed: a gold IWC with what seemed to be an alligator band.

'It's not what they're doing,' he said in continued response to Brunetti's question.

'The first testing is done automatically: for all manner of contaminants, organic and chemical.' He moved a few steps away from the table, drawing the others with him and away from the women before he continued. 'The various conduits that transport water — pipes, streams, rivers — have sensors placed all along them, about a half-kilometre from one another, sometimes closer, from the water source to the delivery points, and if one of them detects anything harmful or dangerous, our system registers it and a technician is sent to collect that particular sensor, replace it with a new one, and bring it back for further examination. The water in the sensor is subjected to a number of analyses to find out exactly what's in it, and in what percentage. Sometimes it's possible to determine from these tests where the pollutant came from.'

Vianello asked, looking back at the women, 'What are your colleagues doing?'

Veltrini turned to look at them, as if he'd forgotten they were there. 'Those are samples we've taken from wells in the area to see if the water's potable,' he said. 'Or if it's safe to be put on the fields.'

'I beg your pardon,' Vianello said, sounding genuinely surprised. 'Aren't they the same thing?'

'Well, we never know what's underground, do we?' Veltrini asked and walked over to remove one of the red-topped tubes, which he did without bothering to ask permission.

The woman continued entering information into her computer.

He went back to Brunetti and showed him the tube, pointing to the handwritten label. 'See? There's the name of the owner of the land, the date and time the sample was taken, the depth of the water in the well and the depth of the well itself.'

Brunetti studied the label and pointed to a row of numbers. 'What's that?'

'The geographical coordinates,' Veltrini said. 'Sometimes a person's land has more than one sensor. If a river runs through their property, there's a sensor every half-kilometre, so there needs to be an identification number to keep one sample from being confused with another.' Brunetti nodded and thanked him.

The lab director walked back and replaced the tube in its slot, then took a paper from the table. This time, when he showed it to Brunetti, Vianello came over and stood beside them to see what was written.

'This is a report of what's in the water,' Veltrini said.

'Where does it say whether it can be drunk

or used?' Vianello asked.

Veltrini looked at him as though surprised to discover that a man in a policeman's uniform could ask a question, no matter how obvious. Putting his reaction aside, he answered, 'It's all here,' shaking the paper. When Vianello seemed confused by his response, the director ran his finger down the column at the left. 'That's a list of the substances we've checked for in these five samples,' he said. Then, moving his finger across the top, he explained, 'Those are the identification numbers of the five samples.' He looked to see if they understood: both men nodded.

He moved his finger to the first vertical column and, running it down the numbers, said, 'That's how much of each of the substances is in that sample. Expressed in parts per million. It's the calculation we use,' he concluded, not bothering to explain the other possible systems.

Vianello put his finger on 'arsenic'. 'Does that mean there's arsenic in this water?' he asked, making it sound as though he feared the poison would leap from the page and burn his hand.

'Yes,' Veltrini answered. 'But it's nothing more than a trace: you can see that by the level indicated.' He pulled the paper closer to his eyes and said, 'This sample has only 0.003 per million, so it's not going to do anyone any harm. The limit for contamination is 0.010 per million.'

'And these other elements?' Vianello asked, pointing to the column.

Veltrini pulled the paper back and studied the entire list, then set it down next to the woman who was working on the tubes and said, 'The only danger here is nitrates.' The woman nodded in affirmation but said nothing, prompting her colleague to say, not bothering to look away from her microscope, 'It's the only problem we have around here.'

Veltrini behaved as though she had not spoken and went on. 'There are 150 parts per million in one of the samples, which is about three times what European law permits.'

'And so?' Vianello, drawn by real curiosity, asked.

'And so we notify the people who own the land about it, and they decide what to do,' Veltrini said and shrugged his shoulders in a rather dejected manner.

'And what happens?' Vianello asked.

'As I said, they decide what to do.'

'Three times over the limit?' Vianello asked.

'Yes,' Veltrini answered. He looked at the name at the top of the paper. 'He's a farmer and puts fertilizer on his fields every year. A river flows through his land. We've been informing him about the increasing level of nitrates for at least five years.'

'Six,' muttered the woman at the microscope, still not having looked away from it.

'And that's just the level of pollution that's leached into his well,' the woman sitting by the test tubes said and tapped again at her keyboard, leaving Brunetti and Vianello to wonder where the rest was going.

Brunetti nudged Vianello's ankle with his foot; the Ispettore stepped away from the table, folding his arms over his chest as he did so.

'Is that where the nitrates come from?' Brunetti asked. 'The fertilizers, or is it there naturally?'

'The only way we can be sure is to test any nearby land that hasn't had fertilizers put on it,' Veltrini said and then asked rhetorically, 'And where can we find a large patch of land around here where that's the case?'

Brunetti remembered the cornfields that expanded on both sides of the autostrada coming north, looking as though they would

196

run to the horizon. 'We saw the corn,' he said.

'Not only corn,' Veltrini said, sounding dispirited. 'They put fertilizer on anything that grows, and up in Friuli, on the vines. And on the apples in Alto Adige. If it grows on the earth, the farmers want to speed up the growth and make it bigger by putting nitrates on it, no matter what it is.' His voice became heated as he spoke until he had to close his eyes to calm himself down. Brunetti noticed that the lenses made his eyelashes almost countable.

In an entirely different voice, somehow managing to sound older, Veltrini said, 'I've heard them call it *medicina*, but that's only the old people. To them, I suppose the earth does need *medicina*: they've farmed all the strength out of it. So now they use nitrates. And babies die of methemoglobinemia.'

He suddenly shook himself. Brunetti had read for years of characters in books who shook themselves free of some feeling, but he had never seen it done. Nothing could better describe what Veltrini did: like a dog, he shook the top part of his body, hands pointed at the floor, fingers vibrating.

It lasted only a few seconds; when he stopped, he turned to Brunetti and said, 'But this isn't what you wanted to ask me about, is it?'

'No, it isn't, Dottore.'

Veltrini looked at the two seated women, who were no longer bothering to pretend interest in what they had been doing and were sitting and listening, hands resting on the table in front of them. Brunetti noticed that one of them was now wearing glasses and was watching Veltrini.

'Perhaps we could go into the *cantina* and have a coffee, then,' Veltrini surprised him by suggesting, and moved towards the door.

They both followed him. Brunetti turned back at the door and thanked the women for their help. The woman wearing glasses met his eyes, pointed down the corridor, and made a waving signal of negation with her right forefinger before returning to her work. Brunetti paused a moment, wondering what her gesture meant, then turned away, convinced that he shouldn't eat in the *cantina,* and quickly caught up with the other men. One after the other, they entered a large room with many tables, all but three of which were empty. A tired elderly woman in a white uniform — far less elegant and far less clean than the white jackets Veltrini and his assistants wore — rose from a chair behind the counter and came to stand at it.

Veltrini led them over, turning to ask,

'Coffee?'

Both nodded.

'*Tre,*' he said in the direction of the waitress.

When Brunetti reached for his pocket, Veltrini put his hand on his arm. 'You're my guests.' They thanked him, and when the coffees came, they took them and followed Veltrini to the table farthest from where the other people sat. Vianello and Brunetti nodded their thanks.

They all busied themselves stirring sugar into their cups, then drank the coffee quickly, Brunetti marvelling and giving thanks that the room was not the usual arctic horror he found in so many private and public offices.

After they'd finished, Brunetti said, indicating the open space that surrounded them, 'Now that we're here, and alone, Dottore, could I ask what you wanted to tell us?' He pushed his cup aside and looked directly at the other man. 'It seemed to me that you didn't want to speak in front of your assistants or in front of Dottoressa Ricciardi.'

Veltrini gave a booming laugh. The attention this drew from the other tables was enough to stop him. 'She wouldn't like to hear it.'

Brunetti stopped himself from leaning towards the man or drawing his chair closer to the table or, indeed, from showing curiosity in any way. 'And why is that?' he asked neutrally.

'All this talk about Fadalto,' the other man said shortly. 'As if I didn't know who Vittorio is. Was.' Then, in a calmer voice, he added, 'He was one of my closest collaborators here.'

Vianello, Brunetti observed, had worked his old trick of rendering himself invisible. Anyone looking at the men at the table would probably remember seeing two of them and not the one who wore the summer uniform of a police officer: blue trousers and a white jacket. Brunetti had observed this for years, even envied the Ispettore his talent. Vianello's hair was a neutral colour, his face had a neutral expression, and he seemed to have grown a part of the chair in which he sat.

As if giving proof of the idea, Veltrini ignored the Inspector, directing everything he had to say at Brunetti. 'She knew perfectly well I recognized the name, but we had to go through the charade that I didn't.'

'Why is that, Dottore?' Brunetti asked.

'Because of what went on between the two of them,' Veltrini said, following the words

200

with a puff of disapproval.

'I'm not sure I understand you, Dottore,' Brunetti said. 'I've no idea of what went on between them.'

'Then why are you here?' Veltrini asked indignantly.

'We came', Brunetti began, hoping to bring Vianello back into existence, 'to find out anything we could about Vittorio Fadalto.'

After a moment's thought, Veltrini asked, the words coming slowly, as though he'd succeeded in working it out, 'About how he died, do you mean?'

'Not necessarily that,' Brunetti answered, 'but anything about him or his behaviour in the days or weeks before his death that might seem . . . unusual in some way or other.'

'Well, he was trying to keep out of Fulvia's way. That's for sure.' There was a note of self-satisfaction in Veltrini's voice, as if he'd finally managed to say something another person might find interesting.

Although he doubted that there were other women named Fulvia working there, Brunetti still asked, 'Do you mean Dottoressa Ricciardi?'

'Of course,' the lab director said and emitted another disgruntled puff of disapproval.

201

'She was so taken with him that she didn't see he wasn't interested,' he added and nodded his chin once, almost defiantly, as if to dare Brunetti to question his words.

'Ah, I see,' Brunetti said. Then he asked, 'How did you come to learn about this, Dottore?'

'Because I bring my eyes to work every day,' Veltrini said and laughed at his own cleverness. 'I'm afraid just about everyone here saw what was going on,' he continued but paused to add something. 'Except for that poor cluck Fadalto. All he could see were his own problems, so he had no idea what was going on in her head.'

'And what was that, Dottore?' Brunetti asked with curiosity he made no attempt to disguise.

'That she'd decided he was the man for her,' he began, then lowered his voice into a mincing chant when he added, 'the man of her dreams.' He glanced at Brunetti to see his reaction, which was a smile and an encouraging nod that were clearly a request for more.

Veltrini looked around the room and, although the others had all left, lowered his voice. 'I was one of the first to see it, but no one would believe me when I asked if they'd noticed anything.' He pushed himself to his feet and said, 'I'm going to have another coffee. Would either of you like one?'

'No thanks,' Brunetti said; Vianello shook his head.

As Veltrini was walking to the counter, Brunetti asked, 'What do you think?'

'I think he's a nasty bastard,' Vianello answered, then asked, 'What do we do?'

'We listen to whatever it is he wants to tell us, and then we find a way to verify it. In either case, one of them is playing a false game.' Just as the returning Veltrini got within hearing distance, Brunetti said, 'Isn't the river always this low at this time of year?' Then, feigning surprise when Veltrini placed his coffee on the table, he looked at him and said, 'Ispettore Vianello says he doesn't remember the river's ever being this low.'

Veltrini ripped open his envelope of sugar and poured it into his cup. As he stirred it in, he said, 'It's July, for the love of God. It's always been like that.' Then, before either of them could speak, he held up his spoon and waved it at them both in turn. 'Don't start with any of that nonsense about global warming.'

Brunetti smiled and shook his head to dismiss such an unlikely prospect. Veltrini returned his spoon to the saucer and took a sip of his coffee. 'When did other people begin to notice them, Dottore?' Brunetti asked.

Veltrini set his cup down so quickly that it made a sharp click in the empty room. 'Maybe two months ago. People told me his wife was very bad, and you could see just by looking at him that he was in poor shape.' He stopped then and began to sip repeatedly at his coffee.

When Brunetti couldn't stand the intermittent slurping noise any more, he asked, 'And Dottoressa Ricciardi?'

Veltrini looked around the room. 'She started by sitting next to him at lunch and asking him how his poor wife was and saying how sorry she was about it and how difficult it must be for him, with the two girls. And then she'd see him in here when he came back from an inspection, and she'd come and have a coffee with him, and I suppose she'd tell him the same things.' He beat time with his spoon on his saucer as he said, almost chanting, 'Poor wife, poor Vittorio, poor kids.'

He dipped the spoon into the cup, swirled up the remaining sugar, and put the spoon in his mouth. When he pulled it out, he went on. 'Soon enough, they were best friends and had lunch together every day.' He puffed up his cheeks and blew air out of his mouth. 'Poor fool probably had no idea what was going on.'

Brunetti coughed a few times, and asked, hoping to sound faintly embarrassed while at the same time unable to control his curiosity, 'Had she ever . . . done anything like this before, Dottore?'

Dottor Veltrini's lips pressed together in what was meant to be a smile and he said, 'Not that people noticed.'

'But you did?' Brunetti asked, making no attempt to keep the admiration from his voice.

Veltrini put the spoon down and folded his hands on the table. 'Well,' he began and hesitated, as if trying to find the right way to say this, 'I was involved in it, you see.'

Brunetti allowed his confusion to show. 'I'm afraid I don't . . .'

It was Vianello who figured it out. 'Do you mean it was you she . . .' Like his superior, the Ispettore was uncertain how to phrase his question, especially, his expression and posture showed, when speaking to a man of science. Finally finding the properly neutral word, he finished, 'you that she befriended?'

Again, the room filled with Veltrini's laughter. 'Befriended,' he repeated, and then again: 'Befriended.' He allowed himself another jolt of laughter before saying, 'You

205

could call it that, although I'm sure there are those who would call it something else, something less pleasant.'

'I'm astonished,' Brunetti said. 'Why, she seems . . .'

' "Normal", did you want to say?' Veltrini asked.

'Well,' Brunetti mumbled. 'Perhaps it's better to say that I thought of her as a professional woman, and such unseemly conduct . . .' Try as he might, he failed to keep his disapproval from his voice.

'It didn't last long, let me tell you,' Veltrini said. 'I realized very soon what she was doing, and I soon put a stop to it.'

'I hope it wasn't . . .' Brunetti said.

'Oh no, hardly,' Veltrini said, sounding like a man who was familiar with this sort of problem. 'I simply said one day that I preferred to eat my lunch alone, that I had a lot of things to think about throughout the day, and that lunchtime was the only time I was free to be alone.'

Brunetti and Vianello both appeared to display sympathy with the awkwardness of the situation Veltrini had described. Brunetti shook his head in wonder, and Vianello made a clicking noise of disapproval with his tongue.

With no warning, Veltrini got to his feet

and reached out his hand. Surprised, Brunetti had no choice but to stand and shake the offered hand; so did Vianello. 'I'm glad I could be of help, Signori,' the lab director said, then turned and walked away.

As if uncertain how Veltrini had succeeded in leaving, Vianello asked, 'How'd he manage that?' When Brunetti didn't answer, the Ispettore asked, 'What now?'

Brunetti stood quietly for a moment, then reached down, picked up a cup and saucer and handed it to Vianello. He picked up the other two, then turned towards the counter. 'We go and talk to the waitress,' he said and started in her direction.

14

The woman pushed herself to her feet as they approached. Brunetti placed both cups on the counter; Vianello was quickly beside him and set down the third. 'Could we trouble you for two more, Signora?' Brunetti asked, adding, 'We have to go back to Venice, and I want to stay awake during the ride. The heat always makes me sleepy.'

She had been busy placing the cups and saucers into the rack of the dishwasher but looked up when he spoke and asked, her astonishment audible, 'Don't you have air conditioning in your car?' She stared at Brunetti, as one would at something that had fallen from the ceiling.

He smiled and said, 'Of course we have it, Signora. But I hate it; I'd rather have the windows open and try to stay cool with the breeze.'

She nodded; assured that she was not dealing with Someone Strange, both her voice and her face softened. 'It's one of the nice things about working here,' she said. 'They aren't crazy with the cold, so I don't have to go outside every half-hour to un-freeze myself.' She smiled then, and Brunetti saw that her smile, too, had unfrozen.

Vianello joined in easily, saying, 'I know how you feel, Signora. I spend the summer getting over colds and headaches and sore necks. No trouble in the winter, only in the summer from the air conditioning.'

She turned away from them, made the coffees, and set the cups in front of them. 'Talking to Dottor Veltrini, eh?' she asked with badly disguised curiosity.

Brunetti poured the sugar into his coffee. He picked up his spoon and, instead of stir-ring the coffee, tapped the back of it against his left palm. 'Strange fellow, I thought,' he said casually.

She nodded.

Brunetti shrugged and returned the spoon to his saucer. He turned to Vianello and said, 'What did you think, Lorenzo?'

Vianello finished his coffee and placed his cup in the saucer. 'No stranger than many we've talked to,' he answered and reached into his pocket. He put three Euros on the counter, at the sight of which the woman said, 'It's only two Euros, Signore.'

Vianello smiled. 'It's to make up for the way he spoke to you,' he said, nodding towards the door through which Veltrini had disappeared silently.

The waitress smiled in return and said, 'If I had a Euro for every time he's been rude to me, or the other women, I'd be rich.' She laughed after she said this, adding, 'But he's a poor thing, really, and we should be sorry for him, not make fun of him.' Her kindness sounded formulaic, the sort of thing one said to induce, even provoke, a question. Brunetti noticed that she swept all three coins into her hand.

' "Poor thing", Signora?' Brunetti asked, making no attempt to disguise his curiosity. 'I didn't find him *simpatico,* even though we spoke to him for — how long was it, half an hour?'

'More like twenty minutes,' she said, words that encouraged Brunetti.

'Well, you know him better than I do. I asked him for information. Maybe he just didn't have time to give me his life story,' he said, speaking in a tone that made a joke of what he said.

She pulled their cups and saucers towards her and said, 'Oh, you'd never get that from him. But you'd certainly get lots of talk about other people. And never anything

210

good,' she added, taking the cups and saucers and giving them a quick rinse before putting them in the dishwasher.

'True,' Brunetti said, as if realizing this only because she had pointed it out to them. 'He certainly didn't have much good to say about Dottoressa Ricciardi.'

'Oh, no; he can't stand her.'

'Why is that?' Vianello asked, drawn back into the conversation.

She had a moment of uncertainty before Vianello smiled and put on the face of the average man. His bland amiability worked its usual magic, and she relaxed and went on. 'He followed her around like a puppy for a few weeks, years ago, when she first came, before the operation.' They watched her looking across the room while thinking back to those times, and Brunetti realized what a strategic location she had: she'd see everyone and have time to gossip over coffee with them, as well.

'Operation?' he asked.

'For a slipped disc,' she said, shaking her head in an expression of sadness. 'Something went wrong, but no one ever admitted that. Anyway, she was still walking when she went in for the operation, but she came home on crutches, and now she needs a cane to walk.'

'Ah, the poor woman,' Vianello said.

'And when she came back?' Brunetti asked, hoping that she'd understand he was asking about how Veltrini behaved and not the woman.

'Oh, he was cured by then.'

This time it was Vianello who gave in to curiosity and asked, 'How did that happen?'

Fighting against a smile, she said, 'I was told that Dottoressa Ricciardi had cured him before the operation. Told him, right out, to leave her alone.'

Brunetti made a humming noise and turned to Vianello as if to ask him a question, but stopped himself just in time.

'What is it?' the woman asked. She had very bright eyes, birdlike in the speed with which they shot from face to face. When she saw that Brunetti was reluctant to answer, she switched her gaze to Vianello.

With seeming reluctance, the Ispettore said, careful to speak only after a long hesitation, 'He told us today that she was the one who showed interest.' He hadn't finished the sentence when she forced out a gruff noise resplendent with disbelief. Then, as if to show she didn't hold Vianello responsible for the remark, she said, 'And I'm Sophia Loren.'

Vianello smiled and said, 'I knew you

212

looked familiar, Signora,' at which she laughed aloud.

Suddenly curious, the woman asked, 'What else did he tell you?'

She had asked it of Vianello, who said, 'That the Dottoressa was interested in the man who died.'

'Vittorio?' she asked, then added, because these were strangers, 'Fadalto?'

Vianello nodded.

'Oh, he *is* a snake,' she whispered in a savage undertone.

Brunetti made himself sound surprised, almost shocked, by her vehemence. 'That's a strong opinion, Signora.'

'Not strong enough,' she answered instantly. Before she could say more than that, the door to the *cantina* opened, and three men entered. They went and sat at a table on the far side of the room. Brunetti and Vianello turned away from the counter and sat at a table nearby.

The waitress went over to the other men, exchanged a few words, and returned behind the counter, where she busied herself making three coffees. She pulled out a tray and set saucers on it, put the cups on them, added spoons and two pieces of cake, and took it over to the men at the table.

On her way back, she stopped at the table

where Brunetti and Vianello were sitting and said, 'I won't ask if you'd like another coffee, Signori.' Both of them smiled in relief; Brunetti asked for two glasses of *acqua minerale*. When she came back with their water, he stood and pulled out a chair. 'Can you join us for a moment, Signora?' he asked.

She gave a quick glance to the other table, then back to them. She sat and placed the empty tray in front of her, as if somehow to mark out territory, and said, speaking quickly, 'All of this is none of my business, Signori. But from what I saw, I believe it was Veltrini who bothered her. Fadalto was nothing more than a man trapped in sadness who found someone who would listen to him.' She nodded, as if to suggest her approval of such a thing.

For some time she said nothing, then she added, speaking slowly, working out how to say what she meant, 'Someone told me he spent a lot of time in her office.' Brunetti watched as memory came to her, causing her to glance nervously aside, as if she'd just now seen something she had overlooked and was uncertain about continuing.

'And between the two of them?' Vianello asked neutrally.

She hesitated a long time before she answered. 'Poor devils: she with her bad back and cane, and Vittorio with his wife in the hospice, and nothing that could be done about either thing. They needed the help of their . . .' she began and then hesitated before adding, 'friendship.' She paused, as if listening to that last word to see if it sounded correct. Apparently satisfied that it did, she pulled the tray towards her. 'If that's all, Signori, I'll go back to my work.'

She placed her palms flat on the table, getting ready to stand. 'Before you go, Signora,' Brunetti said, trying to sound like a friend, concerned for her peace of mind, 'is there anything else you'd like to tell us?' Even as he said it, he feared he had over-played his hand and had scared her off.

She looked at him, waited some time, and then said, 'One of the girls in Payroll told me she saw him come out of the Dottoressa's office, about a week before he died, and she said he looked upset. Like his old self.' She shook her head at this. 'He hadn't been like that for some time.'

Confused, Brunetti asked, 'Like what, Signora?'

'Like he could be. In the past. Before his wife got sick,' she said. Seeing Brunetti's re-action, she went on, 'He had a temper, always had to be right in what he did or said. I saw it happen a few times; it could

215

be embarrassing.' She paused to allow memory to come, then said, 'I saw him in here one day, with a colleague. They were sitting together for lunch. I saw it start. The other man — he doesn't work here any more: he got a better job — he and Fadalto started arguing about something, and the first thing you know, Fadalto was on his feet. He slammed his chair back in place and walked out.'

'Did anything come of this?' Vianello asked.

She shrugged. 'I never saw them together again, and no one ever said anything about it, but I know — you know how it is when you watch people all the time — that some people were always a bit cautious with him.'

Suddenly, as if she'd tuned in to herself and heard what she was saying, she added, 'But I have to say he changed when his wife got sick. People noticed it, too, and things were easier here for him.'

'Why was that, do you think?' Vianello said.

'Because he was suffering, and people are always kind to people who are in pain,' she said simply. Aware that the other men were leaving, she pushed herself upright and, careful to take the tray with her, walked over to their table.

Brunetti made no attempt to stop her. She stacked the cups and plates on the tray and walked back to the serving counter, went behind it, and disappeared into an opening on the left that must lead to the kitchen.

They got to their feet and returned to the violence of the day and their icy ride back to Venice.

The evening temperature showed no mercy. The thought of taking the Number One was unbearable: he'd walk back home by way of the Frari, while Vianello, lucky devil, could take the 5.2 and walk home from San Pietro di Castello. They parted at the car that had brought them back, having discussed — to no conclusion — what they'd been told while in the *cantina*.

Brunetti arrived home a bedraggled remnant of the man who had left that morning. He hated his suit, his shoes, his tie, all the things that had constricted him and trapped him, always upping the temperature until he wanted to do nothing but shower, wrap himself in a fresh towel, and go and sit on the terrace with a glass of white wine. No, he realized as he got to the fourth floor, a glass of water, plain water, no bubbles, with moisture condensing on the outside of the tall glass.

Who was it that Dante tortured with thirst? A maker of false coins? Master Someone: he was sure of at least that, but he remembered no more than the man's mad craving for even a drop of water.

He entered the apartment and, not bothering to see who else was home, kicked off his shoes and went to the bedroom, where he freed himself of his jacket, tie, and damp shirt, removed his socks and trousers and walked down to the bathroom.

Fifteen minutes later, a different, calmer man emerged and, wrapped in an enormous white towel, went back to the bedroom, where he ignored the limp clothing still littering the bed. He changed into loose linen trousers that tied with a string and a light blue linen shirt that hung outside the trousers. He picked up the towel and returned to the bathroom, which now had the humidity of a sauna. He draped the towel over a rack and opened the window wide, then left, this time also leaving the door open.

In the kitchen, he opened a bottle of mineral water and drank two large glasses, then took bottle and glass to the living room and set them on the table in front of the sofa. He toyed for a moment with the idea of going back to the bedroom to pick up his copy of Dante but, accepting the certainty that he was there to take a nap and not to read, he abandoned the idea and sat, then lay, on the sofa. The last thing he remembered was seeing that the window to the terrace was open, which meant someone else was home, but then he ceased to see or understand his surroundings, and his spirit disappeared.

Voices sounded, and Brunetti listened. One said, 'Guido is down here somewhere.' And then two others began an argument, and Brunetti moved closer to them in order to hear, entirely fascinated at the sound of them.

But then his Master spoke and told him how angry he would become should Brunetti remain there, listening to these creatures argue, and he awoke from his dream, still hearing the spectral voice of Virgil and astonished that the memory should be so deeply embedded, even after all these years.

He lay still to await the return of reality, staring at the ceiling and suddenly thinking it was time to get the room painted. That seemed enough evidence of reality, so he reached out his right arm in search of the bottle. No luck. He turned to look for it and, beyond it, saw Paola sitting on a chair, watching him.

219

'You been there long?' he asked.

'Ten minutes. No longer.'

'Reading?' he asked.

She held up her hands. Empty.

Paola sitting in a chair and not reading? Perhaps reality had not fully returned.

'Then what were you doing?'

'Watching you sleep.'

'You get that for free every night,' Brunetti reminded her.

'The way I sleep? The only way that could happen is if you shook me and woke me up, but then you wouldn't be sleeping.'

'You see anything special?' he asked.

'No.'

Remembering that he'd left his watch somewhere, Brunetti asked, 'What time is it?'

'Eight-thirty.'

'Does that mean dinner's ready?'

Paola bent forward and buried her face in her hands. 'You are a monomaniac, Guido.'

'For what?' he asked with limpid innocence.

She laughed and shook her head. 'I've never known anyone who loves to eat as much as you do.'

He shrugged, which was not easy to do when lying down. 'My mother always rewarded us with food.'

She laughed again. 'Is that how I reward you?' she asked, joking.

'Dearest heart,' Brunetti said, 'you reward me by sitting and watching me sleep.'

She sank down in the chair and gave him a long speculative look. 'It just occurs to me that I never know, when you say things like that, whether you mean them or you're speaking in code. Or what you really mean.'

'They usually mean that I love you,' Brunetti said. 'But this one also means I'm hungry.' Before she could ask, he added, 'And that part's not in code.' That said, he got to his feet and headed towards the kitchen.

15

The next morning, just as he turned into the *riva* leading to the Questura, Brunetti saw Griffoni arriving from the direction of Il Ponte dei Greci. He reached the entrance first and stepped into what shade it offered. He noticed that the door was open, a warm breeze flowing from it. The guard stood inside but to the left of the door, out of the breeze, which Brunetti judged hot enough to dry beef.

Griffoni, he was troubled to see, did not look well, even at this distance. Her face seemed sun-starved, and her hair, pulled back from her face, seemed oily and would certainly be unpleasant to the touch. As she neared the door, he saw that her eyes looked dry and lifeless.

'*Come stai,* Claudia?' he asked, trying to mask his concern under an ordinary greeting.

'Not so good,' she said, passing into the

Questura and stopping a few metres beyond the guard. 'I mean I'm fine: I feel all right today, but I had to go home early yesterday.' He nodded in understanding, and she went on. 'It's been hard to sleep the last two nights: I kept seeing her and you, and hearing her.'

Brunetti wondered if he too looked like the survivor of troubled nights. He had tried to keep Signora Toso alive and lost her, but he had not formed a bond with her before she died: Claudia had. Claudia had spoken to her, held her hand, called her 'Benedetta', touched her arm while Signora Toso spoke the few words she gave them. He had tried to keep her alive, and failed, but it was Claudia who had lost her.

'It's difficult,' she said, although it hardly needed saying. 'I keep trying to make sense of what she told us, and then I start thinking about the girls.'

'You shouldn't be here today,' Brunetti said.

She made a noise, leaving it to him to interpret its meaning.

'Let's see what Signorina Elettra's found,' he suggested, hoping it would help them to keep busy.

She looked at him directly, making no attempt to hide her surprise, nor to move.

'The other day it sounded like you were fed up with this whole thing, and now you're interested.'

Brunetti offered no defence, no explanation. He was embarrassed to say he'd made a promise to the dying woman or that having his hands on her heart at the moment of her death had changed everything. Because he didn't understand this, he could hardly explain it to her.

In the face of his continuing silence, Griffoni went on. 'Think about it, Guido: she knew she was dying, she knew she didn't have much time. So why was it so important to talk to the police? What did she think? Or know? Or,' she began and paused, as if waiting for the right words to come. They did. 'What did she have?'

Brunetti didn't want to discuss this here, in the entrance hall, where anyone could pass by and hear what they said. 'Let's go and see what she's found,' he said again. By a conscious effort of will, he kept himself from putting his hand on her arm to calm her.

'Before we do, Guido,' Griffoni said, her impatience audible, 'let's decide whether you're interested in what she's found. Or even if you believe she could have found something. Or that there was something to find.' She started up the stairs: Brunetti, caught off guard by her severity, was slow in following and caught up with her only on the first landing.

Hoping to calm her, he said, 'I've already been out to the place where he worked.'

That stopped her. He watched her absorb it and then consider it. She leaned back against the wall, arms and ankles crossed. The first thing Brunetti noticed was that she looked much better. Her colour had improved, and her eyes were bright again. Relieved, he said, 'Let's see what Elettra's found, all right?'

'And if she hasn't found anything that jumps out of her computer with its hands in the air, screaming, "Murder, murder, murder," then what do you propose to do?'

'To take another look at the whole thing, adding in anything she's found and what I was told by the people where he worked.'

'Good,' she said and gave a small grin that managed to calm them both even more. 'Let's see,' she said and started up the second flight of stairs.

'Ah, good morning,' Signorina Elettra said, smiling in welcome as they entered her office. Then, to Griffoni, whom she obviously had not seen since Signora Toso's death, she added, 'I'm terribly sorry about what happened.'

Griffoni nodded her thanks but failed to speak. Instead, she raised a hand and threw open her palm, as if to release the dead woman's spirit into the air.

The three of them remained silent for enough time to allow that spirit to escape the room, when Signorina Elettra said, 'I've got his *telefonino* records going back a year from both his work phone and his *telefonino;* whom he called, who called him.' She picked up a sheaf of papers and handed it to Brunetti.

Griffoni, seeing the stack of papers, said, 'Good God, now that we carry phones around all the time, we spend our lives using them.' She moved closer to Brunetti as he leafed through the pages, but he turned them too quickly for her to grasp what was on them. Even before he was finished, she asked Signorina Elettra, 'Did you find the total number of calls to each person?'

Signorina Elettra said, 'There's a summary page with that information. Before that, the main list is chronological with the date and time of each call he made, the number called, and how long the calls lasted.' To forestall the inevitable next question, she said, 'The incoming calls are in a

226

separate list.'

Brunetti flipped over the final pages and found that she had also prepared a list of the most frequently called numbers: the first place was held by Fadalto's wife, whom he called every day, sometimes five or six times. Then came numbers identified as various phones at the clinics where his wife had been treated, and those of the doctors who had seen her, the numbers changing on the same day as she changed hospital, although the number of calls he made remained more or less the same. There were calls to the phone listed as that of his older daughter, Daria. In the last week of his life, he had called Dottoressa Donato at least twice a day.

There were regular calls to the landline of Maria Grazia Toso, Benedetta's sister, in whose care the girls had been placed.

In descending order of frequency, there were calls to various fellow employees — all identified, along with job title, by Signorina Elettra — of Spattuto Acqua. There were daily calls to the Ufficio Tecnico, sometimes frequent during a particular day, perhaps to report his changing location; there were calls to the laboratory at least once or twice a week; there was also a series of calls to Dottor Veltrini's *telefonino,* some of these made late in the evening. Towards the final pages were the numbers he called with no frequency, some of them a few times, some only once.

Brunetti found Dottoressa Ricciardi's number towards the bottom of the list: he had called her six times in three months, as many times as he had often called his wife in a single day.

'Who's Dottor Veltrini?' Griffoni asked, looking from the papers to Brunetti.

'He's the head of the laboratory at the place where Fadalto worked.'

'What did Fadalto do?' she asked.

'He was in charge of testing the water,' then, before she could ask, 'to see that no contaminants are in it, either bacterial or chemical.' He flipped back to an earlier page and said, 'I think it's the Ufficio Tecnico that takes care of the flow of the water, regardless of quality.'

'That's why he was in such steady contact with them and the laboratory?' Griffoni asked.

'Probably. If he's out in the field, taking samples, he might have questions for both places.'

She nodded, accepting the explanation.

Brunetti tapped at a name on one of the last pages and turned to Signorina Elettra,

'Why would he call the Ministero dell'Ambiente in Rome, and then call, in the following hour, four more phone numbers in the same Ministry?' He looked at the list again and added, 'He called them from his *telefonino,* not the office phone.'

'I saw that,' Signorina Elettra answered. 'He could have been asking them for information while he was out in the field.' She reached for the papers, and Brunetti passed them to her. She flipped ahead a few pages and pointed to two more listings. 'He called the office of Italia Nostra earlier this month, and then, immediately after he called them,' she continued, pointing to the time listed for the call, 'he called a private number listed for a dead man.'

'I beg your pardon,' Brunetti said.

'Well, the person in whose name the phone is listed — and who is still paying the bills — died three years ago.'

'It could be anyone, then,' Griffoni said, as easily as if she were finishing Signorina Elettra's sentence for her. 'I don't think anyone bothers to change the name any more, not if they have to pay to have the service terminated and then reconnected. Why bother?'

Neither Signorina Elettra nor Brunetti thought this question worthy of an answer.

'How did you find out he was dead?' he asked.

Before answering, Signorina Elettra returned to her chair, as if the nearness of her computer would add weight to whatever she said. 'First, I checked the Telecom files to find whose phone it is and where he lives, then I checked the Ufficio Anagrafe to see if he was still living at the same address, but he died three years ago.'

'Who's living there now?' Griffoni asked.

'His wife — widow — and a man who might be his son, Giacomo Braga, who has the same surname as the dead man.'

'Is the number here?' Brunetti asked.

'You mean, in the city?'

'Yes.'

'On the Giudecca,' Signorina Elettra said.

'Did you find anything about this . . .' Brunetti began, then looked at the paper again and said, 'Giacomo Braga?'

She smiled in return. 'There are seven pages of names, Dottore.'

'Of course, of course,' Brunetti said. Then, including Griffoni, he asked, 'Can we have another copy?'

'Of course, Signore,' she answered. 'I've already printed it out.' She picked up the papers from the other side of her desk and handed them to Griffoni.

Brunetti nodded his thanks, saying, 'We'll go and have a look at these.'

'Of course,' Signorina Elettra answered. 'Let me know if there is more I can do for you.'

'Perhaps you could find out which offices those phone are in, the ones at the Ministry of the Environment?'

'Of course, Signore,' she answered.

On the way to his office, Brunetti explained to Griffoni the probable importance of the dates when Fadalto had made the cash deposits that might have been his attempt to allow his wife another month in the private clinic. The first thing he did when he got to the office was slide his computer to the side and pile up and remove everything else from his desk. Then he unclipped the papers and set them out in a chronological row, running from left to right.

Griffoni understood instantly what he was doing and, on the other side of his desk, dealt out the pages of her copy in the same way. Both of them bracketed the calls made in the week before he had made the three deposits into his own account.

'He tried three banks,' Griffoni said, running her finger down the names of the places Fadalto had called.

'The first one is his own bank,' Brunetti said, remembering the name on Fadalto's financial records. 'He must have called the others when they refused him.'

'So much for customer loyalty from your friendly local banker,' she said.

Feeling awkward at having to defend the integrity of a bank, Brunetti said, 'If the person he spoke to had the records in front of him, they'd see that Fadalto had withdrawn almost all of his savings in the last two months. In fact, Fadalto might well have told them what he needed the money for.'

Griffoni glanced across at him and gave a slow shake of her head. 'Hearts of steel, banks,' she said and moved her attention to the time around Signora Toso's transfer from one clinic to another. Then she asked, 'How do we know which calls are important?'

'They'd probably be the anomalous ones, not to family or friends.'

'Well,' she said instantly, 'the calls to the Ministry of the Environment are certainly that.'

'And the one to Italia Nostra,' he said. Brunetti knew little about the environmental group, but the fact that so many people he disliked for political reasons spoke against it

232

had always prejudiced him in its favour.

He went and stood at the window, thinking about what made them both believe these particular calls were out of the ordinary, when they had little idea of what 'ordinary' calls, aside from those to his family or the clinic and hospice, would have been for Fadalto.

'How long after his call to Italia Nostra did he call this man on the Giudecca?'

Griffoni looked at the lists. 'Giacomo Braga,' she supplied, then added, 'One minute after he hung up.'

'That means they gave him the phone number.'

She nodded in agreement but said nothing. She lifted one of the papers and said, 'You want the number?'

Brunetti walked back to his desk and picked up the office phone: he dialled the numbers as Griffoni read them to him.

On the seventh ring, a man's voice said, 'Braga,' nothing more.

'Signor Braga, this is Commissario Guido Brunetti,' he said in Veneziano. 'I'm calling about a phone call made to this number by Vittorio Fadalto.' He took the paper Griffoni held out to him and added, 'On the fourth of July, at three-twenty-one in the afternoon.'

'Is that meant to be a threat of some sort?' the other man asked mildly.

'No, not at all, Signore,' Brunetti said. 'I mentioned it only to verify that we know Signor Fadalto made the call.'

'Then, since you must be the police, you must also know that Signor Fadalto is dead?'

'Yes, we do,' Brunetti answered in an even tone.

'So I could easily tell you he called to ask me to subscribe to *Il Gazzettino*?'

'Oddio,' Brunetti exclaimed with false astonishment, 'what a very unpleasant thing to say about a man who's no longer here to defend himself.'

The man let out a bark of laughter and then fell silent for so long that Brunetti was led to say, 'I didn't mean to be disrespectful of Signor Fadalto if he was a friend of yours.'

'No, as a matter of fact, he wasn't,' Braga said. Then, in an entirely sober voice, he added, 'But he might have become one.'

'Then I apologize for the remark,' Brunetti said, meaning it.

'There's no need to apologize, Commissario. We spoke only one time and not for very long.'

'Could you tell me about that conversation, Signor Braga?'

After a moment's hesitation, Braga said,

'Not on the phone.'

'Tell me if you'll meet me, and if you will, where and when?'

'Aren't the police supposed to order people around and threaten them that they'll have to come to the Questura when they're told to do so?'

'I think that happens primarily on television,' Brunetti suggested. 'Those of us who work here, in a building without air conditioning, are always looking for reasons to escape.'

'Would you be willing to come to the Giudecca?'

'Only if I can bring a colleague with me. She's Neapolitan, and I try to expose her to as much spoken Veneziano as I can in hopes that she'll blend in here.'

'I could meet you both at the Palanca in half an hour,' Braga said, but then, voice lighter, perhaps with the anticipation of being able to play a joke on the police, he added, 'but only if she's tall and blonde and beautiful.'

'We'll be there in half an hour,' Brunetti said in his most serious voice, then replaced the phone, and waved to Griffoni to show her they were leaving.

16

They caught a Number Two at Riva degli Schiavoni and arrived at Palanca exactly thirty minutes after Brunetti replaced the phone. Not for an instant did it occur to him that anyone would wait outside, either in the *embarcadero* or — more unthinkable — on the *riva*. He led Griffoni from the boat stop directly into the Palanca.

It had been months since he'd been to Giudecca and years since he'd been inside the bar, but the bar at least had not changed. The *tramezzini* he still remembered sat in a glass case, and tired men stood at the bar, drinking either coffee or white wine; even water.

Four women, one wearing an apron, sat at a table towards the back; three adolescent boys sat in a circle at a small round table, each looking at his smartphone, occasionally nudging one of the others and tipping his screen towards him; a solitary, white-

236

haired man was at a table in the back, a copy of the *Gazzettino* folded in front of him.

They approached him. Brunetti asked, 'Signor Braga?'

Braga got to his feet and held out his hand. Clean-shaven and very tall, he had a thick grey moustache and glasses with round metal frames of almost the same colour. He might have been in his early fifties, but he moved with the grace of a younger man. 'Commissario,' he said. 'Thank you for coming to meet me.' He spoke Italian, not Veneziano, but he spoke it with the cadence of the Northeast.

Griffoni extended her hand, saying, 'And thank you for speaking in Italian: it will make it much easier for me to follow.'

'And contribute, I hope,' Braga responded with an admiring smile.

She returned his smile, nodded, and said, 'How kind.'

Braga bent to pull out a chair for Griffoni, while Brunetti pulled out his own. As he recalled, the service at the Palanca kept to its own time zone, so he sat with his back to the bar, hoping that would slow things down even more.

'Shall I begin?' he asked after enough time had passed to show that Signor Braga was not going to speak.

Braga waved his hand.

'Vittorio Fadalto was killed in a traffic incident near Quarto d'Altino. His motorcycle went off the road and finished with its front wheel in a shallow canal at the side of the road: Signor Fadalto went into the water and drowned. His body was discovered some time later by a man who was driving past and saw the light of his motorcycle.'

Brunetti paused to see if Braga had any questions. When it seemed that he did not, he continued. 'The police have asked anyone who might have witnessed the incident to notify them, but no one has.'

A waiter walked past their table, not doing anything as peremptory as asking them if they'd like to order.

The surface of their table, Brunetti noticed, was empty: Braga had not yet requested anything. He looked at the others and asked, 'Shall we order?' It was hardly time for lunch, but he had always enjoyed the *tramezzini* here. The other two asked for coffee; Brunetti asked the waiter to bring a plate of *tramezzini:* any kind he pleased, and a bottle of mineral water and three glasses.

'What do you think happened?' Braga asked after the waiter had returned to the counter.

Brunetti pushed himself back from the table and crossed his legs. 'I have no idea of what actually happened, but I think there are possibilities.'

'Such as?' Braga asked.

'Fadalto was tired and lost control and drove off the road. Someone hit him and didn't notice. Someone hit him and panicked and drove off without stopping. Someone hit him and did stop, but when he saw the motorcycle and Fadalto in the water — if he could see that in the dark — he panicked and drove away. Or,' he added, 'someone followed him, and when they reached a place where there were no other cars on the road, he speeded up and turned into him and drove him off the road.'

Braga nodded; so did Griffoni.

'The last one needs a motive,' Braga said.

'That's what we're looking for,' Brunetti said.

'And you hoped I might provide it?' Braga asked calmly.

Griffoni broke in to say, 'Nobody "hopes" for something like that, Signore, at least neither the Commissario nor I.'

'Why not? It would justify your investigation.'

'There is no real investigation, not at the moment, Signor Braga,' she said, then, before he could protest, added, 'It's possible the conclusion will be that he lost control of the motorcycle.' When Braga did not comment, she added, 'Better for his children, for one thing.'

'I don't understand,' Braga said.

'Because they won't have to go through life suspecting that someone killed their father and didn't bother to stop or that someone wanted to kill their father and wondering why that was.' She waited for him to comment, and when he remained silent, she added, 'And their lives won't be contaminated by the desire for vengeance.'

Braga waved in Brunetti's direction and said, 'Your colleague said you're Neapolitan.' She nodded. 'I've always been told that people from the South sit around all the time, mulling over past injuries and lusting for vengeance.'

'And I've been told that we all beat our women and children and eat nothing but pasta and mozzarella.' She paused a few seconds before adding, 'With our hands.'

Braga smiled and was about to respond when the waiter arrived with their order on a large tray. He placed the coffees in front of those who'd ordered them, set the bottle in front of Brunetti and distributed the napkins, plates and glasses, then put a plate of *tramezzini* in the centre of the table. He went to the women at the other table and asked if they'd like anything else.

From the sides of the sandwiches spilled ham, egg, tomato, tuna salad, radicchio, ruccola, shrimp, artichokes, asparagus, and olives. Brunetti counted them: seven. Was the provocative extra meant to cause dissent, or was it a kind of reverse tip for which they would not be asked to pay?

He filled all three glasses and slid one over to Braga, then said, 'As you understood, we have a record of Signor Fadalto's calls from his *telefonino*. Earlier this month, he contacted the office of Italia Nostra and, less than a minute after finishing his call with them, called you.' He paused, but when Braga did not respond, Brunetti went on. 'Unless he knew you before this and had your number, I'd guess they gave him your number and he called you directly.'

Braga picked up the glass and circled it with both hands. 'That's correct: they gave him the number. He called me after speaking to them.'

This time, it was Griffoni who broke the ensuing silence. 'Why did he call you?'

Braga set the glass down without drinking and turned to her to say, 'I'm a journalist. Or, rather, I was a journalist until two years ago, when I was fired.' He gave a one-sided grin, adding, 'It's incorrect to say I was fired: my contract simply was not renewed.'

'For whom did you write?' she asked.

Braga mentioned one of the national news magazines, known for its left-leaning politics, much given to exposure and denunciation.

'What happened?' Griffoni asked.

Braga pulled the plate of *tramezzini* closer and took one without bothering to see what sort it was. He bit off one corner and grabbed up a napkin to wipe his mouth, then set his coffee cup aside and placed the rest of the sandwich on the saucer. 'I overestimated them, I'm afraid. After years of working for them, I should have seen how much more shocking the headlines were than the stories that followed.'

He shrugged and took another sip of water. 'But I was a true believer and ignored that, as I ignored a number of other things.' He reached for his sandwich but drew his hand back and pushed himself farther into his chair.

'I wrote an article about the lack of success in prosecuting the company that owns the factory that polluted the groundwater near Verona: I named the company, since it was already named in court documents.' He took a long drink of water and finished his sandwich.

'Two weeks later, I was told that my contract would not be renewed because my position was being eliminated.'

When he said nothing else, Brunetti asked, 'I'm not sure I see cause and effect here.'

Braga gave a radiant smile. 'Which is exactly what my union steward said.'

Griffoni asked, 'Would you tell us what the reason was?'

He smiled across at her and raised his glass to salute her. After finishing it, he set it quietly on the table and said, 'I later learned that the conglomerate that owned the factory accused of having contaminated the water also owns the three chief advertisers in the magazine.' His smile was still there, but it had dimmed.

'When I pointed this out to my union, they said they did not see a connection.' He shrugged and tried to smile again, but when that failed, he bent his head to study the plate of *tramezzini* and chose another.

Brunetti waited until Griffoni had taken one and took one for himself. The three of them ate in silence until Griffoni set hers on the edge of her plate and said, 'Did Signor Fadalto call you about the article?'

'He'd read the article and asked me if I was still working on the same subject.'

'Water contamination?' Brunetti asked but only to make it clear to all of them.

'Yes,' Braga said. 'He asked me if I planned to write more about the subject.' He pulled the bottle towards him and, seeing that their glasses were still full, added water to his own.

Neither of them spoke.

'I told him I was no longer working. Because we'd never met, he had no idea how old I was, so he asked if I'd retired. It was the obvious question, I suppose. Two years had passed, after all. I told him no, I'd been fired for having written the article he'd read, and there was no chance I could get any article published after so long a time.'

'How did he react?' Griffoni asked.

'At first he was very angry, but I told him there was no use for anger any more: it wouldn't help. He quietened down when I told him that and asked me if I'd reconsider. When I said that there was nothing to reconsider because nothing would get me my job back, he thanked me for my time and hung up.'

'Did you hear from him again?' Griffoni asked.

'No.'

'How did you learn that he had died?' Brunetti asked.

'I may not be a journalist any more, but I still read the papers and magazines,' Braga answered. 'And you know how the *Gazzettino* loves these stories about possible hit-and-run drivers.' After a moment's reflection, he added, 'Though they usually prefer the ones where it's a child or a grandmother who dies.'

'That's all he asked you — if you'd write another article?' Brunetti asked.

'Yes.'

'Nothing about who he was or what he was doing?'

'Nothing,' Braga said.

'Strange,' Griffoni said, almost to herself.

Braga shook his head. 'It's not strange at all.' Having got their attention with that, he continued. 'He had a purpose when he made the call: to interest me in whatever information he had about water contamination — why else would he ask me if I was going to write another article? And when I said I was not, he no longer had any interest in me because I couldn't be of use to him. So he hung up.' He sipped at his water, set the glass on the table and said, 'It's exactly what I spent my life doing: I found out if people could be useful to whatever story I was writing, and if they weren't, I didn't waste their time or my own.'

Griffoni leaned across the table and tapped his forearm. 'Is that a suggestion that we stop asking questions and leave?' she asked in a friendly voice.

Braga laughed. 'Good heavens, no. Quite the opposite: I was trying to tell you that you don't have any obligation to stay here and talk to me any longer. I'm sure you have more important things to do.'

'Talking to you is important,' Brunetti said. 'It shows us what Fadalto might have been thinking or planning.' He saw no reason not to show his trust in Braga, especially since he wanted to know what the other man thought or suspected about Fadalto.

Griffoni asked, 'How did you hear about the factory in your article?'

Braga planted his elbows on the table and rubbed at both sides of his forehead with his fingers. 'My wife's sister lives out there, and one of her grandchildren has this PFAS thing in his blood. When she told us about it, years ago, she said the factory had been closed for ages, but the stuff was still in the ground and in the water table. A lot of the local kids have it in their blood.' He sank his chin into his hands and said nothing more.

'Is he ill?' Griffoni asked.

'He's been tested for a lot of things. He catches colds easily and doesn't seem to have any energy or resistance to sore throats. He gets sick a lot and can't go to school. But it's not as if there's proof that PFAS is the cause.'

Looking down at the surface of the table, he shook his head a few times. 'It's said to affect adults, too. Hormones, I think. But you know how cautious they are about saying that anything is dangerous: how long did it take them to tell us about cigarettes?' He shook his head, as if to pull himself back to the original question.

'Even though I wrote the article and read everything I could about it, I can't say that it's the cause. No, wait a moment,' he said, waving both his hands in the air as if to prevent a cart from hitting him. 'I can't say it with any scientific certainty, but so many kids — and not only the kids — in the area have the same problems that it's got to be the reason. If we knew for sure, they'd be called symptoms, but all we can do is call them problems.'

He moved his glass a bit to the left, then put his hands in his lap. 'What are the people in all those small towns and villages supposed to do? Quit their jobs and abandon their homes and start a new life somewhere else?' Then, suddenly unable to contain his anger, he asked, 'How are they supposed to pretend they don't know their children are being killed?' That last question seemed to exhaust him and he said, tiredly, 'When I was out there, people told me that even their dogs are sick.'

Brunetti pushed his saucer away from him, no longer interested in the sandwich; Griffoni did the same.

Braga surprised them both by getting to his feet. He leaned towards them and shook their hands with great formality. 'Thank you for listening to me. I wish I could tell you more about Signor Fadalto: it might make it easier for you to draw the connection you seem to want to, but I've told you everything that was said in our conversation, which was very brief.'

They both stood, as well; Braga did not wait to see what they were going to do but walked to the counter and spoke to the man behind the bar. Then he turned to the door and left, not looking back at them.

They finished the water in their glasses, made thirsty by the sandwiches. Their agreement to leave was silent. Brunetti went to the bar and pulled out his wallet, but the man behind the bar held up his hand, palm towards him, and said, 'It's been paid, Signore.'

'I didn't want that,' Brunetti protested, troubled that Braga had paid. He, who considered the lack of generosity the worst of vices, had a horror of not being the one to pay a bill, something he had learned by observing his father who, poor as he was, considered it a dishonour not to pay for a coffee, a drink, or a meal.

He went back to the table and put a five-Euro note under the unfinished plate of *tramezzini*. If he couldn't pay, he could at least over-tip.

17

As they sat in the nearly empty *embarcadero,* waiting for the Number Two that would take them to the other side of the Canale della Giudecca, Brunetti looked at his watch and saw that it was just after eleven.

Looking at Griffoni, he asked, 'Is it time to talk to her sister?' He had avoided it, no doubt from emotional cowardice. Not by accident had he proposed to do the interview while he was with Griffoni. They had been together in situations of great physical danger, yet it was her grace in dealing with people who'd come untethered in reaction to loss or betrayal that had impressed, and steadied, him most. Just about everyone had invaded or conquered Napoli, he thought, so she could easily be the descendant of some Viking warrior, his valour enriched over the centuries and transmuted into moral courage.

'I was waiting for you to decide it was,' she answered, her eyes studying the façades of the *palazzi* on the opposite side of the Canal.

Silenced by that, Brunetti took out his notebook, found the number of Maria Grazia Toso, and dialled it.

After only a few rings, a woman's voice answered. *'Pronto.'*

'Signora Toso?'

'Sì.'

'Signora, this is Commissario Guido Brunetti. I spoke to your sister before her death, and I'd like to speak to you about some of the things she told me before that sad event.' Even to him, it sounded stilted and artificial; a glance at Griffoni's face showed him that she thought so, too.

The woman said nothing, so Brunetti went on. 'I'd like to clarify some of them, and I'd also like to speak to you about her late husband, Vittorio Fadalto.'

'She's not even buried,' she said in a voice suddenly grown harsh, 'and he's already causing her trouble. Wonderful.'

Brunetti waited for her to say more, but she did not. 'It's precisely about this that I'd like to talk to you, Signora,' he said calmly.

'About what?'

251

'The trouble he caused her.'

'Why do you say that?' she asked, her curiosity audible.

'From some of the things she said, I suspected it, although your sister never said anything directly.'

She gave a pained choking noise that sounded to Brunetti like an attempt at laughter. 'Well, that's certainly Benedetta, isn't it? Loyal to the end.'

'I can't say, Signora,' Brunetti said. 'I knew her only a short time, spoke to her only twice.'

After an even longer silence, the woman said, 'Call me back in ten minutes,' and broke the connection.

When Brunetti put his phone in his pocket, Griffoni removed her attention from the façades and asked, 'Well?'

'She told me to call her back in ten minutes.'

Griffoni looked to the right, to the vaporetto approaching from the Redentore stop. 'By the time that gets here and we get to the other side, it will be time to call her,' she said and got to her feet.

Brunetti joined her and waited for the boat, boarded it after her. Griffoni, he noticed, was again entranced by the buildings on the other side. 'We never see anything like that,' she said. 'We can see buildings along the water when we approach by boat, but there's a road with cars and a beach filled with people in front of them, so they never look like real apartments where people live.' She raised her arm and pointed ahead. 'But here they look like buildings on a normal street, as if there were identical ones facing them on the opposite side of the street. Only the street's water.' She shook her head in bemusement. 'And no cars.'

She turned to Brunetti and said, 'I'm used to that now: no cars. No noise, no horns, no *motorini.*' This time she shrugged to emphasize her words. 'Now, when I go back to Naples, I can't stand the noise and the confusion.' Before he could correct her, she said, 'I know, I know, there's too many people here, but there's no noise.' She said this as would a believer at the first sight of the towers of Jerusalem.

'Did you realize, Claudia,' Brunetti asked, 'a year ago, you would have said, "when I go home".'

Her hand reached towards her mouth, but she stopped it in time and grabbed his arm, 'Don't tell my mother.'

Their vaporetto banged against the landing at the Zattere, and Griffoni joined the people getting off. She waited on the embankment for Brunetti to join her. He took out his phone and pushed 'redial' and then turned on the speaker to allow Griffoni to listen.

'Signor Brunetti?' Signora Toso asked when she picked up the phone.

'Sì.'

'I called Dottoressa Donato.'

Resisting the temptation to tell her he thought that was what she'd do, Brunetti contented himself with a soft, 'Ah.'

'She said I can trust you and your Neapolitan colleague.'

'That's very flattering,' Brunetti said, glancing at Griffoni, who gave a thumbs-up signal. 'To have the respect of a woman like that.'

'What do you want to know?' she asked, sounding hurried.

'I think, Signora, that this is not a conversation to have over the phone. Would it be possible for us to come and talk to you, or meet somewhere, if that would be more convenient for you?'

After a pause, she asked, 'Will this help the girls? Whatever I tell you?' Her voice was urgent, worried.

He glanced at Griffoni, who held her hand out, palm down, and flapped it quickly.

254

'It depends on what you tell us, Signora, and on what else we learn. We haven't excluded the possibility that Signor Fadalto was deliberately killed. You're the only person who can judge how this would affect his daughters.'

There was no response. The silence went on for a long time.

Griffoni stepped towards him and wrapped the phone in her hands, making a sandwich of it. 'Tell her Fadalto was working in a good cause,' she said in a low voice and removed her hands.

'Signora, both of us believe he was doing something he thought was good.'

Her reply was instant. 'Men usually do.'

Brunetti was left with no response. 'May we come and talk to you, Signora?'

'Where are you?'

'At the Zattere stop.'

'I live near Tonolo,' she said, naming the legendary *pasticceria*. 'Go past it, over Il Ponte del Chewing Gum. Third house on the left, number forty-two.'

'And the name on the bell?' he asked.

'Toso,' she said and broke the connection.

Brunetti turned to Griffoni to see what she thought and was surprised by her question. 'Guido, how in God's name could I find that house?'

Surprised, Brunetti responded, 'She just told you.'

She looked at him, then tilted her head, first right, then left, the way a curious, or confused, bird would. 'Tonolo,' she repeated. 'All right, I know where that is. I love their pastries. But I don't have an idea about the Bridge of Chewing Gum.'

Brunetti had known it forever: the bridge leading from the University to Piazzale Roma, where students who lived on the mainland went to get their buses home and where, it seemed, many of them stuck their chewing gum on the underside of the railing. Rather than try to explain the reason, he contented himself with saying, 'It's what we call the bridge after Tonolo, the one on the way to Piazzale Roma.'

She walked out of the *embarcadero;* he followed into the battering sunlight. She stood on the pavement, looking down towards San Basilio. 'I'd guess that way,' she said, pointing towards the port.

'Yes, but not along the *riva,* not at this hour,' he said. 'We'd fry.'

He led her towards the bridge but did not cross it, turned right along the canal to the second bridge, left, narrow street, canal popping up from nowhere on the right, another bridge into an underpass, Griffoni

256

following close behind like a weak-sighted servant of the Three Kings, unable to see the star. Brunetti never paused, began to swivel his body a half-step before he reached the corner where he had to turn, glanced across canals at the buildings on the other side, slowed to watch a cormorant dive under the water, and kept going. They crossed Campo San Barnaba, down to Campo Santa Margherita, over yet another bridge, and immediately another to the left, then down to the end and again left, and when they stopped, they were in front of a building with the number forty-two above the door.

He rang the bell, Griffoni motionless with surprise. After a moment, the door opened and they went in. When they reached the third floor, a tall, thin woman with shoulder-length dark hair stood in one of two doorways, the door open behind her. 'I'm Maria Grazia Toso,' she said, holding out her hand. She shook Griffoni's and then Brunetti's and asked them to come inside.

If a painter had done a portrait of Benedetta Toso's face, the finished painting would surely have recalled the beauty of her un-ravaged youth. If he had painted this woman, the features would have been less well defined. Brunetti had no idea whether she was younger or older than her sister, nor could he estimate how many years separated them, but there was no doubt that they were sisters: the eyes and mouth told him that.

Both visitors asked permission before stepping through the door. The first thing Brunetti noticed was the temperature, for the apartment seemed hotter than it had been outside, though that might have been no more than their response to having climbed the stairs.

He was facing the back of the building; from the large windows at the end of the long hallway he saw, looking over the roofs of three short buildings that must run along the nearside of Rio San Pantalon, part of the tower in Campo Santa Margherita and the rooftops surrounding the *campo.* Because he saw them through a series of windows framed in wood, it seemed at first like an enormous *trompe l'oeil,* and it was only by looking carefully that he saw it was nothing more than the normal beauty of the city.

Given the reason that had brought them here, he could not compliment Signora Toso on the beauty of the view and instead entered the room into which she led them and looked around for a place where they might sit and talk.

At first he couldn't believe what he saw. The floor was covered with a light-coloured plastic laminate that didn't even bother to pretend it was wood. An obese green velvet sofa stood just in front of the window, turned away and looking back into the room, where it faced three red plastic chairs. The sideboard was also plastic, dark, with ferocious thin black metal legs.

There were reproductions of paintings on the walls: the Van Gogh sunflowers; one of Vermeer's waiting women; a Rembrandt portrait of an old woman; and, much to his surprise, *The Raft of the Medusa*. Brunetti felt sorry for the people in the last, that they had survived the sinking only to spend the rest of their lives looking at that sofa.

It was all very clean; the glass knick-knacks on the plastic cabinet against the far wall glittered in the light that flooded into the apartment. Three sad-faced glass tore-adors waved their glass capes in the same light.

He took a seat on one of the chairs, thus forcing Signora Toso to sit opposite him. Griffoni took the chair next to him.

'I want to thank you for agreeing to talk to us, Signora,' he began formally and took his notebook from his inside pocket.

'Could you tell me what you want to know?' she asked, sounding more abrupt than she had on the phone.

'I'd like to know anything you can tell me about Signor Fadalto,' Brunetti answered.

She waited some time before answering. 'I knew him for more than fifteen years. That's a lot of knowing.' She spoke in a level tone that gave no indication of the feelings that prompted the response.

Brunetti saw the strain in her face as she answered; her mouth pulled itself in each time she paused in speaking, as if to prevent herself from saying too much or telling a lie.

'I know about him only by speaking to the people with whom he worked,' he explained, saying nothing about having seen his employment records.

'And my sister, didn't she tell you anything about him?' He listened for positive or negative verbal clues in this question, but he detected none.

'By the time I spoke to her, she was too sick to say more than a few words at a time, Signora. She told me only that her husband had had something to do with "bad money" and that "they" killed him, although she didn't make it clear whom she was talking about.' To say something that might bring

260

solace, he added, 'Her last thought was for her girls.'

'What do you mean?' she asked. 'Dottoressa Donato didn't say anything about this.'

Griffoni broke in to explain. 'The last time we saw her, there was a sound at the door, and she thought it was the girls.' Signora Toso's face grew calm at this. 'But it was Dottoressa Donato.'

Brunetti cast his memory back to that scene and tried to recall the expression on Benedetta Toso's face when she spoke of the girls, but he recalled seeing no happiness, only resistance to pain. But Griffoni had been closer, so she must have seen.

His thoughts were interrupted by the dead woman's sister, who said, 'Good. She's been a friend to us both.' Then, sadly, 'To all four of us.'

'How are they?' Griffoni interrupted to ask.

'Orphans,' she answered, then put her hand to her mouth and whispered, *'Scusate, scusate.'* Her hands sought out one other and locked themselves together on her lap. 'It's very difficult. At the moment.'

'They're staying with you, aren't they?' Griffoni asked.

For the first time, Signora Toso gave something resembling a smile. 'Luckily. My

261

husband and I could never have children, so we've always been very close to them. And they to us.' Then, as if superstition warned her against saying anything else about this, she repeated, 'It's a blessing. For us all. They're young, and we can only hope that . . .' Her voice trailed off at the enormity of the task of naming what hope she had in mind for them.

With this talk of the girls, Brunetti realized, the mood had changed and the original tension had ebbed from the room. She was a woman of sorrow and acquainted with grief; no wonder she did not welcome the police into her home.

'Could you tell us more about Signor Fadalto?' Brunetti asked, suddenly aware of how little he understood the man about whom they had been speaking.

'He was a good father,' she answered immediately. 'The girls adored him as much as they did their mother. So these weeks, when first he, and then she . . . left them have been terrible.'

'Have they changed?' Griffoni asked.

'Livia — she's only twelve — doesn't want to go out much any more. I have to take them out to Lido to go swimming or arrange for them to visit friends. Daria's older — she's fourteen; I try to get her to see her friends, but she doesn't want to talk to them or have much to do with people.' Then, after a pause, she corrected that to, 'Except me and Livia, that is.'

She explained, 'It started with their father's death. They knew where their mother was and what that meant, not that you can ever prepare for death, not really.' She let that hang in the air for a moment and then added, 'Especially if you're a child.'

She sighed deeply and turned to look out the window. Brunetti couldn't stop asking himself if she even noticed the beauty of the scene, but called himself back from this speculation to say, 'It's unimaginable.' He raised his hands helplessly and could say only, 'I'm sorry.'

Signora Toso tried and failed to smile. 'Thank you,' she said.

Before the silence between them expanded to make further questions impossible, Griffoni said, 'Your sister really did tell us those things: about "bad money" and that someone killed him. Can you think of anything that could explain this?'

This time Signora Toso closed her eyes: Brunetti was uncertain whether she did this to concentrate her attention or to block out possibilities, or perhaps to stop herself from saying what she knew. She pulled her lips together, and Brunetti thought she was going to cry. Time passed and she said, voice very soft, 'She told me the same things.'

After some time, Griffoni asked, 'Did you believe her?'

The Signora shook the possibility away with her head, grabbing her legs just above the knees and squeezing them. 'Of course not,' she said adamantly. 'I didn't and I don't.'

'Then why would she have said such things?' Griffoni asked, managing to sound confused.

'Drugs,' came the answer, too loud. 'You were with her. You know what state she was in. It wasn't my sister lying in that bed: it was someone who'd been heavily drugged for a long time.' She tried to calm herself by taking deep breaths and said, 'Vittorio would have nothing to do with "bad money", no matter what it means.' She thought for a while and continued. 'You can say many things about him, but not that.'

'We were told that he was quick-tempered,' Griffoni said, making it sound almost a compliment.

'It's true,' Signora Toso said with no hesitation. 'He was a perfectionist. In everything: his work, the girls' homework, whether the doctors were doing the right thing for Benedetta, how fast other people should drive on the autostrada. Everything had to be the way he thought it should be.' Before either of them could ask, she added, 'If not, he lost his temper and told them. Or if he saw someone doing something wrong: smoking in a restaurant, getting on the vaporetto without a ticket — things like that — he'd stop them and tell them they couldn't do that. He couldn't accept dishonesty, no matter how minor.' She stopped again and finally said, 'I think I exaggerated on the phone. The only person he caused trouble for was himself.' Then, after a very long pause, she said, 'Sorrow leads to anger, I'm afraid.' Brunetti chose to take this as an explanation of her own behaviour as much as of her brother-in-law's, and smiled to acknowledge it as such.

She looked at her hands again and then said, as if she were talking to them and not to Brunetti, 'He tried to stop doing it, reacting like that, especially in the last year, when he saw how it affected Benedetta.' She raised her hands and let them fall back on to her lap. 'He did stop it with her and with the girls and,' she added, sounding almost guilty, 'with us.' Finally, as if to set Fadalto free of the accusation entirely, she added, 'He was a good man.'

'Was he a good husband?' Griffoni asked. Brunetti instantly wondered how Paola would answer that question, were it ever put to her.

'I think so. Yes.' Then, to explain, she went on. 'He was honest in everything he did and taught this to the girls. He did his best to control his temper, and in his last months he succeeded. He was trustworthy.' At the edge of this list, Brunetti heard the small voice of 'but' trying to push itself into the conversation. Better to leave it there and not call attention to it by asking a question, he decided.

'And he loved Benedetta beyond words or thought. That's why I think you're both wasting your time here, Commissario,' she said.

'I beg your pardon?' Brunetti asked.

'You're here because you think he was killed. Murdered. Aren't you?'

Before either of them could think of answering, she continued. 'There's something you should know.' Her voice sounded broken, as if they'd beaten her to the point where she had to say this. 'A week before he died, he told me he didn't want to live without her.' This time, she raised her hand to stop them from interrupting. 'I told him he couldn't do that to the girls, but he said his life was hell: he said he'd destroyed everything between them and become a liar and a cheat, and he couldn't bear it.'

Her voice changed and Brunetti heard the threat of tears. 'I told him not to be a fool, that one dead parent was more than enough for them to have to endure.' She shook her head as at the memory of something stupid she had done. 'I told him to leave, that I wouldn't listen to such talk. And,' she added, suddenly looking across at them, 'a week later he was dead.'

18

Into their silence came the sound of a closing door. A girl's voice called down the hall, *'Zia Maria Grazia, siamo qua.'* Both Brunetti and Griffoni turned in their chairs and saw them arrive, a tall girl with her mother's eyes and nose and a shorter one who had the same vagueness of feature as had her aunt. They wore jeans, cleaned and pressed and with no open holes cut in them, and T-shirts, Livia's with horizontal stripes, Daria's vertical, as if reflecting the difference in age and height.

They stood stock still at the door, unable to hide their surprise at the sight of strangers. 'Come inside and say hello,' Signora Toso said. 'This is Dottoressa Griffoni and Dottor Brunetti: they've come to tell me how sorry they are about what's happened. They knew your mother.'

The older one, Daria, said, 'I don't remember either of you.'

Both got to their feet, and Griffoni said, 'We aren't old friends. We met your mother only at the end of her life. We also met Dottoressa Donato.' The girl's posture relaxed at the name of the doctor, and her gaze grew less intense. 'We wanted to do as your aunt said, come and tell you how very sorry we are. She was very brave, your mother, and even when she was very near the end, she could still make people laugh. Especially Dottoressa Donato.'

Livia came alert at that. 'Did Mamma tell jokes?'

'No, but she asked the doctor how she was, and she answered, "fat".'

'But then the doctor made the joke,' Daria said.

'But Mamma made the joke possible,' Livia insisted, to Brunetti quite reasonably.

'I still think it was the Dottoressa's joke,' Daria insisted, reminding Brunetti of what had been said about their father.

Brunetti turned to Signora Toso. 'Thank you for your time, Signora,' he said. 'We'll leave you alone with the girls.' He looked at his watch and said, 'It's time for their lunch.'

'For ours, too,' Griffoni said lightly, then turned and thanked Signora Toso for talking with them.

With no introduction, Livia asked, 'Did

Papà send you?'

'Excuse me?' was the best Brunetti could say.

She started to repeat what she had said. 'Did Papà . . .' she managed, but before she could continue, her older sister poked her in the arm, and she stopped.

'No, he didn't,' Brunetti answered. 'But I hope whoever he sent comes to visit you.'

'Thank you, Dottore,' Livia said and, shooting an irritated glance at her sister, gave what looked very much like a curtsey.

'Oh, Livia,' her older sister moaned, 'you are such a baby.'

Offended, the girl turned to her sister and said, 'Mamma and Papà said it's always right to be polite and show respect to older people.'

'Not bowing. That's not respect. It's just stupid.'

'It's not bowing. It's a curtsey,' she said, pronouncing the English word as though it were Italian. 'It shows respect. You use it with old people.' She turned and walked down the corridor. After a brief hesitation, her sister followed her.

Griffoni walked over to Signora Toso and offered her hand. The girls' aunt held it while she said, 'Thank you both for coming. I think it helps.'

270

'To talk?' Griffoni asked.

'Yes.' She released Griffoni's hand but turned instantly back and placed a hand on her arm. 'It almost brings them back,' she said. 'In a way.'

Griffoni nodded and turned to follow Brunetti to the door. They paused there and said polite things again, then the two of them were down the steps and out into the *calle*. To escape the sun, they moved quickly to the underpass just before the Bridge of Chewing Gum.

'What now?' she asked.

'Lunch?'

'I'm not hungry,' she said. 'I usually don't have two *tramezzini* for breakfast.'

'We can go and get the vaporetto at San Tomà and go back,' Brunetti suggested.

As they were approaching the Questura, Brunetti caught a glimpse of a man who resembled Pascalicchio just slipping into the doorway and quickened his pace. Griffoni remained behind, apparently reluctant to behave in such an insane fashion at midday, the sun at its highest point.

Inside, Brunetti called to what was indeed the Magistrate just as he was starting up the stairs. 'Salvatore. Salvatore.'

Pascalicchio turned at the sound of his name and smiled when he saw who it was.

He came down a few steps, greeted Brunetti with a strong handshake and a few pats on his arm. 'I'm glad to see you, Guido. I came to talk to you,' he said, leaving unstated his unwillingness to use the phone.

'Where have you been?' Brunetti asked.

'On the trains,' Pascalicchio said. 'Between here and Treviso, trying to sort this mess out.'

'Mess?'

'The girls.'

It took Brunetti a second to understand that Pascalicchio was speaking of the two Rom girls, not Fadalto's daughters. 'What's gone wrong?' he asked.

'One of them turns out to be pregnant,' Pascalicchio said, then added, 'The older one.'

'But they're minors,' Brunetti said, revealing a great deal about himself with the remark.

Pascalicchio held up his hands in a sign of helplessness. 'Nevertheless, she's four months pregnant.'

'And so?'

'So she has to be sent home. Social Services called the mother, and when she didn't answer, they sent her a message to come and collect the girl.'

'Good,' Brunetti said. 'If she's pregnant,

sitting in a jail cell is hardly the place for her to be.'

'Jail cell?' Pascalicchio asked with undisguised astonishment. 'Where have you been?'

The question confused Brunetti. 'Not in Treviso, apparently,' he answered. 'Tell me.'

'Because they're minors, they were living in a separate place.'

'What sort of place?'

'An apartment. Two women police officers were living in the same place with them.'

Pascalicchio was using the past tense, but Brunetti let this pass and asked, 'To keep an eye on them?'

'More or less.'

'Could they go out?' Brunetti asked, using the same tense but now curious to learn why this was necessary.

'Only if one of the officers went with them.'

'Salvatore: there were two girls and two officers.'

'It's an experimental project,' the Magistrate said, straight-faced.

'Designed by someone who can't count beyond two?'

Pascalicchio turned and started up the steps again. Over his shoulder, he said, 'It

273

didn't work.'

Brunetti ran up a half-flight so he could reach the other man and wished he had not. 'What happened?'

'They're gone, both of them.'

'How?'

'They went out this morning with one of the policewomen,' Pascalicchio began, and then added, in a more tentative voice, 'They said they wanted to go to Mass.'

'And both policewomen,' Brunetti began with special emphasis on the first part of the last word, 'believed them?'

Ignoring Brunetti's question, and his tone, Pascalicchio said, 'The one who went with them is twenty-one, Guido, and this is her first job. They left about fifteen minutes later and started towards the centre of town.'

'And?'

'A car pulled up and stopped. They both got into the back seat, and the car pulled away.'

'Did she get the licence plate number?'

'She had her phone in her hand, so she at least took a photo of the back of the car. With the number.'

'That's something,' Brunetti said. 'And?'

'It was reported stolen two days ago.'

'I see,' Brunetti replied. 'So they're gone

and probably already back here and at work again.'

They stopped at Brunetti's floor and continued on towards his office, Brunetti setting the pace, conscious of the sweat on various places on his body. He followed the Magistrate into the office, appalled by the heat.

'Does the Vice-Questore know about this yet?' he asked.

'No,' Pascalicchio told him. He lowered himself into a chair, and Brunetti went around his desk to take his own seat.

'So what do we do?' the Magistrate asked. 'You know him better than I do, so you'd have a better idea of how he's going to react.'

'Let's not worry about his reaction,' Brunetti said. 'Let's see how to resolve the situation.'

'What do we do?' Pascalicchio repeated.

Brunetti gave a deep sigh. 'It's only a matter of a few days now. The magazine was on the news-stands today, so — if the Vice-Questore is correct — people will have forgotten about it in two or three more days.'

'Why is that important?'

'It's not exactly important,' Brunetti admitted. 'But it tells us how long this is going to be a problem.'

'Isn't it always a problem? Professional pickpockets who can't be arrested?'

'That's a legal problem,' Brunetti said. 'But what we're dealing with is an image problem, and for the Vice-Questore that's much worse. So for the next two or three days, even if we can't arrest them, we can at least neutralize them.'

'That's a very military-sounding word, Guido.'

'I know, but it's the right one.'

'What does it mean?'

'It means that we authorize special personnel, at least two extra plain-clothes men, or women, who will find these girls — by now everyone on the force has seen their mug shots so often, they could recognize them in a dark room — and they each single out one of them and walk beside them all day long, or at least until the girls are so fed up, they leave.'

'You think that will work, keeping an eye on them?' Pascalicchio asked, failing to disguise his scepticism.

'If the officers are told they have the right to warn people away, and the interventions they make when the girls are getting too close to tourists are moderate, it should work.'

'They aren't lepers,' Pascalicchio said.

Brunetti refused to respond to the provocation.

The Magistrate considered this for some time and finally asked, 'In what language?'

'Good question. We need people who can do it in both Italian and English, but all they need to know is, "Be careful with your bag, madam," or "Be careful with your wallet, sir." If they say it enough times, the girls will give up.'

'You sound very sure.'

'Gypsies aren't violent, Salvatore. You know that. They might steal, but they don't usually hurt people. They'll just wait until we get tired of it, and then they'll go back to work.' He looked to see how Pascalicchio was taking this, but the Magistrate seemed to be calm in the face of the situation.

'So,' Pascalicchio said, and Brunetti knew exactly what he was going to say. 'If you have one police officer for every pickpocket, then the crime would be stopped?'

'It would be very nice to be able to think that,' Brunetti said. 'But we don't have that many people on the force, and pickpockets are like raspberries: no matter how many you pick, the branches are always full again the next day.'

Pascalicchio put his elbows on Brunetti's

desk and linked his fingers together into a cup. He rested his forehead in it and stared at the surface of the desk. 'It's only three days. It's only three days,' he muttered.

It was not until late in the afternoon that Pascalicchio and Brunetti had managed to sort out the problem of what they ended up calling 'baby-sitters' and found two officers to assign to the Rom girls. It took considerably less time to find the girls themselves, for they were back at work, and some of the officers on patrol had already reported seeing them. A general request to the uniformed officers — who were told to make themselves continually visible to the girls — tracked them back and forth from Rialto to San Marco twice before two plain-clothes officers, a man and a woman, took over.

There ensued something that Brunetti — perhaps because he could picture the scenes being played out in the midst of tourist-crowded streets — envisioned as a scene from *commedia dell'arte.* Each time one of the girls got close to another person, the officer following her stepped up beside her and politely warned the potential victim to be careful of purse or wallet or shopping bag. It took the police almost an hour to drive the two girls — the future mother had

278

returned to work with her colleague — to screams and threats and claims that their legal rights were being infringed upon by the forces of order. The officers ignored their protests and continued warning people of their approach. Finally, in exasperation, one of the girls raised her hand to one of the policemen, only to have it pulled down by the older one. Conceding defeat, she led the way to the Rialto vaporetto stop and on to the Number Two to Piazzale Roma without bothering to buy tickets.

The policemen followed, they too failing to acquire tickets, and remained near them, vaporetti being places of high risk. Standing on the deck of the crowded boat, the older girl pulled out her iPhone and made a call. They left the boat at Piazzale Roma and went to the kerb where only buses were meant to stop. After some time, a sad-looking, trunk-heavy blue Fiat pulled up in front of them; a man got out of the passenger seat and pulled open the back door to allow the two girls to climb in. The man slammed the door after them, got into the car and slammed his own door, and the car drove away slowly, its motor protesting at the weight of the passengers.

Some time after the girls got into the car,

Brunetti was sitting on his terrace in an old pair of shorts and a T-shirt he'd taken from Raffi's closet, drinking a glass of lemonade and reading *The Eumenides*. He had read and considered *The Libation Bearers* the last two nights and had been left unsatisfied by its vision of justice as mere vengeance, though he had to admit to having, when younger, felt an atavistic tingle at the idea.

This time he was reading the plays with none of the urge forward that had characterized his student reading, sometimes even his most recent reading: find out what happened, follow the plot, learn their destinies. Instead, he tried to consider each line, occasionally failing, victim of translation or distraction or the giving in to his old habit of wanting to lurch ahead.

Brunetti had never liked Agamemnon, rejected husband of Helen and leader of the Greek forces against Troy. His fleet landlocked by contrary winds, the windbag commander was impotent to lead the Greek army off to conquer Troy in revenge for the abduction of a guilty woman. He dared not desert his allies, abandon his fleet; not he, the Destined Leader. So the gods, their sense of timing truly divine, sent the order. What better way to solve the problem than to slit the throat of an innocent girl, his

280

daughter? The deed was done, and the winds of war were freed.

A decade later, Agamemnon got what was coming, cut down in his bath by his wife; then she got hers, cut down by her son. So where was justice? The play was meant to tell him that. But so many wanted it, first Clytemnestra's ghost, demanding justice because, 'At the hands of nearest kin I suffered death.'

He raised his eyes from the book and saw that it had grown darker while he sat there. He returned his attention to the page, and Clytemnestra tried to bribe the Furies, reminding them that 'my hands have fed your lapping tongues with a sacrifice other than wine'. No, not something he wanted to read just now.

Brunetti closed the book and tossed it on to the seat of the chair next to his. He stretched out his sandalled feet and braced them against the wall of the terrace, took a sip of lemonade and tipped his chair on to its back legs, something the children were forbidden to do.

'They knew a thing or two, those Greeks,' he said out loud. He let his chair slap down on the floor, picked up his glass and the book and wandered back to the kitchen to

see if he could find something to tide him
over until dinner.

19

Brunetti spent a half-hour the following morning — after being brought coffee in bed — lying and staring at the ceiling. He listened to the other three people leave the apartment, recognizing each by the way they opened and closed the door, though not understanding how or why he did.

The ceiling was not particularly interesting but, if he stared at it long enough, was capable of causing Brunetti a certain amount of self-reproach. Water had leaked from the roof three years before, and the stain remained. It was the size of a salad plate, though with the passage of time he had become accustomed to it and had to hunt for it in order to see it, and when he did, he was irritated at his own laziness in not painting it over or having it done.

Turning his eyes to the windows, he considered things that he had heard and seen, wondering what he was failing to notice or understand about Vittorio Fadalto and Benedetta Toso. Fadalto was a perfectionist and had a temper; aside from this, Brunetti did not have a clear picture of him. Benedetta Toso was even more out of focus. She loved her husband and her children. She had a degree in history from the university and had, for some years, before her illness, taught in a middle school: this information was in one of the documents Signorina Elettra had unearthed. Her birthday was a few days before her husband's death, so that was probably when he took the 'bad money' to the hospice, perhaps telling her she could now go back to the private clinic.

He shifted around in the bed and turned on his side. Fadalto had confessed to his sister-in-law that he was a liar and a cheat, and then he was dead a week later. Fadalto was a technician and a man who apparently admired exactness, for certainly his work demanded that. Driving his motorcycle off a road into a ditch while wearing his helmet — as the accident report had made clear — was not the sort of suicide chosen by a man who admired precision. Crash into a pylon. Into the cement wall of an embankment. Into an oncoming truck, although the law-respecting Fadalto would have been reluctant to do that. But don't go off the road into a ditch where there is no certainty that you will die. As it turned out, he did die, but because he fell into the water, unconscious. Without that, he might still be alive.

If it had not been a successful suicide, it had to be something else, and Brunetti had already led himself through the possibilities. He pushed himself up on one elbow, took his *telefonino* from the night table, and found Vianello's number.

An hour and a half later, they were back in a car, with the same driver, going to the same place. 'I didn't pay particular attention to it at the time,' Brunetti said to Vianello, 'but one of the women in the lab seemed to want to or was attempting to tell me something about Dr Veltrini. Or about the *cantina.* I'm not sure, but I'd like to talk to her.'

'And is my job to lure her from the laboratory?' Vianello asked.

'No. Dottoressa Ricciardi has agreed to do that for us.'

'Just like that?' Vianello asked.

'I called ahead this morning and explained to the Dottoressa that I'd like to speak to one of them but didn't know their names. I told her which desk the woman was using and that she wore glasses, and Ricciardi knew which one I meant.'

'And so?'

'When we get there, I'd like you to go to the laboratory and ask Dr Veltrini for more information and keep him occupied for some time.'

Vianello gave his friend a long look and asked, 'Information about a particular subject?' In the face of Brunetti's silence, the Ispettore asked, 'Or should I ask him for the name of a good restaurant in the area?'

Brunetti thought he heard a noise from the front seat, but when he glanced in the mirror, the driver's face was still, his eyes directed at the traffic ahead of them.

'You could ask him for a map of the places where they have the sensors that sample the water. And you could ask him for the geographical coordinates of those samples of water he showed us that had arsenic in them.' Brunetti tried to imagine the placid Vianello talking to the lab director, who had not seemed a very patient man.

'I don't know how much time I'll need with her,' he continued, 'so try to keep him as long as you can.' He added, 'If you think you need more time, ask him about other substances in the water: copper, lead, mercury.'

'All right,' Vianello agreed, then said, 'What do you want to ask her?'

'Well, if the waitress has things right, Veltrini can't be much liked by his colleagues.'

As he said this, it came to Brunetti to wonder why he had never asked Signorina Elettra to have a look at Spattuto Acqua's personnel records. Even as he thought this, he was struck by the cavalier manner in which he assumed she could simply 'have a look at them', in order to avoid being delayed by the time it would take to receive them through official channels.

Vianello nodded, and Brunetti pulled out his phone and called Signorina Elettra to ask her to see if she could find her way into the Spattuto personnel files. Did he hear her give the same dry chuckle he thought he'd heard from the driver? Ignoring it, he said he'd like to know what sort of evaluations had been made of Vittorio Fadalto and Eugenio Veltrini. And, as an afterthought, he added Dottoressa Ricciardi's name.

He turned his head and looked out at the omnipresent corn. He had no idea what it was being grown for. In his youth, corn was grown for forage and for polenta. His grand-uncles had told stories of the corn harvests of their own youth: setting the cobs in the sun for days until the kernels were dry and rock-like, then stripping them and taking them to the mill to be ground, then waiting there, chatting with friends, always keeping careful watch to see that the corn that went into the mill was yours and that the weight that went in was the same weight that came out, minus what might have blown away or fallen to the floor.

Polenta, he knew, was what had kept his ancestors alive through the winter, polenta and the great wheels of cheese and the salami and prosciutto into which their pig had been turned. There were herbs and plants from the fields, as well, plants that had names only in dialect, plants no one named or remembered any more. They'd spoken too of tisane made from rose hips that had helped with colds and were believed to protect against disease.

Only later had he learned that rose hips were rich in Vitamin C and so probably helped keep away colds and flu through those endless winters. People had still starved to death, well into the Fifties, in some of the poorer villages in Friuli. And so his mother's family had come to Venice, his grandfather to be a waiter and his wife to take care of five children.

The car stopped, and Brunetti returned to the present. They were in front of the main building of Spattuto Acqua and Vianello was looking at him, a mild expression on his face.

'I always wonder where you go when you disappear like that,' he said.

Brunetti snorted and raised his eyebrows. 'I never know, but usually into the past and what my grandparents and uncles and aunts told us about how it was to live then.'

'They were farmers, weren't they?'

'Yes.'

'Then they probably lived in that enormous Friuli village: *Povertà.*'

Brunetti smiled and answered, 'They did,' opened the door and got out of the car.

The same receptionist was there, and she led them immediately to Dottoressa Ricciardi's office. When the Dottoressa saw them, she gave them the sort of smile a member of the management of a large company would give at the sight of two police officers returning to question members of the staff for the second time. Brunetti decided to make the best of it, smiled amiably, and thanked her for her cooperation in arranging conversations — he called them that — with two employees.

She told the receptionist that she would take Dottor Brunetti to the conference room and asked her to show the Ispettore

289

the way to the laboratory.

When the other two were gone, she pushed herself upright and, one hand flat-palmed on the desk, used the other to take the cane that was hanging from the back of her chair. Steadied by that, she started towards the door: Brunetti followed. She favoured her right leg, he saw, either from pain or from some difference in the length of her legs. She would be forever unsteady on her feet, always fighting that strong list to the right. At the door, he stepped around and ahead of her, pulled it open, and closed it after them. She moved down the corridor and opened a door on the right; Brunetti followed her into the room.

She pointed to the rectangular wooden table at the centre and invited Brunetti to have a seat. 'I'll phone Antonella from my office and ask her to come here,' she said and left.

Brunetti studied the room. It was, he thought, a place where people were meant to sit around a table and make decisions: it could have been in any small city in Europe; perhaps in Asia or South America. There was a square opening in the centre of the table where various devices could be plugged in and a medium-sized whiteboard on one wall that would serve for writing or projecting images. Three black-and-white photographs of waterfalls hung on the other walls. The absence of colour from the photos had, he feared, removed most of their beauty. They, too, could have been anywhere. He walked over and looked out of the window, into the parking lot. Most of the cars were foreign and almost all of them grey, one a large Mercedes.

After a few minutes, there was a light knock at the door.

'*Avanti*,' Brunetti said, quite as though he were in his own office.

The woman who had been working with the test tubes, the one with glasses, entered the room and gave him a nervous smile.

Brunetti walked over to her, smiling, extending his hand. 'How kind of you to agree to talk to me, Signora. My name is Guido Brunetti, from the Venice police. My colleague and I are here again because we're looking into the death of Vittorio Fadalto.'

She shook his hand and said, 'I know.' Then, more politely, 'Antonella Sala. *Piacere*.' She nodded her head a few times and looked nervously around the room.

'I'm sorry, Signora Sala, not to have known your name or the name of your colleague, but Dottor Veltrini didn't bother to tell me them,' he said sternly, using the

291

plural to show that he disapproved of the discourtesy directed at the two women. Then, turning towards the table, he said, 'Please, Signora, take a seat so we'll be more comfortable while we talk.' He pulled out a chair for her, then went around to the other side and sat. He opened his notebook, something that seemed to reassure people.

He wrote her name at the top, and the date. Thinking it best to begin with the impersonality of facts, he smiled and said, 'I'm very interested in what it was that Signor Fadalto did, Signora. Could you tell me something about his work and when and why he brought in samples?'

She folded her hands neatly on the table in front of her, cleared her throat, and began. 'He worked in the field. When a sensor in the aqueduct system, which is linked to our office, signalled any sign of a problem — too much or too little current, contamination, the presence of too much organic material in the water — he went to see what was going on and, in a case of contamination, brought back the sensor. All he had to do was remove the one containing the contaminated sample and replace it with a new one.' Brunetti wrote all of this down. Seeing this, she paused between phrases and spoke slowly and with great precision.

When she saw that he had finished noting what she said, she went on. 'If it was from one of the sensors located in a river or stream, he went to that spot and did the same, then brought them back for analysis.'

Brunetti finished writing what she had said and looked up. 'Am I to understand — from what Dottor Veltrini told us — that the geographical coordinates of every sample are recorded?'

'Of course,' she said, then asked, 'How else could we identify them?'

'Thank you,' Brunetti said and made a note of this. 'And how did he pass these samples to you and your colleague?'

She tilted her chin at this question, but then, no doubt realizing that what was normal procedure in a laboratory would not seem so to someone unfamiliar with the system, said, 'He brought the sensors back, entered their identification numbers in the log, and then gave them to whichever of us was in charge of the sensors along that particular part of the river.'

'And why was that?'

'Why was what?' she asked, genuinely confused.

'Why were you in charge of specific sensors?'

'Ah,' she said, understanding the question

now. 'Dottor Veltrini thought it would be better if the three of us always dealt with the same places.'

'Three of you, Signora? I saw only you and your colleague.'

'Oh,' she said, 'I thought you understood. Dottor Veltrini is the third person. Each of us is responsible for testing samples from particular sensors in particular places.' Suddenly hearing herself and perhaps not wanting to be unclear, she said, 'We test samples from one hundred and twenty-nine sites and from about one hundred and eighty-three sensors. Some sites have one sensor; others have more than that, depending upon the length of embankment that runs through the property where the sensors are located. It works out that each of us has about the same number of sensors we're responsible for. Whenever there's need for manual verification of the readings, we do the ones from the sensors that are our responsibility.'

Brunetti thanked her for the clarification, and made a note.

She smiled and continued. 'That way, we're familiar with the patterns of change in certain substances and the ups and downs of traces in the water in our own sites, so we can be quicker to react. Or,' she added, 'slower to react if it's part of a normal cycle.'

'Could you give me an example, Signora?' Brunetti asked.

'With nitrates. What we talked about the other day,' she began.

He nodded and turned a page.

'At the time when we know the farmers are spreading fertilizers, and if there's rain soon after that, then we expect greater concentrations of them in the samples from the rivers.' When Brunetti gave her a quizzical look, she said, 'Because of the run-off.'

He nodded to show that he understood and muttered, 'Of course.'

'It's generally nothing to be alarmed at,' she said.

Brunetti was not sure he understood her reason for this opinion: if there were elevated quantities of a contaminant in the water, there might be reason for alarm: repetition hardly reduced risk. But she had said 'greater', not 'dangerous', and she was the professional.

'Thank you,' he said. 'This log, does it contain the results of the analyses?'

'No, no: they're completely different processes: the log registers when and where a sample was collected.'

Brunetti held up his pen and asked, 'Could you explain how that's done,

Signora?'

She looked pleased at his questions and the interest he was taking in what she spent her life doing. Her face softened; even her voice grew warmer. 'Each sensor has an identification number, and that number is entered in the log. It also appears on the report — like the one Dottor Veltrini showed you — that contains the results of the analysis.' She paused until his writing caught up with her words and then added, 'The identification label is at the top, both of the sample and of the report.'

'Of course,' Brunetti agreed, and then asked, 'What happens to the containers that hold these samples? They looked to me like they were glass.'

'They are, Dottore. They have to be.'

'And why is that?'

'Because one of the things we check for is plastic.'

'In the water?'

'Yes.'

'I see. Glass, then,' he said and made a note of this. 'Do you reuse them?'

'Yes. We have an autoclave like they do in hospitals, and we clean them and use them again. But with new lids.' Before he could ask, she added, 'Rubber.'

'And the labels?' Brunetti asked.

She paused and gave him a strange look, obviously confused that a policeman would ask such questions. But still she answered it. 'We remove them before they go into the autoclave so that new ones can be put on.'

'I see,' he said. 'So — let me make sure I've got this right — the permanent record is what you put into your computer as you're examining the samples, and that's what gets printed out, with all the percentages of any contaminants.'

'Exactly.'

'And the actual analysis of the water to see what specific contaminants are in it,' Brunetti began: 'who does that?'

'We three.'

'No one else?'

She hesitated a moment and then said, 'I suppose Signor Fadalto could have done it, as well.' In a confiding voice, she added, 'It's really not very difficult: the machines do it all.'

'Fine,' Brunetti said with a warm smile. He turned a page and said, 'I'd like to ask you a few questions about Signor Fadalto but only if you have no objection.' The question was formulaic: once people had started to answer questions, they assumed a responsibility to continue.

She nodded but said nothing to acknowledge his question or to encourage him.

'Would you say he was an honest man?'

Her mouth fell open. 'Vittorio?' she asked.

'Yes.'

'Why, Vittorio was honesty personified. If he found five Euros on the floor, he'd ask everyone he saw if they'd lost it.'

'And if no one claimed it?' Brunetti asked with a smile.

She hesitated and then said, laughing this time, 'I made that up, Signore, just to show you how honest he was.'

'How nice, to learn that there are still people in the world like that,' Brunetti said, thinking that he probably did believe this. 'So you can't think of him doing anything dishonest?'

'Impossible,' she said strongly. 'He might have been difficult at times, and some people might not have liked him, but he was an honest man.'

'What didn't some people like about him?' Brunetti asked, allowing real curiosity to colour his voice.

'Oh, nothing important, really: telling them to go outside to smoke — standing at the open window of their office wasn't enough for Vittorio. He'd remind them to put their snow tyres on or remark that they'd gained weight.' She stopped talking for some time, and Brunetti looked up and across at her. She had suddenly grown nervous: he saw it in the way her hands were clasped in front of her.

'What is it, Signora?' he asked softly.

'No one will find out what I tell you, will they?'

'Of course not, Signora. This is privileged information.' It wasn't, but Brunetti was an easy liar.

'He'd never punch anyone else's time card for them,' she said and moved her hands into her lap and studied them.

'Ah, that old trick,' Brunetti said neutrally. 'I've been told it's pretty frequent.'

'Not here, it isn't,' she said defensively. 'There are a few who do it, but we all know who they are. Some of them will still do it in front of us, but they wouldn't do it if Vittorio was there. He'd tell them he'd report them if they did it again.'

'And would he?' Brunetti asked, interested in this.

'He did it once. That's why no one would do it in front of him.'

Brunetti made a note of this; as he was still writing, he heard her gasp. When he looked up, she was sitting with her palm pressed to her lips, her eyes wide with fear. 'That's not what happened, is it? That someone drove him off the road because he reported them?'

'No, Signora,' Brunetti said easily and smiled. 'That's not a possibility we're considering.' When he saw her relax, he said, encouragingly, 'Only a few more questions, if you'll have patience with me, Signora.'

She nodded.

'Where is this logbook kept?'

'In a cabinet near the door to the laboratory,' she said. 'That way, the first thing he did was enter the number of any samples he brought in.'

'I see, I see. So those would be handwritten,' Brunetti said, continuing to write. 'And the reports you prepare?'

'Oh, they go directly into the system. We still print out a copy of the complete analysis: we have a permanent file of those. And that's the last we see of them.'

'I understand,' Brunetti answered. 'And who has access to this system?'

She propped her chin on her palm, looked across at him and made a humming noise. 'I never thought about that, Signore.' She made the noise again and finally answered, 'The three of us here in the lab, and then anyone in the company who has access to that part of the databank.'

'I see, I see,' Brunetti said and wrote down

what she had said. He closed his notebook and folded his hands on top of it, saying, 'You've been wonderfully helpful to me, Signora.' Then, not bothering to explain why or how this might be true, he added, 'I needed to have a clearer sense of how these things work, you see.'

Then, as if he'd suddenly remembered something, he said, 'When I was leaving the lab the other day, you made a gesture to me. For a moment, I thought you were warning us about the food in the *cantina*.' He paused and gave a broad smile, hoping to put her at ease, but he saw that his question had had the opposite effect. Her face was rigid, and he watched her flail around to find an answer. She turned quickly to the door, as if she needed to be sure it was closed. Knowing she was now unlikely to tell him, he had to go ahead with it and asked, 'Could you tell me what you meant?'

Her face un-froze, but not completely, and she said, 'Yes, it was the food. It's terrible. I didn't want you to eat it. And then go away from us with a bad impression.' As if aware of how much she was talking, she put her hands on the table and pushed herself to her feet.

Brunetti smiled again, got up from his chair and slid it back into place under the table. He hurried to get to the door before she did, opened it and stood aside to let her pass into the corridor first. She stopped and held out her hand to him. He shook it, thanked her again, and watched her until she reached the end of the corridor and turned to the left. Then he went back towards what he thought must be the front of the building to wait for Vianello.

20

The Ispettore sat in one of the two chairs to the right of the receptionist's desk, chairs placed near enough for her to overhear what visitors said while preventing the visitors from seeing what she wrote. Vianello had somewhere acquired a copy of *Il Gazzettino* and was reading the second section, local news. Brunetti had almost reached him when the Ispettore looked up from the open pages of the newspaper and said, 'The leader of the Rom community says he is bringing a case against the city government before the European Court of Human Rights.'

The receptionist's glance was not unlike that of a doe, startled by a noise on the first day of hunting season.

Vianello made a lot of paper noise in folding back the page, the better to bring it close enough for Brunetti to read. ' "Against the Commune of Venice for acts performed by the police and other members of the administration that are damaging to the persons and reputation of members of our community",' he read aloud.

'*O Dio mio,*' a phrase of high discomfort, escaped Brunetti's lips. 'Who did what?' He took the seat next to Vianello, the better to see the paper.

Vianello pointed to the second paragraph of the article and said, 'That's not made clear, but it seems that photos of the two girls — in colour and very clear and looking very much like mug shots — have been posted on every vaporetto stop in the centre of the city. Beside each photo, the word "Thief" is printed in red in six languages. As well as "Be careful".'

Rather than comment on the notices, Brunetti asked, 'What languages?'

Vianello bent over the page and studied it again. 'Italian, English, German, Mandarin, French, and Japanese,' he said, lowering the paper to his lap and asking, 'Why do you want to know?'

'It tells whom they want to scare.'

'Ah, of course,' Vianello said, folding the paper closed and getting to his feet.

Vianello started to walk towards the door, turned back and said, 'We'll talk in the car.' Then he looked at the receptionist and said, quite amiably, *'Buon giorno, Signorina.'*

Outside, bonhomie and irony disappeared, and Vianello asked, voice tight with anger, 'Can you believe that? That he'd bring a case?'

Brunetti was reluctant to discuss this, even with Vianello: there was no safe remark anyone could make, no safe opinion. What would the next posters look like? he wondered. The same photos with a red X across the faces? Or covered with narrowing circles like those on hunting targets? In the new Italy, such things were entirely possible. He was sure the arc of comment would run from the demand that the girls be paid damages to suggestions of violence against them. He also wondered what twists and turns the legal case would follow. For the moment, this might keep the girls out of the city until after the article had been published.

Once they were in the car, heading back towards Venice, Brunetti said, speaking loud enough so the driver would hear, 'I wonder why we don't see Wanted posters in the *embarcaderos* of the men who planned MOSE to protect us from the floods.'

Vianello gave a snort and shook his head.

From the front seat, the driver said, 'If I might comment, Commissario . . .'

'Of course,' Brunetti told him.

'If you steal billions, you get a chalet in Cortina and an apartment in Rome.' He moved into the left lane and increased their speed. 'Those girls should have aimed at something more lucrative than picking pockets.'

Brunetti let a few minutes pass in silence after that and watched the buildings replace the fields. Finally he turned to Vianello and asked, 'What happened with Dottor Veltrini?'

'I told him we'd come back to ask a few more questions and made it clear that I didn't much like having to do it. Nor did I show any real interest in the questions I asked him and didn't bother to write down his answers.' That said, he pulled his phone from the inner pocket of his jacket and held it up for Brunetti to see. He recalled Griffoni switching her phone on before they entered the room in which Signora Toso was so soon to die.

'What did you ask him?'

'What you told me to: if he could give me a copy of the map of the area where they found the . . . I made it obvious that I had to think a while before I remembered it was arsenic. He said there would be no problem and, even before I could say anything else, asked my email address and went to his computer and sent me the map.

'Because we were right beside the computer, I asked him if he could do the same for places where they'd found copper and lead, and he entered those requests and smiled at me. I looked impressed. I suppose he thought I'd never seen a computer in my life.' Vianello smiled after he said this. 'He found them and sent them, and I stopped myself from falling to my knees and crying, "Miracle, miracle."

'I went through the business with my notebook again, flipped a few pages to show how unimportant I thought any of this was, and asked if he could do the same for mercury.' Vianello came to a halt, as if he were the chorus changing posture to indicate that there would be a matching change in the events.

'The word jolted him. He didn't move or say anything for some time, but he recovered and told me he wasn't sure if they'd checked for that recently and would have to look at the records. He said he'd run a check through the system and send the map tomorrow. I thanked him for having been so generous with his time and said there was no great hurry. I thought about telling him it made no sense to me that you were asking all these questions, but I suspected it would be too much, so I just thanked him again and said I'd wait for the results.' Vianello, who had a fine dramatic sense for story-telling, made a long pause here.

'All right, all right, Lorenzo, let's hear the big secret.'

Revealing nothing with his expression or tone of voice, Vianello said, 'We had been walking towards the door when he told me that, but once we were outside the laboratory — and out of hearing of his assistant — he said he'd just remembered that there had been some sort of error in the system, and the map, even the numbers from the last report, hadn't been accessible the last time he looked for them.'

"An error in the system, eh?' Brunetti asked. 'Like, "The dog ate my homework"?'

'Exactly. I smiled and said it probably didn't matter at all, and I told him that I had no idea why you were asking for all of this stuff.' Vianello waited for that to register and then added, 'I think he believed me.'

'It doesn't sound as if he's very good at it.'

'At what?'

'Lying.'

'No, he's not,' Vianello said dismissively, making no attempt to disguise his contempt for Veltrini's being such a clumsy liar. 'He couldn't hide his reaction when I mentioned mercury. He was frightened and said the first thing that came to him: blamed it on the system.' He pressed his lips together and raised his eyebrows to show his opinion of so paltry an attempt. 'The idea of mercury upset him.'

Before Vianello could suggest it, Brunetti said, 'Signorina Elettra.' Other agencies of the government had their sudden response units, their task forces, uniformed young men who rappelled down from helicopters: the Questura had no more than Signorina Elettra Zorzi, who would suffice.

Brunetti's mind wandered off from the many competencies of Signorina Elettra and returned to the news that Vianello had given him: mercury. Years ago, he had seen a book of photos that contained a Japanese Pietà. He remembered it still: the mother, head wrapped in a piece of cloth, submerged in a large wooden bath, her naked, agonized adolescent daughter racked by disease and lying across her lap. Mercury poisoning, the company knowingly dumping wastewater into the bay for decades, aware of what they did while denying what they did, and eventually paying for what they had done. As if that were possible, Brunetti told himself.

To Vianello, he said, 'And the woman in

the lab? What happened when her colleague left to talk to me?'

'He ignored her, and she seemed busy with her microscope.' Changing the subject, Vianello asked, 'What about you? Did you learn anything?'

Brunetti shrugged. 'Veltrini and the two assistants each have specific sensors they're in charge of. It allows them to become familiar with what causes the repeated increase or decrease of certain elements in the water where their sensors are. She told me that Fadalto was implacably honest and that some people disliked him as a result.'

He sat back in his seat and studied the corn in the fields, still looking as if its goal were to reach the horizon. 'The last time, the one I spoke to, Signora Sala, started to tell me something, just as we were leaving, but she changed her mind. And when I asked her about it today, she said it was to warn me about the food in the *cantina.*'

Vianello shrugged and said, 'I didn't notice it.'

Deciding not to pursue this now, Brunetti said, 'You know, Lorenzo, the more I learn about this Fadalto, the less I find to like about him.'

'What?' Vianello asked, puzzled, curious.

'He interfered with people, told them they

shouldn't smoke, reported their infractions to the company.'

'What's wrong with that?' Vianello asked.

'Nothing's wrong with it, Lorenzo, nothing at all. But the person who told me this seemed bothered by it, and that suggests it was as much his manner as what he said or did.' When Vianello remained silent, Brunetti added, 'Remember that judge from Torino who was here a few years ago?'

'The one with the thick glasses?' Vianello asked.

'Yes. Remember how he always had to give a sermon at the end of every trial? Explaining just how the accused had broken a law and what the purpose of the law was?'

Vianello nodded.

'He didn't last a year, did he?' Brunetti asked. 'And they sent him off to Sardegna, I think.'

'And your point is?' Vianello asked.

'That people don't like to be preached at, even if they agree with what the preacher is saying.'

'You don't know this for certain about Fadalto, do you?' Vianello asked.

'No, I don't, but it sort of leaks out of what people say about him.'

' "Leaks out"?'

Brunetti realized how difficult it was to

explain what he meant. After all, he had never met the man, never even seen a photo of him, had heard of him only after his death. Nor could he recall a precise expression or tone in anything that had been said about Fadalto that had led to this impression or, now that he'd voiced it to Vianello, opinion.

How unpleasant to hear the voicing of one's own negative judgements; how difficult to hear your own intolerance. The best Brunetti could do was shrug and lift a hand and turn to study the seemingly endless fields of corn.

After lunch, when he returned to the Questura, Brunetti was to discover the same 'leaks' in some of the remarks contained in the files that Signorina Elettra had managed to 'procure' — her new word of choice — from the files of Spattuto Acqua.

The idea of personnel records or comments about fellow employees had always made Brunetti more than a little sceptical: regardless of how secret these things were sworn to be, most people assumed that any remarks they made could and would be traced back to them. And now, in these times of grinding economic decline, who would be willing to compromise their own position by telling the truth about another worker or reporting the misbehaviour or aggression of a superior? Lie low, lie low. And wait.

Thus, Fadalto was 'an example of integrity', 'a firm colleague', and 'a model to younger workers', Dottore Veltrini was described as 'precise' and 'supportive', 'intelligent', and 'a good leader', while Dottoressa Ricciardi was 'pleasant', 'helpful', and 'a source of inspiration'. Brunetti allowed himself some time to graze through the other flowers that adorned the names of various members of the administration and found them unfailingly 'supportive', 'helpful', and 'intelligent', men — they were almost all men — 'of integrity and vision', as well as 'examples of industry and commitment to excellence'.

His mind swerved towards the Questura, imagining what would be said in a similar account about the performance of those in charge there. What words of praise would rain down upon Patta? What celestial graces would be discovered in each feature of Lieutenant Scarpa's behaviour? He paused and accepted the fact that, were he obliged to comment upon the Vice-Questore, he would assuredly turn to phrases like 'establishes the tone of the Questura', 'treats all colleagues with equal courtesy', and might even fly so close to the wind as to risk 'wasted no time in earning his current rank'.

He saw that there were a few pages left, but he lacked the stomach to read them. He tossed the papers on his desk and turned his mind to gossip. Fadalto had been Venetian: Veltrini and Ricciardi both sounded as though they were: from the Veneto, at least.

He called down and asked Signorina Elettra if she by chance had found their CVs; she said they would be in his inbox within minutes. Were this woman's colleagues asked their opinion of her, the pages would blaze with light. A soft boing heralded the arrival of her email.

Dottor Veltrini had earned his degree in Chemistry more than thirty years before. His work history was normal: two previous jobs in firms manufacturing chemical products, each lasting about ten years, both in the Veneto. He was not married.

Dottoressa Ricciardi had a degree in Psychology from the University of Padova and had worked as a counsellor for the school system, helping girls who left school upon becoming pregnant. Her superiors spoke very well of her. After more than ten years, she had risen to the position of vice-supervisor of the department, only to resign to return to school.

She had gone back to the university and earned an advanced degree from the Department of Psychology and Socialization and, with her new title, taken the job with Spattuto for a salary significantly larger than that of her previous position. She had been there for three years. She was divorced, without children.

Almost without thinking, Brunetti dialled Paola's number and told her he loved her.

'That means you want something.'

'The name of the guy who teaches Psychology at Padova. All I can remember is Renzo.'

'Renzo Pandolfi,' she said, 'and I suppose you want his phone number?'

'Yes, please.'

'I'll find it and text it to you,' she said and hung up.

A moment later, a number appeared on the screen of his phone and he called it.

After five rings, a man's voice said, 'Pandolfi.'

'Hello, Renzo, this is Guido Brunetti, Paola's husband. I'm calling about a professional matter.'

'I'll come quietly,' Pandolfi said. No wonder Paola liked him.

'No, this time you're safe. I'm calling

315

about a woman who took a Doctorate there about three years ago in something called Developmental Psychology and Socialization.'

After a very long pause, Pandolfi asked, 'How would you respond if I said your degree was in "something called Law"?'

'I'd be offended,' Brunetti admitted. 'In the department of Developmental Psychology and Socialization.'

'Sounds much better. Name?'

'Ricciardi, Fulvia.'

'I assume you aren't interested in her grades.'

'No, I'd like to know anything that would work in her disfavour, or in her favour.'

'Regarding anything in particular?' Pandolfi asked, and then added, 'Speaking as a psychologist, I find it interesting that you put "disfavour" first.'

'I was testing you,' Brunetti responded in a sober voice.

'*Oddio,*' escaped Pandolfi.

'Anything you can tell me about her might help,' Brunetti said. 'The little I know is that she had a slipped disc, was operated on, and finished with a limp and a cane.'

Pandolfi let some time pass and then said, 'I'll ask around: I know a few people who teach there. Anything else?'

316

'No,' Brunetti said and then, 'Thank you.' Pandolfi made a noise and broke the connection.

Brunetti's thoughts turned to Dottor Veltrini, but he could think of no person who might know something about his life beyond the laboratory.

Because he was at his computer, he idly typed in 'mercury' and read a bit about what it was used for, and what it did to those who came in contact with it or, worse, consumed it in some form.

Continuing his search, he came upon the photo that had been imprinted on his memory so many years ago, evidence of what he had just read. The image of the teenaged girl in the pool floated towards him, her mother cradling her backward ever-arching body, as if trying to save her spine from snapping. *'Maria Vergine,'* he whispered. Loss of coordination, memory, hearing, strength, speech. And, inexorably, life. Minamata.

21

The next morning, Brunetti awoke early, his arm draped over what he thought was his wife but turned out to be a pillow. Hers. She was missing but soon returned with two cups of coffee, sat on the side of the bed, and held one of the cups towards him.

He shifted on to his back and pushed himself up against the headboard. He took the coffee and sipped at it. 'Bless you,' he said, meaning it. 'You have no idea how much I love this, to lie here and have this simple pleasure given to me.'

'I assume you're talking about my presence,' she said.

He was going to joke about this, but he thought it better to tell the truth. 'Of course. Your presence. But it's also the fact that, day after day, year after year, you still do this for me.' Then, continuing with the truth, he added, 'Sometimes.'

Her tone shifted, growing more serious.

'It's easy to do because you take such pleasure in it.' As if she were afraid of falling into sentimentality, she got to her feet and said, 'It's already hot. Is there any way you might avoid wearing a jacket?'

He set the cup and saucer on the table beside the bed and wiggled himself closer to a sitting position. 'Remember the Raj,' he said.

'I beg your pardon?' Paola asked, picking up his cup and saucer, but not yet turning towards the door.

'If you look at the early photos of the men who went out to the colonies — the Englishmen, that is — they're wearing, summer and winter, their woollen uniform jackets. So I think I can wear a cotton jacket today.'

'You're mad,' she observed and took the cup back to the kitchen.

'So were they,' Brunetti said, but he said it softly, and only to himself.

Half an hour later, as he emerged into the *calle* leading towards the boat stop at San Silvestro, Brunetti thought again of those thousands of men who went out to the colonies, persuading themselves that they were there to labour for the Empire, for the Queen and Empress, and no doubt for the salvation of the souls of the subject population. He had no idea what they actually desired: some wealth, some power, some the opportunity to do good. Perhaps.

His own country had not behaved particularly well with the few colonies it had managed to grab in modern times. From what his father had told him, they had proclaimed the same desires as had the English; no doubt all conquering armies made the same declarations. How fortunate, in these modern times, to have been a second-rate colonial power.

Suddenly overwhelmed by the growing heat, he shed these thoughts, boarded the Numero Uno, and went inside to take a seat. It was not yet nine, but he was already regretting his insistence on wearing a jacket and folded it over his knees.

A few passengers got off at San Tomà, after which at least thirty people boarded the boat, most of them choosing to remain outside. Brunetti often caught this boat and so recognized some of them: the well-dressed woman with the red glasses who always got off at Accademia and who, he thought, must work at the Museum; the young man wearing the 'Help Venice' T-shirt whom he had seen in the Piazza, selling food for the pigeons; and the old woman wrapped summer and winter in a tartan woollen scarf who spent her days sitting under the balcony of the Palazzo Ducale, watching people pass in front of her. He had never seen her anywhere else in the city and wondered where she spent her nights.

He got off at San Zaccaria and, hooking his finger in the loop of his jacket, started towards the Questura. Before he had gone a hundred metres, he wished he could tele-transport — though he had no idea how — himself to the Questura and up the stairs to his office, but only if someone had gone in an hour before to open the windows. His pace slowed; he found himself holding each breath the length of four steps, reluctant to pull more sodden air into his lungs. *Il Gazzettino* gave, each day, the level of pollution in the air, and each day Brunetti turned his eyes away in helpless alarm. What did it mean, so many particles to the cubic metre of air? What, exactly, was he pulling into the moist coating of his lungs, and what would that lead to in future years?

It used to be the winter that people feared, with heating systems turned on in the city, and little or no rain to beat the particles out of the air. But summer, he realized, was far worse. People were outside much of the time, breathing the air, no longer fresh but digested and spat out by the cruise ships that passed with alarming frequency; air conditioners at so many windows; more vaporetti than in the winter, more tourist-filled cars and buses arriving at Piazzale Roma; and the same wind from the west, pushing towards them the pollution of one of the areas of highest industrial production in Europe.

He turned just before the Greek Church and looked down the *calle* leading to the Questura. Never had the *tricolore* hanging from the balcony of Patta's office seemed such a shining beacon of safety. As he'd hoped, the temperature dropped a little just inside the door. He spared the officer on duty — thinking about how many times he must have heard comments on the heat — any mention of it, simply said good morning and went up to his office.

No one had opened the windows, so he dropped his jacket over the back of his chair and went across to do so. When he turned, he was delighted to see the breeze lift papers from his desk and scatter them over the floor. He stood, back to the window, and held his arms out to the sides, hoping the breeze would dry his shirt and back and lift his spirits.

He was standing like that, eyes closed, when he heard a sound at the door. Keeping his eyes closed, he thought about whom he would be least annoyed to see there.

He opened his eyes and, just as the slight coolness of the breeze had soothed his spirit, so too did the sight of Signorina Elettra, framed by the door and standing full in the blaze of light coming from the east.

'Bon dì, Dottore,' she said and started towards his desk. He noticed that she was wearing wide-legged black trousers and a pair of Stan Smiths, no socks, her linen shirt the same green as the tags on the heels of the sneakers. He saw, then, the manila envelope in her hand. He walked over to her and accepted the envelope, which was sealed.

She started to turn away, but he held up a hand to stop her. He ripped open the flap and extracted three stiff pieces of paper, turned them over, and saw that they were photographs. The first showed the back of a man who appeared to be wearing a uniform; Brunetti looked closer and saw that it was a police uniform, the dark blue winter jacket. The man was speaking to two women: at least the right and left thirds of two feminine forms were visible, bisected by his body. In the absence of faces, there was nothing to distinguish them but their thick jackets and enveloping scarves, long skirts and what looked like scuffed shoes peeking out from under them; well, one shoe each.

To take the second photo, the photographer had shifted a bit to the left, and so now one of the females was entirely visible, while almost all of the other was blocked by the man's broad form. The third photo had been taken from even farther on the left, and now he could see both women, bodies and faces entirely relaxed, and recognized them instantly as the two young women in the fake wanted posters at the boat stops in the city centre. The officer with whom they were speaking, now clearly seen in profile, was easily identified as a smiling Lieutenant Scarpa.

Keeping his voice calm, Brunetti asked, 'How is it you come to have these?'

'They were in the bar down at the bridge. I stopped for a coffee this morning and Sergio gave the envelope to me, said someone left them there yesterday and told him there was no hurry, but they were for you.'

Brunetti looked more closely at the photos, trying to identify the location. He turned to his desk and set the three of them in a line, then stood aside so that Signorina Elettra could see them.

She moved a step or two closer and, recognizing the Lieutenant, whispered, 'Ma-

ria Santissima.' She studied them for some time, her head a searchlight going back and forth. She reached forward and tapped at the first photo. 'Campo Manin,' she said. 'There's the chain, and behind it you can see the steps of the monument.'

Imitating her, Brunetti bent and tapped his finger on Scarpa's jacket in each photo: one, two, three. 'It's in autumn, or winter.' She nodded, and he added, 'So it was long before their photos went on display at the vaporetto stops.'

'And well before much attention was being paid to them,' she agreed.

'Exactly,' Brunetti added, staring at them lined up there, and repeating the visual flow from anonymity to revelation.

Anticipating his question, she said, 'Sergio didn't remember anything about the man except that he wore sunglasses and a hat.'

Brunetti nodded and began to consider why the Lieutenant would stop, or allow himself to be stopped, to talk with these girls. So far as the law was concerned, they were two girls walking in the city with every right to do so. They had been detained numerous times, but they were minors and had been released each time, so they had the right to pass unimpeded by the forces of order. Not that Scarpa gave any indica-

325

tion by his posture that he was interested in impeding them in any way, Brunetti thought. Quite the opposite. The side of his mouth, in fact, was turned up, perhaps in a smile, as though he approved of something one of them had just said.

For their part, they appeared entirely relaxed and comfortable in his company: they did not smile — in fact, he could not now remember ever having seen any of the Rom he'd dealt with smile — but their expressions were far from the resentful uneasiness he saw in the faces of the frequently arrested. In fact, shorten their skirts and cut their hair, put Scarpa in a pair of jeans and a leather jacket, and they'd be any three people chatting on the street.

But who had taken these pictures and, more interesting, why had they thought to send them to him?

He looked at Signorina Elettra and asked, 'Is there any way you can . . .' but left the question unfinished because he wasn't sure what he'd like her to do.

She crossed her arms and leaned back against his desk, her stance and expression just as relaxed as those of the girls in the photos. 'I can begin by checking who's looked at the reports of their arrests.' Seeing his confusion, she explained, 'The system keeps track of the names of people who consult arrest records,' something he hadn't known and found profoundly disconcerting. She re-crossed her ankles and looked down as if to admire her shoes, saying, 'Anyone who comes to visit them or comes to claim them here has to present identification, which is scanned. If the person being held is a minor, the visitor has to be a relative or guardian appointed by the court and must present proof of that fact.' Then, as if having read his mind, she said, 'There's no record kept of our personnel who might visit or speak to them while they're here, only the signature of the person who approves their release.'

Brunetti considered all of this and said, 'I want to know who visited any time they were held here and what their relationship to the girls is. And I want the names of the people who came to pick them up every time they were released. Age, sex, relationship, criminal records, citizenship. I'd also like to know if the Lieutenant ever arrested them or any of the people who came to visit them or to take them home.'

When it was clear he had nothing further to say, Signorina Elettra pushed herself away from his desk. She nodded and went off to carry out his instructions.

He stacked the photos and slipped them back into the envelope, deciding in the instant to get them out of the Questura and to do it now. He left the building and chose the narrow *calli,* avoiding the grill that the *riva* had already become.

The faces of the Rom girls were still to be seen in the city, yet someone had noticed Scarpa with them as long ago as the autumn and found the trio worthy of a photograph. The social opinions of the Lieutenant were not known for their expansiveness, nor yet for their elasticity, so his smiling ease in the company of two young girls of Rom origin was unlikely to go down well in the circle of his friends. Or, failing those, his acquaintances.

But standing with them in a public place was hardly a crime. In fact, the ease and — yes — amiability of the man in the photo suggested that he could be their older brother or their uncle; most definitely their friend.

As he walked through the crowded streets, Brunetti thought again of the posters with the faces of these same girls, and he thought of the bold declaration: 'Thief.' They had at least been apprehended in the act of thievery: Scarpa had been apprehended by the anonymous photographer standing and talking to two young girls. He was guilty of no crime. As yet, there was no law prohibiting either friendship with Rom, or talking to them in a public place.

He stopped, stepped into the doorway of a house, and dialled Signorina Elettra's number.

'*Sì*, Commissario?'

'That last request I made to you before leaving, about finding some information about a person we know . . .'

'*Sì?*'

'I'd like you to forget I asked you to do it.'

'Of course, Signore,' she said, and Brunetti realized he had hoped she'd say more. After a moment, she did. 'I'm pleased you called.' And then she was gone.

At home, he slipped the envelope into the bookcase in Paola's study, between the two volumes of *The Atlas of Nineteenth Century London*. That done, he hunted for and finally found a collection of the poems of Leopardi and, deciding there was no sense in returning to the Questura, read them until lunchtime.

22

The afternoon passed without event or interruption. Brunetti divided his time between casting his eye over — it would be too much to call it reading — staffing plans for the following month and requests for information from other agencies of the state. A colleague in Rome wrote to say he was being given early retirement. The last time Brunetti had seen him — his colleague having taken the train up from Rome to have lunch with him and back to Rome the same afternoon — the man had asked him if he knew anything about the years a secretary to the Minister of Finance had spent in Venice, working as a lawyer for one of the construction companies involved in the MOSE project and who was now under criminal investigation.

Brunetti had begun by telling his colleague what the official opinion of the lawyer was and what high praise he had received in the newspapers and from both sides of the apparent gap between the political parties. And then, because they had worked together on a case, years before, and unsuccessfully, Brunetti trusted him enough to divulge part of his own opinion, which was not complimentary and was based almost entirely upon gossip and insinuation, those Venetian twins of truth.

The man he'd spoken to was only a few years older than Brunetti — three years at the most — and he was already being retired. Thinking of his own future, Brunetti wondered what it would be to hand back warrant card and service weapon, no longer to ask questions of anyone he chose, nor to spend his days solving problems, understanding mysteries, and occasionally initiating the process that would lead to the arrest of the criminal and the punishment of the . . .

His mind wandered away when he failed to find the correct word. Most of the people he arrested were weak creatures who gave in to passing temptation or impulse, meaning to do no real harm and then, afterwards, stunned by the consequences of the actions they'd never planned or the devastation they had caused.

He'd retire; someone would take his place,

and people would continue to harm and cheat and kill one another. Brunetti stopped himself there, knowing no good could come of going down this path. He concentrated on the paper he was reading but was instantly struck by a sudden restlessness and the equal need to resist it. He quickly skimmed the remaining reports on his desk and only then accepted the fact that there was nothing else he had to read.

The only thing remaining was the video of a young officer conducting his first interrogation of a suspect. An optician in Frezzeria had been robbed three nights before, and yesterday a man had been arrested while trying to sell new Ray-Bans in Campo San Luca.

Brunetti did what he always did when watching these videos: he looked at it first without sound so that he could see what the body of the suspect, and the interrogator, told him. By the second viewing, his brain had usually formed an impression of the person being questioned, as well as of the person asking the questions, although he tried not to let his response pass beyond the physical and intuitive. He watched them as he would people who were waiting to board the same plane or who sat in his line of sight in a restaurant.

He watched the suspect's eyes as they shifted to and from the face of the man interviewing him, saw the confusion, the nervous shakes of his head at what must be observations or new questions, and he saw the moment when, listening to the officer speaking to him, he realized he had no hope. His expression became weak and furtive as his mind scurried in search of an excuse, an alibi, a justification, anything that would obviate whatever it was the officer had just told him. Finally he put his hands over his ears, as a child would at the sound of a reprimand. He followed that by closing his eyes, as if that would help stop the sound of the evidence the police had against him.

The officer waited without speaking. The suspect put his hands on the table and opened his eyes. The officer, face calm and one hand raised in an easy gesture, spoke to him for a moment, perhaps offering something in exchange for collaboration.

The suspect closed his eyes again and pulled both hands into fists. He pushed at his lips with one, while the other man sat facing him quietly, hands folded on the table in front of him.

This is when he'll break, Brunetti thought, and this made it happen. The suspect nodded, folded his hands, and rocked back and forth a few times. He lowered his head and spoke for a long time, occasionally glancing up at the officer, who nodded silently. The suspect stopped speaking; the officer said something and stood. He spoke again to the suspect, who stood and followed him from the room.

Brunetti told himself there was no real need, now, to watch the interrogation a second time, listening to their voices, but still he began. He watched for five minutes, and nothing he heard in any way went counter to what he had inferred from watching the silent figures.

He was halfway through when his phone rang. He stopped the video and answered. 'Brunetti.'

'It's Renzo Pandolfi,' the professor said. 'I've spoken to a few of my colleagues.'

Brunetti closed the screen of his computer and asked, 'About Dottoressa Ricciardi?'

'Yes,' Pandolfi said, adding, 'Except it's not Dottoressa. She took a Master's degree and is still enrolled in the doctoral programme.'

Brunetti thought of the university system, clogged with non-attending students and people who seldom bothered to take exams. 'Enrolled and likely to finish, or merely enrolled?'

'Enrolled and likely to finish, but she hasn't chosen a topic for a doctoral dissertation yet.'

'And?'

'Two men who'd had her in their classes said she was intelligent and was widely read.'

'You sound hesitant,' Brunetti said, for want of another word.

'Her one female professor said she was a student with an excellent memory but perhaps not suited to work in psychology.'

'Did she say why?'

'Not on the phone. But we've known one another for a long time, so she suggested we meet for a coffee.'

'And?'

'And she said she thinks the woman is a narcissist and probably always has been.' Pandolfi lapsed into silence after that, like a guilty man before confession, until he finally said, 'I probably shouldn't be telling you this, but I trust Paola, so I suppose I can trust you, too.'

'Thank you,' Brunetti said.

'Ricciardi was a student in my friend's class. She was a very good student: bright and attentive, but had trouble working in a group, at least a group where she was not in charge.' Had Paola heard the remark, it occurred to Brunetti, she would have smiled and asked Pandolfi if he'd ever heard the same judgement passed on a male student.

A more temperate Brunetti said, 'Interesting.' He waited for Pandolfi to continue, but had to nudge him by asking, 'Only that?'

'She said she noticed it in the tutorials, that Ricciardi most often spoke about herself, saw everything through the lens of her own experience and importance.'

After saying that, Pandolfi stopped speaking; Brunetti decided to wait him out. After what seemed a very long time, the professor continued, 'My friend is a good teacher and an experienced psychologist.'

'Do you think she'd speak to me?' Brunetti asked.

The answer was immediate. 'No.'

'Did you tell her I was a police officer?'

'Yes. I told her that before I asked her any questions.'

'And she still answered?'

'She said she'd tell me, but she wouldn't speak to the police. She doesn't trust them. You.'

'I see,' Brunetti said. 'Then that's that, I suppose.'

'I'd say so,' Pandolfi agreed; 'at least as far as I can be of help.' When Brunetti didn't respond, Pandolfi said, 'Say hello to Paola for me,' and ended the call.

After getting to his office the following morning, Brunetti turned his attention to the sky visible from his window and wondered if this was the endless blue that shipwrecked mariners saw from their lifeboats. Though there had been storms on the mainland, it had not rained in the city for some time, and the usually cheerful blue had begun to menace him with the threat that it might never change. What happens if it doesn't rain? he wondered. Do we simply stay here until the water is gone? If the rivers disappeared and the aquifers ran dry, the seas on either side of the peninsula would be no help at all, and Venetians could not drink the water that had given their city life.

Mention of the water situation had been frequent in the two papers, one local and one national, that he read every day. In the bars, as well, he heard people express concern about the bizarre contrast between the torrential rains and flooding of only a few weeks ago and the ensuing lack of rain; a few had even suggested that consumption should somehow be limited. In the past, Brunetti had heard people — always women — ask a barista to turn off the perpetually running water in the sink, a request that had always caused trouble, as if one of the perks of working in a bar or *pasticceria* was the right to waste as much water as one pleased.

Recently, though, *vox pop* had switched to the side of the public, leaving angry baristas isolated in their wastefulness. Brunetti, however, allowed himself no optimism about these trace elements of behaviour, not with a daughter who, on the subject of the environment, was as grim as any of Dante's damned.

Where did the water they drank come from, anyway? The mountains, the rivers? He had no idea. Still thinking of water, Brunetti closed his eyes and tried to remember what Dottor Veltrini had explained to him about the apportioning of responsibility to the three people in the lab. Each was in charge of specific areas and would thus note fluctuations in pollutants or contaminants in their areas. What happened when a permissible level of pollution was exceeded? he asked himself, not allowing himself to consider what 'permissible pollution' might mean. To whom was it reported? Signorina Elettra had been as busy as Santa's little helpers with the files and records of Dottor Veltrini's laboratory, but Brunetti had not had time to ask about them.

He leaned forward and lifted his phone to call her.

'Sì, Signore?' she answered.

'Who does the lab at Spattuto have to report to if they find polluted or contaminated water?'

She paused for a moment, and he heard a few keys click. When that noise stopped, she said, 'To the branch of the Carabinieri who deal with environmental crimes, the Forestry Police, and, if there's any evidence of Mafia involvement, the Anti-Mafia Directorates.' After another moment she added, 'The Ministry of the Environment might be involved, but it's the Carabinieri who do the first investigations.'

'Did you find the reports from the lab?'

'I'm just finishing with the last two months, sir. It might take me another fifteen minutes to retrieve all of them.' Before he could ask, she added, 'They're the results of all of the tests performed on water samples

340

in the various areas.'

'Good. Send them when you can.' Then, before she could end the call, he added, 'Is it possible for you to arrange the reports according to who performed them?'

'Any way you'd like it, Commissario. By contaminant, by seriousness of the contamination, by date, by zone, by geographic coordinates, even by time of day,' she told him, audibly proud of her capacity.

'By zone, then,' Brunetti said. He replaced the phone and went back to the consideration of the sky.

A fair bit of time passed; it would not be incorrect to say that Brunetti's thoughts drifted away from the Questura as his head fell forward on his chest, where it remained until it was yanked upward by the ping that announced an incoming email. He pulled back his feet and scootched his chair closer to his desk, shook his head a few times, opened the mail from Signorina Elettra, then the attachment.

There were eleven pages, listed by the name of the person responsible for the geographic zone, giving the readings made in the last two months from samples of contaminated water detected by the various sensors placed in the territories under Spattuto's authority. He read through them, then again, more carefully.

He picked up the phone and called Signorina Elettra.

'*Sì,* Signore?'

'The quantities of the pollutants that they find in these samples, how does a non-chemist know how dangerous they are?'

'Ah,' she said in a long breath. 'Of course.' She was silent for a moment, then said, 'Give me five minutes, and I'll send it to you again. I'll list the toxicity for you.'

'Good. Thanks,' he said and hung up to leave her to it.

While he waited for her email, he looked at the results listed for the sites overseen by Signora Sala during the first of the two weeks preceding Fadalto's death. Traces of animal faeces had been found on the second day, traces of iron on the third, copper on the next and arsenic on the last. The levels were so low that the sensors apparently registered them without sending an alarm.

He flipped to the sites checked by her female colleague during the same period and saw much the same results for the first two substances as well as mention of microplastics, though there was no evidence of arsenic.

The results for the sensors in Dottor Veltrini's zone were much the same for the first week, save for the brief appearance of Bisfenolo in one sample on the fourth day.

The ping of his computer stole Brunetti's concentration as it announced the arrival of the newly added information about the level of toxicity. He reread all of the entries for the first week and saw that the only substance that had earned a rating in the table of toxicity that Signorina Elettra had added was Bisfenolo.

It was when he started looking at the records of the next week, the one before Fadalto's death, that Brunetti became confused. At the beginning of the week, mercury, like the god after which it was named, made a sudden appearance in one of the sensors, only to disappear entirely by the time the next reading had been registered. The same sensor that had registered the mercury noted, four hours later, vinyl chloride, although that too had disappeared before arriving at the next sensor.

He looked at the wall, imagining possible scenarios. He opened his server, found the files of *Il Gazzettino* and checked for the exact dates of the heavy rains that, he remembered, had fallen farther north in those days. None had fallen in Venice, but there was an article about torrential rain near Belluno and the resulting erosion of the banks of the Piave, flooding, and damage to crops. There was also a photo of a car floating upside down in the Piave near Susegana. Succeeding editions of the newspaper also carried stories about the rain, which continued all through the week, always falling near Belluno and refusing to move south.

That might explain, Brunetti reasoned, the lessening — even the disappearance — of contamination in the samples as the flooded river diluted the elements present. But what explained the anomalous readings? How was it possible for these substances to have appeared, only to vanish so quickly?

Nothing similar was registered in the following week; indeed, the results were similar to those of the previous month, save for the cameo appearance of arsenic, whose very name frightened Brunetti, until Signorina Elettra's rating of 'low' for the toxicity of the recorded quantity put his spirit to rest.

Certain that Signorina Elettra's curiosity would have been provoked as much as his own, Brunetti closed the file and went down to speak to her. She greeted him with a nod and returned her attention to her computer, saying, 'It doesn't make any sense to me, either.'

Hands busy on the keys, she said, 'I'm checking to see if they reported it to the Carabinieri.' While he waited, Brunetti wondered how she might access this information. She'd already burgled Spattuto's system, so she had access from there: child's play to see if they'd sent it. Entry into the database of the Carabinieri, a branch of the state police that often dealt with matters of some importance, should have presented her with some obstacles. It was possible that, like a pianist wanting to keep in shape, she might have chosen to have a go at them. The seals and letterheads that appeared on the screen suggested that she had, and successfully.

After some minutes, she stopped scrolling. 'There it is,' she said neutrally, never one to call attention to her skills.

He read the document, which bore the Carabinieri letterhead and referred to a Spattuto mail, copied below it. Earlier that month, the company had reported a malfunction of their sensor #B287-B-2H5. The sensor — the geographical coordinates followed — when extracted and examined, showed signs of corrosion on two internal circuits and had been replaced. The two readings, the Spattuto mail continued, which had caused the sensor to be removed and taken to the laboratory for examination, should thus be considered the result of error and ignored. The readings from the next sensor downstream — which had been examined and shown to be in working order — in no way corroborated these readings and thus were further evidence that the first readings were the result of malfunction. The report bore no signature but was issued by the Analytic Laboratory of Spattuto SpA.

'What do you think?' Brunetti asked, straightening up and stepping away from the computer screen.

Her eyes still on the document, Signorina Elettra answered, 'Until I can go back through their correspondence and see if anything like this ever happened before, I'd say it sounds entirely convincing.'

'Do your friends ever tire of your scepticism?' Brunetti asked.

She turned and graced him with her warmest smile. 'Given the country in which we live, Commissario, I suspect they have come to expect it.'

'Indeed,' was the only answer he could find. Then, before he could ask how long it would take, she said, 'Why don't you go down to the bar and have a coffee, Signore?

I should have it by the time you get back.'

Brunetti nodded and started towards the door. 'Don't forget to drink some water, Signore,' he heard from behind him. 'This heat is too much.'

Brunetti took his time and had a second glass of mineral water after his coffee, lingered to read the copy of *Il Gazzettino* on the bar, and spoke with the Senegalese barman, whose family had recently joined him in Italy. These normal things distracted and calmed him.

He stopped at the door to Signorina Elettra's office on the way back to his own; she smiled and waved him in, saying, 'I've checked their records for the last two years. Nothing like this had ever happened.' Before Brunetti could ask, she said, 'I'm running a check on the two years before that now.'

He went over to her desk but didn't bother to check the screen of her computer: she'd tell him. She pushed her chair back and turned to look at him. 'I think you've ruined me, Commissario,' she said, sounding and looking serious.

Not sure whether he should be alarmed or not, Brunetti asked, 'In what way, Signorina?'

'I've become suspicious about human behaviour. If I read in the paper that a man backed out of his garage and hit and killed his wife, I begin to wonder whether he planned it; if I go into a jewellery shop, I start working out how best to rob it; whenever a person is interviewed on television, I assume they're lying about something.' She held up her hands in a sign of helpless surrender.

'I'm not sure whether you're angry with me, Signorina, or want to thank me.'

She lowered her head and considered the state of her right thumbnail. 'I share your uncertainty, Commissario,' she began. 'It interests me that Vittorio Fadalto was in charge of the inspection and maintenance of the sensors,' she said, looking up to meet his glance. 'It's in the information they sent in response to your request,' she added, not bothering to apologize for reading his mail.

Brunetti considered this: Fadalto, around whose death all of this had begun. He nodded towards her computer and asked, 'Can you show me a map of where the areas are, and where the sensors are?'

She gave him a long look and moved closer to the computer; she brought new pages into view. From where Brunetti was standing, the glare from the screen prevented him from reading the documents.

She typed in requests, but nothing that came on to the screen pleased her. She muttered something under her breath, hit a few more keys, and a satisfied 'Ah' escaped her lips.

Brunetti took a step closer and saw a map bisected by a crooked blue line that meandered from upper left to bottom right. It wasn't until he bent even closer and read the name 'Ponte di Piave' that he had any idea of the location. Smack in the middle of the floodplain of the river Piave, the town was at perpetual risk from the erratic rise of the waters.

Signorina Elettra hit a few keys, and the map changed: three parcels of land, separated by thin dotted lines indicating different ownership, appeared on the eastern side of what tiny letters identified as the Piave River. The rectangular shape of a single building stood in each parcel. She hit another key, shrinking the size of the buildings and greatly expanding the area displayed. She moved the cursor and hit a few more keys, and what looked like a series of tiny red microphones appeared in the river passing through the zones.

'The sensors?' Brunetti asked.

'Yes, sir,' she answered. 'I have no idea what they look like, so I thought microphones would at least suggest a resemblance.'

'They do,' Brunetti said. 'And nicely.'

'Thank you,' Signorina Elettra said in quite a normal way. 'I've put one at each of the geographical coordinates of the sensors.'

Brunetti waved his hand across the three rectangles of property. 'Is there any way to learn what these buildings are and what's in them?' he asked.

She put her left elbow on the desk and rested her chin in her hand, and began to peck at her keyboard with the fingers of her right hand. She studied the document that replaced the map and pecked some more.

Suddenly she sat upright and began to type with both hands, and Brunetti felt himself disappear. That is, Signorina Elettra ceased to be aware that he was in the room with her. He was sure of this. He could have begun to pirouette, gone to sleep on the floor, walked to the window and jumped: she would not have noticed. He walked over and sat on the windowsill, the better to watch her work.

Type and pause, type and wait, type and study, type and type, nod, smile, type again, stop, look across the room and smile. 'I've found everything except for a small office in one of the buildings, but that's because it's un-rented at the moment.'

one of the buildings, but that's because it's imprinted at the moment

24

Brunetti walked over to have a look at the screen. It now showed an aerial view of the three buildings, photos of their façades taken from the other side of the street, and a second aerial view from a greater height that included the area behind them, extending down to the river. When Brunetti looked more closely at the aerial photos, he saw that each building had a parking lot behind it, small cars parked obediently between white lines.

Using the cars as a rough measure, he estimated that the buildings were about a hundred metres from one another, perhaps less, with only low grass growing on the land between them. Each had a footpath leading from the back of the parking lot to the river: the path behind the building at the far right of the photo was lined by a tall, well-trimmed hedge that ran as far as the river and provided a welcome touch of green to the otherwise barren landscape.

'This is one of the areas that Dottor Veltrini oversees,' Signorina Elettra said, waving towards the one with the hedge.

'What sort of businesses are they?' Brunetti asked.

She brought the information on to the screen. The building at the far left was a distribution point for a supermarket chain: this would explain the many trucks reversed against the loading dock at the back of the building.

The second was a warehouse for a distributor of parts for trucks, tractors, and motorcycles. The trucks backed up to its loading dock looked smaller than those of the supermarket.

The last was a factory producing wire cables and automobile parts, specializing in custom-made upholstery for luxury cars. A few trucks were backed up to the loading dock.

'That's all, eh?' he asked.

She nodded.

'Could you print me a copy of the owners and tenants?' he asked, tired of looking at surveyors' drawings on the screen. He still found print to be, somehow, more real. He thought of Chiara's and Raffi's willed commitment to a paperless world and was proud to concede them the ecological high ground. But still he preferred paper. What was it St Augustine had said, 'Lord, make me pure, but not yet'?

He waited while she did it, his thoughts turned from his daughter's desire to save the natural world to some of the things his fellow citizens were capable of doing to destroy it. A week didn't pass but he read of forest fires, small and large, all the result of arson, and of the cavalier disregard with which his countrymen treated their jointly owned patrimony. His memory flashed back to the refrigerator he and Griffoni had seen hauled out of the Rio dei Lustraferi.

When Signorina Elettra handed him the papers, he said, 'I'd like Vianello to read this. Could you send him a copy?'

She seemed surprised by his request and asked, 'Did you look at today's roster?'

Brunetti seldom did but thought that an inadequate excuse. 'I didn't have time. Why?'

'The Ispettore is in Mestre today and will be again tomorrow, perhaps even the next day,' she said, providing no explanation.

'Why?'

'He's been summoned as a witness in a trial,' she began and instantly corrected herself. 'It's really a hearing, not a trial.

354

They're minors, after all.'

Thinking of the plague of adolescent crime that had afflicted the city for months and the arrest, a week ago, of four members of the 'baby gang' who had been mugging and robbing children their own age, he asked, 'How can there already be a hearing? They caught them last week.'

'I'm sorry, Signore, but it's not that gang. These are the ones who were caught two years ago.'

'And the hearing is only now?' he asked mildly, unable to be surprised. 'They must be eighteen by now.'

'I should think so,' Signorina Elettra answered with equal calm.

'Perhaps you could send it to Claudia,' he asked, intentionally not using her surname.

'I've already done that, Commissario,' she said.

He nodded, and went on. 'See if you can get us a roster of Spattuto's employees and the names of anyone mentioned in the newspaper accounts of Fadalto's death.'

Signorina Elettra folded her arms across her chest and looked at her computer screen. Brunetti thought about whether a creature with more sensitive hearing — a dog, say — would be able to detect the sound of the gears turning in her head.

She looked up, smiling, and said, 'Interesting possibilities, sir.'

Brunetti nodded at this. 'There are pieces lying all over the place,' he said, 'but no way of putting any two of them together. Little things: Fadalto's job was to collect samples of contamination, but the lab has no report of contamination. Fadalto's wife said "they" killed him, but there's no "they", and now she's dead, too, and we'll never know what he found or knew. There's talk of "bad money", but there's no sign of money. A man considers himself a Don Giovanni, but two women think he's anything but.'

Smiling, Signorina Elettra said, 'How rare, Signore.'

He raised the papers between them, saying, 'Thank you for these,' and turned to leave her office.

'I'll have another look,' she said. He was disappointed not to hear the sound of hunting horns in her voice as she said this.

'Whatever you can, Signorina,' he replied and went back upstairs.

He set the papers on his desk and pulled open his drawer to look for a highlighter pen, then began searching for the names of the owners and tenants of the three buildings. There were quite a few, and Signorina

Elettra had somehow managed to find the names of the employees of most of the companies, as well. Brunetti highlighted the names in green as he found them and kept at it until he had twenty-six, eight of them Chinese.

He turned to the varied pieces of information she had — he struggled over the verb — 'accessed' from Spattuto. There was a document giving the name of Fadalto's wife and children and the name and number to call in an emergency. He highlighted all of these names in pink.

Dottoressa Ricciardi's information was already familiar to him; he read through it nevertheless but found nothing new.

He read the files of the two lab technicians, Antonella Sala and Elisa Guttardi, but nothing written about either woman seemed of use to him.

Last was Dottor Veltrini, whose first wife, Vittoria Cavallini, received a payment of seven hundred Euros taken directly from his salary every month. Brunetti stopped at the name and went back to the list of the employees in the three buildings. He found her in UMBIS Elements, the automobile seat cover factory behind which was the sensor that had signalled the excessive quantities of mercury and vinyl chloride, where she worked as an accountant.

'*Dio mio,*' Brunetti whispered. He reached for his phone and dialled Griffoni's number.

'*Sì?*' she said.

'You've seen the name?' he asked.

'Yes.'

'What do you think?'

'It could be an innocent coincidence.'

'And just as easily a guilty one,' he replied pleasantly, then asked, 'Shall we go out there so you can talk to him?'

'When?' she asked.

'I'll come up and get you,' he said. 'Not long.'

'Good,' she said and hung up.

He gathered the papers into a pile and stared down at the top sheet. He sat for a while, casting his memory back to their last visit to Signora Toso, when she told them her husband 'Took the results'. There had been no time to ask her more: what results? How did he find them? Where were they? The arrival of Dotoressa Donato had put an end to questions. Signora Toso had mistaken the footsteps and believed her daughters had arrived. He stared at the page for a long time, replaying the scene. He remembered the long silence spiralling out from whatever Griffoni had asked her, something about the results, although he failed to recall her exact words.

Then the long squeal of the opening door announced the entry of Dottoressa Donato into his memory. Brunetti shoved his chair back and got suddenly to his feet. Leaving the papers on his desk, he left his office and went quickly up the stairs to Griffoni's.

She turned when he reached her door, surprised perhaps by the speed of his footsteps. 'Do you have the recording you made in Signora Toso's room?' he asked with no introduction.

Clearly surprised at his question, she answered calmly, 'Yes, I do.'

'Could I hear it?' he asked, immediately amending that to, 'Could we, I mean. Towards the end.'

'Of course,' she said, reaching for the phone lying on her desk. She picked it up, then touched the screen a few times, responding to whatever possibilities the phone offered her. Without looking away from the screen, she stood and moved beside her chair, allowing Brunetti to squeeze past and replace it before sitting on the chair on the other side of her desk.

She sat, placed the phone in the middle of the desk, and gave one final tap. 'How did Vittorio get the money, Benedetta?' Griffoni's recorded voice said into the silent room.

Then came the series of long, deep breaths, each one, now, sounding like a preparation for the last one, so soon to come.

Finally the puzzling answer, so long delayed, 'Took the results.' He felt again his pounding desire to help Griffoni ask the question; she had not needed his help. 'Do you have them, Benedetta?'

'No.'

To hear the lack of delay between that answer and Griffoni's next question was to hear his colleague at her most relentless, using her seducer's kindly voice. 'Can you tell me where they are?' Griffoni was too sly to ask her if she would tell her. Instead, she tried to enlist the help of a woman she knew to be close to death. 'Can you', as if it were only a question of will or energy, for surely Benedetta Toso would want to answer that question, wouldn't she?

Brunetti leaned forward in his chair, as though he feared he would not be able to hear the sounds he knew were coming. The door squeaked, a long sound that ended when it was fully open. He counted to himself the silent seconds that were still to elapse. One, two, three: perhaps not seconds, but surely long pauses, certainly enough time for Signora Toso to see that the girls, as she had agreed, were not there.

360

And then it came, that clear declaration, 'The girls. The girls.'

Then a long silence that ended with the doctor's question, 'How are you today, Benedetta?' and the now unbearable reply, 'Alive.'

Griffoni tapped the screen, and the room grew quiet.

'Do you hear it?' Brunetti asked.

'Hear what?' Griffoni asked, obviously confused.

'You ask her where the results are. Then the door opens, but she's already decided that the girls aren't going to come that day. The door opens, and there's plenty of time for her to see that the girls obeyed and aren't there. And then she says, "The girls. The girls."'

'Yes,' Griffoni confirmed, still not understanding, still not hearing.

'She's answering your question, Claudia. She's telling you where the results are. They're with "The girls. The girls."'

Griffoni froze, one hand halfway to her cheek to push back a strand of hair. She redirected the hand to the phone and tapped it a few times, and the sound picked up again with her own voice asking, 'Can you tell me where they are?'

The knock, the endless squeak and then

361

the even more endless time before she identified her children who were not there, and then the doctor's cheerful arrival.

Griffoni tapped the phone to silence and said, 'Of course.'

Brunetti suggested that Griffoni make the call. Signora Toso answered, and Griffoni asked how she and the girls were. When the woman began to answer naturally, Griffoni made a thumbs-up signal to Brunetti and continued to listen for some time, occasionally murmuring in wordless agreement or sympathy. After letting Signora Toso speak for a long time, she asked if it would be possible for them to come to talk to her again; in response to a question, she explained that they had new information that might be helpful.

'We could come after lunch,' she suggested to whatever Signora Toso answered. When the girls were more likely to be at home, Brunetti assumed, again marvelling at the amiable perfidy of Griffoni's mind.

After a lunch neither of them paid any attention to, they had Foa drop them in front of the church of San Pantalon, for whom, Brunetti remembered, his mother had had a strong devotion — something to do with a bath of lead, or was it a floating stone?

On the *riva,* Griffoni chose to go to the right, instead of the left, but at the end of the *calle,* in front of Tonolo, she turned left and led him unerringly towards and over the bridge. At the top, she paused. 'I came back and found it, but there was no chewing gum under the railing,' she said, sounding almost disappointed and then starting down the steps.

He rang the bell and they walked, this time more slowly, to the third floor.

Signora Toso was at the door and shook hands with both of them, stepped back to let them in. On the way there, Griffoni and Brunetti had discussed how to say what they had to say without disclosing the circumstances in which it had been said, neither of them wanting to subject this woman to hearing her sister's voice so soon before her death.

The smells from lunch lingered in the apartment: lentils, something with peppers, and fish. 'The girls are resting,' she said, stepping back to let them come in.

When they were back in the room with the view over Campo Santa Margherita, Griffoni explained why they had returned. 'After your sister said that she didn't have the results her husband had found,' she told Signora Toso, 'I asked her if she knew where they were.' Brunetti prepared himself, his memory still stinging from the sound of the four words shouted by the dying woman.

'And she said, "The girls, the girls",' Griffoni continued, her own voice as calm as she could force it to be.

Signora Toso closed her eyes, leaned against the back of the sofa, and, in the manner of a small child, pressed the fingers of her left hand against her mouth. She shook her head a few times, as in regret or recrimination.

Her eyes opened and she looked at Brunetti, then said, abandoning the language of law and speaking Veneziano, their own language, 'Is this what she said?'

'Yes.'

'You heard her say it?' she asked him in the same language. It was not that Signora Toso didn't see the other woman. She could have reached out and touched Griffoni's knee: she was that close. She simply discounted the fact that this foreigner was there.

La go sentio,' Brunetti said, telling a truth. He had heard it.

Signora Toso closed her eyes again and, with the decorum of childhood, folded her hands on her lap. Once she pressed her lips together in a sign of disappointment or

364

resignation, or both. Once she brushed a strand of hair back behind her ear.

With no warning, she got to her feet. Brunetti, without thinking, stood and moved aside to give her greater freedom of movement. She slipped around him and went to the door where the girls had last stood. She opened it, closed it, leaving them to make of her behaviour what they would.

Neither spoke; neither moved. Brunetti finally went over to the window. Only then, looking down into the unsparing light in the *campo,* was he conscious of how hot the apartment was. He slipped his left hand inside his jacket: his shirt was soaked all the way down to his belt. The jacket had become so much his second skin that removing it would not have changed anything.

Because it was not his home, he could not open the windows, though for the life of him he could not understand why they were left closed during the worst of the day. He turned back to Griffoni, but she was sitting, arms propped on those of her chair, mouth pressed against the steeple of her fingers.

He turned back and looked again at the *campo.* Even the dogs had no taste for play but walked tiredly beside their owners, most of them choosing to be shadowed by their legs. If you were wearing your fur, he reflected, then even that little bit of shade might help.

He heard the door behind him open and her footsteps cross the floor. When he turned, she was setting what appeared to be a navy blue rucksack on a low table at the end of the sofa.

She turned to face him and said, 'Daria brought it home the evening before Vittorio died. 'I have no idea what's inside. She told me he'd given it to her at the hospital and asked them to keep it safe.' Before either of them could ask, she continued, 'That's all she said. She put it in the bottom of her closet. She says that she and Livia have told no one about it.'

'Did they open it?'

'He told them not to,' Signora Toso said, thinking this was an answer. Brunetti let it be.

Suddenly Griffoni was beside him.

'Signora,' Brunetti said. 'Please thank the girls for us. I think they did the right thing.' Before she had a chance to speak, he said, 'I'd like you to go back to them, Signora.'

Both women seemed surprised by his request, but it was Signora Toso who asked, 'So you can see what's inside?'

Brunetti answered in Veneziano, 'And so that you don't know what's there.'

She appeared to consider what he said, nodded, and went back towards the door. When it closed, Brunetti, ignoring the rules regarding the treatment of evidence, opened the flap of the bag and loosened the strings that held the top together. He pulled it fully open and bent to look inside, then pulled out a sealed brown manila envelope. With no hesitation, he ran his finger under the flap and opened it; he reached inside and drew out a stack of hundred-Euro notes bound with the white paper band that banks used to wrap large sums of money. Then he reached back in and pulled out another.

He placed them on the table. 'It looks like twenty thousand,' he said and peered into the backpack to see if there was more, but there was not. He and Griffoni stared at the money. It seemed so innocent lying there, so inert. Who would think it could have been the cause of so much trouble? And green, the colour of hope.

Brunetti turned the backpack on its side and inserted both hands. With some jockeying back and forth, he extracted a flat black plastic case that looked like a toolbox. He pressed the clasp and raised the lid. Inside he saw a long tube the size and shape of a cucumber lying flat in a hollow cut in a piece of black Styrofoam. A similar hollow was cut in the lid. He lowered it over the tube and clicked it closed. The fit was perfect.

He opened it again and bent to look at the tube. The bottom was made of smooth black metal, the top thick, transparent glass. It appeared to be filled with water; a serial number was cut into the steel ring dividing top from bottom.

Brunetti held the backpack up to the light, the better to peer inside; a legal-sized envelope lay on the bottom. He pulled it out; unlike the manila envelope, it was unsealed. He opened it and saw that it contained a single sheet of paper bearing the Spattuto logo at the top. He set the empty backpack on the floor and placed the paper on the table beside the open toolbox, then moved aside, an invitation to Griffoni to come and have a look.

The page had a serial number and then a date and time at the top. Griffoni bent down and ran her finger along the number on the paper: both of them saw that it was the same number as on the tube, which Brunetti realized was one of the sensors.

There was no mystery here, no need for great scientific knowledge to read the report: the time was 3 a.m. the readings were the names and quantities of the materials contained within the tube. Some were strangers: clorato, beta estradiolo, and microcistine. Present were also his old friends mercurio and vinyl chloride, but because he now understood how to interpret their presence per billion, he saw that they registered an unsetting reading of 3 per billion of mercury and 2.2 per billion of vinyl chloride.

Beside him, Griffoni leaned over, almost as if she thought that seeing the information from closer up would clarify her understanding of the numbers. Her head went back and forth, turning into a golden beacon in search of truth or trouble. Finally she stood upright and said. 'I give up, Guido.' Her arm arched over the box and the paper and she said, 'All right. What happened?'

'Someone dumped mercury and vinyl chloride into the river.'

25

It took Brunetti a few minutes to explain his theory and tell Griffoni about his visit to Spattuto Acqua. If the torrential rains had leached the chemicals from land permeated by years of leaks and dumpings, the rise would have been slow, gradual, and consistent, as would have been their disappearance: subsequent readings would have shown a gradual diminution of the two substances, and it would have been impossible for the incident to have gone unreported. But by the time the substances were carried to the next sensor, the racing water would have diluted them down to innocuous quantities, and they would have continued unnoted towards the Adriatic.

'You mean someone carried this stuff down to the edge of the river and simply dumped it into the water?' Griffoni asked, making no attempt to disguise her disbelief.

Brunetti tilted his head and raised his

eyebrows, as if to suggest resignation to the inevitable. He picked up the single sheet of paper and placed it on top of the plastic case to give his hands something to do. 'I don't see any other way to explain what's in this report,' he said.

As if Brunetti had not spoken, Griffoni asked, 'That's when the fish died, isn't it?' She glanced away, eyes fixed on the past, and added, 'Carried down to the mouth of the river. About the same time. Thousands of dead fish.'

Brunetti remembered reading about this during the time of the heavy rains. 'It was never explained, at least not in the papers.'

Nodding towards the backpack, she said, 'What's in there explains it.'

'And the money? What does that explain?' he asked her, wondering if she would make the same connection he had.

The question caught her full attention. Brunetti watched her figure it out. 'If it's Fadalto's backpack, it means the sensor and the lab results are proof of what happened.' She followed the trail this idea laid down, slowed to consider closely, and said, 'And he used it to blackmail them for the money his wife called "bad"?'

'I think so,' Brunetti answered, then continued. 'The "bad" money he never got

371

to use to pay his wife's bills,' he said, closing the circle of their reasoning.

After some time, Griffoni said, pointing at the backpack, 'But then they should have had the sensor and the report back.'

Brunetti had wondered about this himself as well, and said, 'Maybe that was just a down payment.'

Her response was instant. 'It would be reason to kill him, wouldn't it?'

He picked up the backpack, saying, 'Without having this, it's unlikely they'd risk it.'

She didn't look persuaded. And leaped ahead to ask, 'Dottor Veltrini?'

'I can't think of anyone else,' Brunetti answered.

'And so?'

'And so we go and talk to him.'

Smoothness disappeared from her face, and she said, 'Even if he admits it . . .' and stopped. Starting again, sounding angry. 'Did you hear what I just said? "If he *admits* it." ' She looked across at Brunetti and waited for him to answer. When he failed to do so, she went on, voice tighter, ' "Admit", as if he'd stolen a chicken or a pair of socks.'

'What would you prefer to have said?' Brunetti asked.

'Confess,' she said loudly. 'He's committed a crime, for God's sake. He's let people

372

dump — or done it himself — poison into the water we drink.' Then, with the slowness that comes with newly accepted truths, she added, 'They're killing our children.'

In hopes of preventing further verbal excess, Brunetti said, 'My children, perhaps.'

Her head whipped around and she said, angry now, 'What's that supposed to mean?'

'That it puts real children at risk, not rhetorical children.'

'Whose?' she demanded.

Brunetti suddenly realized that this conversation had wheeled out of his control and they were speaking, if not arguing, at cross purposes. 'I'm sorry, Claudia; I meant my real children, not your rhetorical ones.'

She froze. Seeing this, he said, hoping to quieten things down, 'I'm sorry, Claudia. I didn't mean to offend you. I'm afraid I was being too literal-minded.'

In an entirely different voice, Griffoni said, 'My child isn't rhetorical, Guido. My daughter's nineteen.'

My God, what had he done? Had he insulted her, offended her, forced her to tell him something he had no business knowing?

Brunetti, bent on preserving whatever fragment of normality remained, closed the black case, picked up the backpack, and tried to reinsert the case. His hands were perhaps less steady than they usually were, for the case would not fit horizontally through the opening at the top. Griffoni took the backpack from him, loosened the strings further and pulled the opening wider. Brunetti slipped the case in, slid the papers on top of it, retrieved the packs of money and placed them on the papers, and pulled the top closed.

Neither of them spoke for some time, as if each were waiting for the other to say or ask something. Finally Griffoni asked, pointing to the backpack, 'What are you going to do with the money?'

'Give it back to the girls,' he said. 'I don't know what else to do with it.'

'If we're going out to Spattuto, we could ask the driver to stop at the Casinò for twenty minutes and lose it all.'

Brunetti recalled how it had been when he was still a child and believed in God and all that he had been told by the priests and sisters. Each time he emerged from the darkened cave of the confessional, after logging in his mini-sins and being absolved of their weight, his spirit had been exalted by the belief that he was free of sin and thus was free of guilt. He felt the same lightness of heart now with Griffoni's joke: he had not wounded her by forcing her to speak of her daughter; he had not done something wrong and painful.

He went to the door Signora Toso had used, opened it and called her name. When she came, he told her they'd had a look at the backpack but had left everything there. He asked her to make the girls renew their promise not to open it. Without asking any questions, she agreed and went to pick up the bag. 'You can trust them,' she said, then backed out of the room, and closed the door.

On the way downstairs, Brunetti pulled out his phone and punched in the number of the Mestre Questura and asked how long it would take to have a car waiting for him and Commissario Griffoni at Piazzale Roma.

When he had the answer, he turned to her and said, 'There's time to go down to Tonolo and have a coffee; then we can go back to Piazzale Roma. You know the way now.'

This time, she paused at the top of the Bridge of the Chewing Gum and looked first to one side, then the other. Saying nothing, she patted his arm as they started down the steps. As they turned into Tonolo, she said, 'I think I'll have the chocolate

bigné: the big one, not the small one.'
Brunetti was gratified to learn that his colleague had been returned to good spirits
and attributed it to the lure of chocolate.

They had a different driver this time, an
older man who kept his eyes on the road.
Brunetti decided to arrive unannounced.

It seemed to him that they travelled more
quickly than they had the other times. The
receptionist remembered Brunetti and
paused to give Griffoni the sort of look a
beautiful young woman gives a woman a
generation older who still presents serious
competition.

'And who is it you'd like to see,
Commissario?' she asked.

'Dottor Veltrini,' Brunetti answered.

The receptionist paused, as if waiting for
more information; Brunetti smiled and
provided none.

'Of course,' she said after a moment. 'I'll
call him.' She stood, saying, 'If you'd like to
sit over here, Signori,' and walked towards
the chairs where Brunetti and Vianello had
waited. When they were seated, she asked if
they'd like something to drink: coffee, water.
They smiled, thanked her, and said they
were fine.

She went back to her desk and picked up

her phone. She spoke for a short time, replaced the handset and came back to them. 'He'll be here in a moment.'

'So kind,' Griffoni said glacially.

The chill drove the young woman back to her desk again, where she turned slightly away from them and consulted her computer.

After a few minutes, Dottor Veltrini appeared at the door of the corridor leading to the back of the building. He paused a moment, saw that Brunetti was not alone, and walked towards them.

Both stood. Brunetti watched Veltrini's face as he approached; he had eyes only for Griffoni. He and Brunetti shook hands, and Brunetti presented 'Commissario Griffoni', without further explanation.

'And how can I be of help?' Veltrini asked, smiling at Griffoni, as though the question were meant for her, and holding her hand in his longer than necessary.

'We'd like to talk about some tests that were conducted — or not conducted — in your laboratory,' Brunetti said.

Confusion played momentarily across Veltrini's face, but he said amiably, 'I'm not sure I understand, Commissario, but perhaps we could go to my office and talk about it there.' He stepped aside and waved his hand to the right, then moved up to walk beside Griffoni.

Brunetti, left looking at them from behind, took the opportunity to study Veltrini's clothing. He wore his shoes, brown tasselled loafers, without socks, no doubt in concession to the heat. His jacket, a very pale blue, might have been linen and silk: only by touching it could Brunetti have been sure. His jeans had been cut narrow in the leg, this time a concession to style, but a style better suited to a man some decades younger. The watch, Brunetti had already noted, today was a square Piaget with a malachite face. His thoughts returned to the Mercedes sedan in the parking lot, and he wondered if it belonged to Dottor Veltrini.

Halfway down the corridor, Veltrini stopped in front of a room on the left, waited for Brunetti and opened the door, then waited while they entered his office. The wood of the doctor's desk was so light that it might have been pear; on it sat a computer so sleek that, had she seen it, Signorina Elettra would have been compelled to drape her own newly arrived model in a chador.

Three Scandinavian chairs with steel tube framing and black leather seats and armrests faced the desk from the opposite side. Dottor Veltrini hesitated for a moment, as if uncertain where to place himself, but decided quickly and went behind the desk to sit in the position of command.

There were a few lithographs on the walls, beautifully framed. They were city views by Bernard Buffet, an artist Brunetti had never much liked. He gave them an admiring glance and went to look closely at one before taking his seat. His interest did not go unnoticed by Dottor Veltrini.

When they were all seated, Veltrini said, no attempt made to disguise his curiosity, 'Tell me about these tests, would you, Commissario?'

Brunetti made his smile as hesitant and embarrassed as he could. 'I'm afraid things have got reversed, Dottore. I've come to learn about them, not to tell you about them.'

'I understand that,' Veltrini said quickly, almost sharply. 'But before I can give you any answers, I have to know which tests you're talking about.' He gave Brunetti a moment to answer, and when he did not, Veltrini tried smiling and asked, 'Well?'

'Of course. I'm referring to a series of tests that were performed here at . . .' Brunetti paused, took his notebook from the pocket of his jacket and flipped it open. '. . . just a moment, please,' he said, flipping one page, another, then turning back to the beginning. 'Ah, here it is,' he said. 'At 10:36 of the morning of the fourth.' Before Veltrini could ask, Brunetti said, 'A Tuesday.'

Veltrini punched some keys and waited while his computer obeyed his will. He moused around for a while, then looked up in apparent surprise and said, 'Of course. How stupid of me. I wasn't here: I was on vacation.' He signalled them to come and have a look: Brunetti joined him behind his desk, Griffoni choosing to remain in her chair.

There it was: Tuesday the fourth. His calendar, for each day of the week, listed only the word *'Ferie.'*

Veltrini kept his eyes on the screen, shaking his head in wry amusement at his own forgetfulness.

Brunetti did not glance at Griffoni, nor she at him. Instead, he glanced down at his notebook, then across at Dottor Veltrini, and asked, 'Could you tell me, Dottore, who would have or could have conducted these tests? At 10:36 that morning?'

Calmly, as though pointing to the self-evident, Veltrini replied, 'Either of my colleagues. But to be sure, I'm afraid you'll have to speak to them, Commissario.'

'Anyone else?' Brunetti asked.

'Anyone who had access to the laboratory and who knew how to conduct a sophisticated chemical exam, I suppose.'

'Could Vittorio Fadalto have conducted those tests, Dottore?' Brunetti asked with the same calm amiability of the previous questions.

Veltrini tried, but failed, to disguise his shock. He looked at the door, almost as if he feared the arrival of Fadalto's ghost, but he failed to speak. He laid his right hand on the keys of his computer, but it was not an attempt to use it so much as a search for help from a totemic object.

Brunetti had never played chess, but he was fascinated by what he had read: the best players could look ahead and predict the next move of their opponent, make a move to counter it and force an inescapable response. And then again, they adjusted their own strategy every time the other player did something unexpected or took a risk. That risk was what he hoped for now.

Veltrini snatched his hand back from the keyboard and folded it together with the other. 'I'd like your colleague to leave the room,' he said.

Bluff or new rules? Griffoni surprised him

by getting to her feet, pushing her chair
back in place, and walking over to the door.
She closed it quietly.

'Now we can talk,' Veltrini said.

Brunetti didn't speak, waiting to see what
the other man's first move would be.

'Let's make a deal,' Veltrini said.

26

With Griffoni's departure, Brunetti was interested to see, Veltrini had grown discernibly calmer: both his body and his face had relaxed. Did the man think it would be easier to negotiate with Brunetti if there were no woman for them to try to impress?

Brunetti decided to say nothing and see if he could wait the other man out. He looked at one of the lithographs, sure that his dislike of the black, self-important lines would force an expression of intense interest on to his face. He moved his eyes to the next, this one of a bridge so stark and cruel that the viewer would see it only as a locus, or impetus, for suicide.

'What do you want from me, Commissario?' Veltrini asked in a conversational voice.

'I'd like you to tell me what you know about the lab tests conducted on the fourth of July on a sample taken from behind a factory on the bank of the Piave, where you are in charge of performing the tests.'

It was evident to Brunetti that the other man was surprised by the question, although he recovered quickly and said, 'If they were taken from any of our sites, then they were conducted in the normal manner by whoever performed them.'

Brunetti let that pass and asked, 'Are you aware of the results of those tests?'

'No, but I'm sure the records will tell you that.'

'Which records?' Brunetti asked.

'I beg your pardon?' Veltrini asked with seeming confusion.

'If you're referring to the ones that are in the files of your laboratory, I have no doubt that they contain normal results,' Brunetti answered. But then, as if suddenly recalling something, he added, 'But perhaps other analyses performed on the sample taken from the sensor would have given different results.' He was suddenly tired of playing cat and mouse.

Veltrini reached out and pulled a sheet of paper towards him, as though he might find Brunetti's meaning there. Apparently failing to do so, he picked up a pencil but set it back on the desk without using it. Tired of the game as well, he spread his palms on the desk and asked, 'How much do you know?'

'Enough,' Brunetti said.

'Do you have the sample?'

'Yes,' Brunetti told him. 'As well as a report of what was found in the water.' He waited a moment to let that information register. 'The water is still in the sensor,' he added.

Veltrini nodded and studied the back of his left hand. With the other, he pushed back the sleeve of his jacket and looked at his watch. Brunetti had the strange sensation that he was not checking the time so much as assuring himself that he still wore that watch, still owned that watch, was still the man who had been able to pay for that watch.

'I didn't know you had it,' Veltrini said, eyes still on the face of his watch.

'And more,' Brunetti told him. 'As I said, I have the report.'

Veltrini nodded more times than necessary. He pushed himself back in his chair, and Brunetti saw his sleeve fall back, covering the face of his watch again. Finally he said, sounding tired, 'I think it's time for us to come to an agreement, Commissario.'

Brunetti shifted in his seat and toyed for an instant with feigning indifference by returning to his study of the lithographs, but he decided not to waste time and kept his eyes on Veltrini. 'What do you mean?' he asked.

A new expansiveness came into the lab director's voice. 'Giving you something in exchange for something you'll give me. Isn't that what an agreement is always about?'

'And that's why you asked my colleague to leave?'

Veltrini smiled at this. 'If you accepted my offer to bargain, her company would have been inconvenient.'

'You seem convinced that we are going to come to an agreement.'

'I believe that's possible, yes,' Veltrini said.

'As you please,' Brunetti answered tersely. When Veltrini remained silent, Brunetti asked, 'What is it you have to offer me?'

'I can tell you who killed Vittorio Fadalto.' There had been no preparation, no hint, but there it was, the possibility that had been ever present through all of this.

'*You* didn't?' Brunetti inquired softly, forcing himself to smile as he asked. Behind that smile, he ran at, and through, the things he had heard and learned in the last days, struck by Veltrini's calm certainty that Fadalto had been killed.

'Good heavens, no,' Veltrini exclaimed and

tossed his hands in the air to show his astonishment at such a thought. 'Why ever would I do that?'

'Because he blackmailed you for twenty thousand Euros,' Brunetti said with equal calm, as though he'd been asked to tell the time and was doing so.

'Ah, yes, the money,' Veltrini said with surprising mildness and steepled his fingers in front of him. 'That complicated things.'

'How?' Brunetti asked, making no attempt to disguise his curiosity.

Veltrini pulled his hands apart and used one to wave away the question. 'It doesn't matter, Commissario. Believe me.'

'If we're going to come to an agreement, Dottore,' Brunetti said with easy certainty, 'then I need to know.' When Veltrini did not answer, Brunetti asked, man of the world that he was, 'Don't you think?'

'The money wasn't mine. That is, the money that he received didn't come from me.'

'But you gave it to him?' Brunetti asked.

'Yes. But it came from another source.'

'Which was?'

'That's not important,' Veltrini answered, and Brunetti heard the adamant refusal. In the face of Brunetti's silence, the other man went on, 'If he hadn't got the money, he would have caused trouble, and that would have caused more trouble.'

Brunetti re-crossed his legs and wondered what this 'trouble' would have been and who, aside from Veltrini, would have felt it. Signorina Elettra's researches had assured him that Spattuto's record was clean, which left few suspects other than the owners of the factories behind which the sensors were placed.

'Would you have been arrested because of the evidence he had?' he asked. 'Was the "trouble" the likelihood that you'd go to prison?'

'Come now, Commissario,' Veltrini said condescendingly. 'When do people like me go to prison?'

'It depends on what they do.'

'An environmental crime,' Veltrini said dismissively and gave a tiny flick of his fingers to show its insignificance. 'That's what I would have been charged with.'

'It's still a crime,' Brunetti said, uncomfortable at the way he was losing control of the conversation.

'And what would the punishment have been? For polluting a river? Ten thousand Euros? Twenty? A hundred?' With a puff of wind Veltrini blew away the irrelevance of those sums. 'And the sentence? A year?

Two? Three? I don't have to remind you, Commissario, that no one who's given that brief a sentence goes to jail: the jails are already full of people who sell drugs. People like me — and if I might expand that and say people like us — we never go to prison. They give us a sentence of house arrest and a fine, and that's the end of things.'

He paused here and offered Brunetti the chance to comment, but in the face of the truth of what he had said, there was no convincing response Brunetti could make.

Pushing himself higher in his chair, Veltrini said, 'So shall we return to what we are supposed to be doing?'

Brunetti nodded. And waited.

'As I said, I will give you both the name of the person who killed Fadalto and sufficient proof to win a conviction.' Again, he paused for long enough to allow Brunetti to speak, but when he didn't, Veltrini went on. 'In return, I want you to give me the sample: the actual sensor, with the serial number intact, and the box that holds it. And the report on the contents.' He paused there, and studied Brunetti's expression; it seemed to Brunetti that the man was hoping to discover how much more he could ask for.

The next thing he will demand, he told himself, is the money, for money was the basis of all of this. Why else had Veltrini done what he had done and allowed what he had allowed?

Into this reflection came Veltrini's voice, saying, 'There's the money. You're the only one who knows where it is now. Fadalto told me he wanted it to pay for his wife's care.'

Brunetti dug in his heels and told himself that he would at least force Veltrini to, if only once, acknowledge the truth. 'Do you want that back, too?' he asked neutrally.

Veltrini considered this before saying, 'No, I don't. Of course I'd like to have it, but if I took it from you, I'd be adding something more to what I asked you for, and that doesn't seem . . .' He stopped speaking for some time until he finally found the word he sought and said, 'correct.' He paused again as if debating whether that had indeed been the right word and, apparently satisfied that it had, continued: 'I asked for the sensor and the lab report. That's enough.'

Brunetti would be left with the money, he realized. Worse, it would leave him with the obligation to explain how he came by it. After that, where would it go? He had been reading for years about massive hauls made during the arrests of Mafia leaders, but he had never read anything about just where that money went. Presumably, into the possession of the state. After that?

'Commissario?' Veltrini said, and Brunetti looked across at the man as though he'd been following what he said.

'Yes?'

'I thought I'd lost your attention,' Veltrini said, sounding half offended.

'No, not at all,' Brunetti assured him. 'I was trying to understand why you'd do this.'

'The money, of course,' Veltrini said and gave a puzzled grin, as if he'd been asked to explain normal behaviour.

'No, not because of that, not at all,' Brunetti said, speaking truthfully. 'I don't understand how you, a scientist, could be part of this. If you were an . . . accountant . . . I could understand it . . . or a banker,' he added as the idea interrupted his thoughts. 'It would make sense because you wouldn't understand, perhaps wouldn't even know, the consequences of what you were allowing.'

'But I *am* a scientist,' Veltrini answered.

Brunetti tried to shake this away with his head, as if hearing an unpleasant sound. 'And yet you allowed this. For all I know, you started it.'

'You could say I inherited it, Dottore.'

'I don't understand.'

'I took this job ten years ago. A friend of

mine had been working here for some time, and when he was offered a better job, he called me to ask if I'd be interested in replacing him. When I said I was, he recommended me.' He waved his hands around the office to demonstrate the outcome.

'And?'

'After I'd been here for a month, I had a call from a man who said he'd like to discuss freelance work with me.' Veltrini wiped both palms across his desk before he said, 'It wasn't at all like any job interview I'd ever had.' He gave Brunetti a friendly glance that invited him to laugh.

Brunetti listened, marvelling at the sort of man who could speak so calmly of what he had been offered, and of what he had done.

'We met for dinner to talk things over, and he explained that there was the possibility of some collateral income.' Seeing Brunetti's expression, he held up his hand and added, 'He never said it directly, but I assume he had had this agreement with my predecessor.'

'Why was that?'

'He told me repeatedly that no one who worked for the company was to suspect what was happening. He knew a great deal about how the system worked and what went on in the lab.' Seeing Brunetti's expression, he added, 'I realized he had to have got his information from someone: my predecessor was the obvious choice.'

'What did he ask you to do?' Brunetti asked.

'Occasionally — usually during periods of heavy rain — he'd call and tell me which sensor would give what he called "incorrect readings" and the time when those readings would take place. They would not always be in the same location: their only common point was that they would be in an area under my control.' Seeing Brunetti's curiosity, Veltrini explained. 'That way, I would examine the sample and write the report.'

'Of the new sensor you used to replace the one that registered the higher level?' Brunetti asked.

Veltrini nodded in approval of Brunetti's surmise and went on quite easily. 'All I had to do was dispose of the samples and make the written results congruent with the previous and subsequent readings.'

'So the elevated amount,' Brunetti began, automatically eliminating words like 'pollution' and 'contamination', 'would not have taken place?'

'Exactly.'

'But how,' Brunetti continued, 'did you prevent the warning from being sent automatically to the Carabinieri?' He infused real curiosity, the sort that leads to admiration, into his voice.

Lowering his eyes in the appearance of modesty, Veltrini said, 'Because I knew when the higher quantities would be registered, minor adjustments to the program running that part of the system stopped the alarm from sounding for a time, but then it resumed after the sensor had been replaced.' Brunetti smiled to himself at the way Veltrini slid effortlessly into the passive voice, as if some other person or entity had done all of this, or perhaps it had done it by itself.

'And in return?'

'I would be paid a sum every month.'

'How much?' Brunetti asked, curious to know what the price would be for what Veltrini had done.

'That doesn't matter, Commissario,' Veltrini said in a voice suddenly grown severe. He tilted his head to the side, as if struck by a sudden thought. 'You don't need to know most of what I did, Commissario. Not really.'

'Did you know?' Brunetti shot back.

'Know what?' Veltrini asked, obviously confused by the question.

'What you were doing?'

'Of course. I just told you,' he answered,

still confused, perhaps beginning to be irritated, by Brunetti's failure to understand.

Brunetti decided to spell it out. 'Did you actually test the samples?'

He saw the question register on Veltrini's face and watched him scurry around to find a way to ignore its meaning and avoid answering it. He could lie, he could tell the truth. It came to Brunetti that it didn't matter in the least which Veltrini had done, tested them or not. One was no worse than the other: neither could change the numbers.

The silence extended, and Brunetti chose to hear in it all the silent voices that let things happen because understanding was too much trouble or would cause a moment's inconvenience. 'It doesn't matter,' he surprised himself by saying, and followed this with a return to practicality by asking, 'You wrote these fake reports?'

When Veltrini nodded, Brunetti asked, 'Is some permanent record kept of the readings that the sensors register?' Best to ask this question and plant the idea that the police had no understanding of the situation at Spattuto.

Veltrini's face blossomed into the smile of every expert asked a question by a person not familiar with the subject. 'Yes, there is.

They're kept in our database.' Brunetti was thinking that this sounded sure enough when Veltrini added, 'It can be corrected by anyone familiar with the computer program.' Then, as if unable to restrain his pride, he added, 'It was quite easy.'

Still curious, Brunetti failed to stop himself from asking, 'Did you do this often?'

'That's another thing you don't need to know, Commissario. I'll discuss only the sample Fadalto collected and which now is in your possession.'

Ah, how Veltrini loved to talk. How he loved the pose of man of the world.

'I need to know how Fadalto came into possession of the sample,' Brunetti said, then added, 'And the money.'

For a moment, he feared that Veltrini would also judge this irrelevant, but apparently he did not, for he said, 'It happened when I was on vacation. I'd told my contact that I would be away, but he must have forgotten. And then those rains came, and the floods. He called me at midnight to tell me that the three o'clock sample would need work.' This time, Brunetti noted, Veltrini's use of jargon to disguise what he was doing sounded almost natural: the sample would 'need work'.

Veltrini's voice, however, was suffused

with irritation he couldn't forget; Brunetti watched as he fought to keep it from changing into something stronger.

'When I told him I was in France, he said I'd have to get someone to replace the sensor before six that morning because it was too late for him to stop things.' When he saw that Brunetti didn't understand, he explained, 'When the sensors register certain levels, they open a tube to a smaller chamber inside and seal some of the water in that. As long as the sensor's in place, the contamination is locked inside.' Veltrini paused and took a deep breath before continuing. 'I couldn't access the alarm from my computer in France, so I couldn't turn it off. That meant, when it went off, the Carabinieri would answer the call, and then we'd have them on our necks.' He wiped at his face, as if to wipe away the memory of his fear. 'There would be no way for us to change the numbers or deny that something had been in the water. And then there would have to be an investigation of the area.' Then, caught out at failing to have mentioned a detail, he added, 'That's why, whenever they called me, I went and changed the sensor.'

'I see,' Brunetti answered. 'What did you do?'

'I had no choice,' Veltrini continued. 'I phoned Fadalto and told him there'd been an emergency and that he had to replace a sensor immediately.'

Veltrini had been watching Brunetti's face as he spoke and said, 'He was the only person who could do it.' Then, reflectively, 'I suppose I acted rashly, but it was all I could think of.'

'Couldn't you persuade the man who called you to delay things, perhaps until after the rain?'

'That's just it,' Veltrini said, impatient with Brunetti's refusal to understand. 'It had to be done during the flooding. That's what washes things away fastest.' Seeing that Brunetti still looked as though he did not understand, Veltrini explained, 'So the dead fish get carried downstream, and it's impossible to determine where they died.'

'Ah,' was the only thing Brunetti could manage.

'I took the first plane the next morning,' Veltrini went on. 'I got to the lab at noon on the fifth, came right from the airport. Luckily, Signora Sala didn't come to work that day because the basement of her house was flooded, and Signora Guttardi — she was covering for me while I was away — hadn't had time to check the readings from my area yet.' Veltrini's face changed here and grew calm. 'I hadn't managed to talk to Fadalto again, so I had no idea of whether he'd succeeded in removing the sensor or not. Signora Guttardi said nothing, so I could assume only that things were fine.'

Knowing he shouldn't say it but unable to stop himself, Brunetti said, 'How lucky for you.'

Veltrini was so enmeshed in his story that he heard only the words and not what propelled them. He nodded in response, looking almost grateful for Brunetti's ability to understand.

'There was no sign of the sensor in the lab, and the numbers in the databank were normal, so I knew Fadalto had got there and exchanged it for a new one.' He shook himself, as at the memory of a close call on the autostrada.

'Fadalto came into the lab at about six that evening, after Signora Guttardi had left. He was very direct, told me he'd brought the sensor in after he changed it and tested the water himself and knew what was in it.

'When I told him he had to bring the sensor back, he said it was in a safe place with the sample still in it, so anyone who wanted to could duplicate his results. He said he wanted twenty thousand Euros or he'd go to the Carabinieri.'

Veltrini stopped and pulled his hands into fists and set them on the desk. 'It was like a cheap police serial on television. Blackmail.' He sounded scandalized.

It took Brunetti a moment to realize that Veltrini's indignation was real. When he accepted that, he asked, 'What did you do?'

'What *could* I do?' Veltrini demanded.

Brunetti wished he'd started keeping track the first time he'd heard a suspect ask that question, but he had not, nor did he remember how many times he'd heard it.

'Indeed,' he affirmed.

'I called the man I dealt with and explained the situation and that the person who had the sensor wanted money,' Veltrini said, and then his face softened as he passed into deep thought. 'You know, what he said was strange, maybe the strangest thing about this whole affair.'

'And what was that?' Brunetti asked in his most priestly voice.

'He said it wouldn't be a problem and he'd meet me that evening to give it to me. And it wasn't until then that he asked how much.'

27

Brunetti could think of nothing to say in response save to ask, 'And is that what happened?'

'Yes. We met at a bar in Conegliano. It was the same man who'd interviewed me,' Veltrini said, using the vocabulary of ordinary life, normal events. 'He gave me a manila envelope with the money inside. Twenty thousand Euros.' Wonder burnished his voice as he spoke the number.

'Did you talk about it?'

'No. He offered me a drink, had a glass of wine. We talked about the weather and when it would stop raining, and then he paid for the drinks and shook my hand and left. The envelope was still on the table.'

Brunetti knew better than to ask about the man or the transaction. The expression on Veltrini's face showed nothing more than confusion at the strangeness of human behaviour.

Their exchange of information had come to a stop, Brunetti realized. What he had heard from Veltrini left him with the certainty that the man had not for an instant considered the dimensions of what he was involved in. Or didn't care. The fact that his contact could blithely hand over twenty thousand Euros without bothering to ask about it apparently had not made him curious about the scope of what was going on: all he could do was judge it to be 'strange'.

'Tell me again what it is you want,' Brunetti said, although he knew. Veltrini was asking him to do what he had sometimes done himself: change the truth in return for a reward.

Apparently relieved that the conversation had returned to safer ground, Veltrini said, 'You give me the sensor and the report. And you stop there: no arrest, no investigation.' He moved his lips in what Brunetti thought to be a smile and went on. 'In return, as I said, I'll give you the name of the person who killed Fadalto and evidence that will prove it.' After a moment's thought, he added, as if this were a sale and he were offering Brunetti the chance to buy one and he'd throw in another one free, 'I retire in six months; if you agree, I'll give you my word that I won't . . .' He let the words run

402

out as he thought of a polite way to say what he wouldn't do. 'Won't change any more lab reports before then,' he finished, having found the suitable euphemism.

'Your word?' Brunetti asked.

Veltrini raised his eyebrows in what seemed a genuine demonstration of surprise. 'I'm willing to take yours, Commissario, that you'll give me the sensor and the sample and not arrest me, and I'll give you his killer. Had you forgotten that?'

Brunetti did not bother to answer.

'You will have put an end to my lawbreaking,' Veltrini said rather pedantically.

Then, in a warmer voice, he asked, 'Isn't that what police officers are supposed to do?'

'We're supposed to begin the process by which the guilty person is arrested and punished, Dottore,' Brunetti answered, sounding no less pedantic.

Veltrini's eyes contracted, but after a moment he seemed to remember the part he was playing, smiled broadly, and said, 'How pleasant it is to discuss something with a person who's obviously studied logic.'

Neither man spoke for some time, until finally Veltrini asked, 'What do you think, Commissario?'

Ironing all expression from his face,

Brunetti said, 'Before I decide anything, I need to know how you learned the name of the killer, and I need to know what evidence you can give me.' He spoke dispassionately and could have been bartering wheat for eggs.

Veltrini, put at ease by Brunetti's calm, nodded and said, 'That seems reasonable enough.' He started to say something else but stopped himself and rubbed his right hand across his eyes and forehead.

Finally he said, 'On the night of Fadalto's death, I was working late, writing performance reports of the people who work in or for the laboratory. It's a complicated process because I have to consult time sheets and memos from other members of staff before I write my own report. I had just finished when I heard raised voices out at the back of the building, in the parking lot. I was curious about who would have been working this late — it was after ten — when the voices got louder. I turned off my desk lamp and went over to my window to have a look.

'Fadalto was standing by his motorcycle, with his helmet in his hand. He was looking back towards the building and speaking to some other person I couldn't see from where I stood. I couldn't hear what he was saying, but I could tell he was angry. More than that. Once he put his hand on his heart and asked — I could hear the single word because he shouted it — "Me?" Then he repeated it and put on his helmet and fastened it closed.'

Veltrini paused here and added, 'That caught my attention: he was in a rage, but he still remembered his helmet.'

Brunetti sat and waited.

'That made me curious, so I went down the back stairs that led to the parking lot.' Veltrini looked at him and gave a faint smile, as if asking Brunetti to be complicit in his reaction.

'I admit I was curious. I had no idea who Fadalto's friends were at work, or his enemies, or even if he had any, so I wanted to see who could get him to act like that.'

Brunetti nodded in understanding. Of course Veltrini would be curious about Fadalto then: the other man had a hold over him. What more normal than to want to find out if someone had power over Fadalto?

'After I got used to the darkness, I went down the corridor and stood by the door to the parking lot. I figured I'd recognize the voice of whoever he was shouting at, but the only thing I heard was the sound of his motorcycle starting, and then he drove out of the lot.

'I waited, but no one came back towards me. I stuck my head out of the door and heard another motor start, and then a car drove towards the exit.'

'Did you see who was driving?' Brunetti asked.

'No,' Veltrini said, 'because of the lights.' As Brunetti watched, a soft, illegible smile passed across Veltrini's face. At first, Brunetti was confused, but then Veltrini's eyes narrowed and the smile was revealed as the very face of malice.

He tried to control the smile, but he gave in to it and let it expand, then said, 'But I recognized the car.'

Veltrini's expression had interested Brunetti, as did the careful timing of his remark. The only response he permitted himself was to raise his chin inquisitively.

'It belongs to Dottoressa Ricciardi,' Veltrini said, delighting in the effect the name had on Brunetti. 'Our own dear crippled saint, off in fast pursuit of yet another man who didn't want her.'

Oh my, oh my, oh my, Brunetti thought; now I know what Paola means when she says that men hate women. Didn't this man ever listen to himself? Was talking so seductive to him that he had lost any sense of what it could reveal?

As if he'd freed himself of venom, or sickness, by saying that, Veltrini returned to his normal voice and manner. 'I don't know what alarmed me, but I didn't hesitate to get into my own car and follow her.'

'You weren't afraid she'd notice?'

'I kept the lights off. I know the roads around here, after all these years. There's almost no traffic after ten. I caught up with her and followed the car. Her driving was so erratic that at first I thought she'd go off the road and I'd have to stop to help her, but she must have calmed down because it grew more normal.'

'Could you see if she was following Fadalto?'

'There's only one road that leads to the autostrada, and if he was going back to Venice, that's the road he'd have to take.'

'She didn't notice you?'

Veltrini shrugged his shoulders. 'I have no idea. She kept going, but she used the brakes a lot. She knew the road very well, so she must have been upset to drive like that. Then, when we were about three kilometres from the autostrada, a car passed me and cut in front of me so fast I had to drive on to the shoulder and slow down to keep control of the car. When I finally got back on to the road, there were no tail lights in front of me, so I thought I might have missed the turn-off to the autostrada.

'I pulled over and looked at my phone to see where I was and if I'd missed the turn. When I found that I hadn't passed it, I sat for a while, telling myself what a fool I'd been to try to follow them. After a few minutes, I started the car and got back on the road, still without my lights on. All I wanted to do was go home. Then, after only a few minutes, I saw a car parked at the side of the road ahead of me. Its lights were on.'

This time, when he looked at Brunetti, he put on a serious expression, and his eyes seemed to grow even larger behind his glasses. 'Yes. It was hers.' Then, as if one fact led inexorably to the next, he went on, 'I still had my phone in my hand, so I slowed down and took a photo of the car.' His voice grew even more serious as he said, 'I sent a copy to myself, to establish the time. I've got a GPS in the phone, so it registered the exact place where the photo was taken.'

'Why did you do that?' Brunetti asked, marvelling at the calculation of the man.

Veltrini smiled again, and Brunetti realized how much he was coming to dislike that sudden flash of teeth. 'I've no idea, Commissario,' he said with every expression of awkward embarrassment. 'Perhaps because it seemed so strange, to see her car there.' He shrugged, almost as if he thought the gesture would add to his appearance of sincere confusion.

Or, Brunetti found himself thinking, because he had seen her drive Fadalto off the road and was already thinking of some future use to make of it. 'Was she in the car?' he asked, leading Veltrini away from whatever plans he might have had for the photo.

'Of course, Commissario. It's a slow process for her to get in and out of the car because of the cane and her bad leg.' He dragged his voice up to those last words, as if to demonstrate his compassion.

Then he put on another smile, this one to indicate that he was finished.

'And then what did you do?' Brunetti asked.

'I went home, Commissario,' he said calmly. 'As I drove past her, I saw that she was sitting with her hands on the wheel, facing forward, so she seemed all right.'

'You didn't stop to see if she needed help?'

With an embarrassed look, Veltrini said, 'I'm afraid I'm the last person Dottoressa Ricciardi would take help from, Commissario.'

'And why is that?'

'As I told you when we first spoke,' he began, allowing a tone of reproach to slip into his voice at Brunetti's having forgotten such a thing, 'I told you that Dottoressa Ricciardi developed a completely mistaken interest in me.'

Brunetti nodded briefly, as though repetition was hardly necessary, so deeply had he incised that information on his memory.

'So she would not be pleased to discover that I had been following her.' Before Brunetti could protest, Veltrini said, giving a small sniff of disapproval, 'Her behaviour to me since I unburdened myself of her attentions has been barely civil. As I'm sure you've noticed.'

Brunetti nodded because he was being urged to do so.

He sat back and told himself to start thinking like a policeman and not react to Veltrini's malice. The fact that her car was photographed on the road where Fadalto was found didn't prove anything much, he thought, except that they were taking the same route from work. Not unless Veltrini had seen her run Fadalto off the road, in which case it was his legal obligation to stop and try to give aid to the victim. There was no witness other than Veltrini to the conver-

410

sation between the two people in the parking lot behind their place of work; no one
else had heard Fadalto's raised voice nor
seen the two leave at the same time. As to
the story about Dottoressa Ricciardi's interest in Veltrini, and then in Fadalto, there
might be gossip, but gossip was not proof.

Into the expanding silence, Brunetti said,
'I'm afraid you're offering me a bad bargain,
Dottor Veltrini.' Strangely, the other man
did not appear to be surprised to hear him
say this. Brunetti gave him a few moments
to speak, and when he did not, continued,
'You've told me you were involved in a
series of crimes — well, one crime, although
it's obvious there have been others — and
in exchange for my not arresting you, you
offer me a story that depends on your account of an event with no witnesses.' He
paused for a while, then added, 'And, if I
might say so, without evidence of any kind.'

He shook his head to demonstrate his
puzzlement that someone would put up
such paltry stakes. He was at a loss to
understand how Veltrini could have thought
this information, even if true, could suffice
as proof that Dottoressa Ricciardi had been
responsible for Fadalto's death. Speculation, lack of witnesses, an easily manipulated
photo: Brunetti wondered why he was wast-

ing his time listening to this man, when what he should be doing was obtaining an order to arrest him.

Veltrini grinned with almost childlike amusement; his eyes warmed in enlarged delight. 'I'm not finished, Commissario,' he said with false deference.

Had Veltrini been a dog that, up until then, had wagged a friendly tail, Brunetti would have stepped back from him now. Malice had come forward and brushed away amiability. Veltrini allowed his smile to remain while he said, 'I told you I have proof.'

28

'What do you know?' Brunetti asked.

Veltrini pushed himself back in his chair and crossed his legs, as if to give himself the opportunity to relax and enjoy the sudden attention. 'I have to preface this by explaining that I listen to the news every morning while I'm shaving,' he began. 'The morning after I followed them, I heard that a motorcyclist had gone off the road near where her car had been the night before but that no one had seen the accident. The rider was dead, and the police were investigating the circumstances. While I shaved, I had time to think about what might have happened. We've heard it a thousand times: perhaps it was *un colpo di sonno* and he fell asleep, or perhaps he was hit by *"un pirata della strada"*, who fled the scene without trying to help his victim.' He paused here to check that his listener was still attentive. Brunetti obliged.

'It didn't take me long to create another scenario,' Veltrini said, sounding inordinately proud of himself.

'Which is?' Brunetti asked with polite curiosity.

Veltrini showed his teeth again. 'I think that must be obvious. To anyone. She followed him, she pulled up beside him and gave his motorcycle a tap with the right fender of her car, and he went off the road.' When Brunetti failed to answer or comment, Veltrini said, voice pitched a bit higher, 'It's what anyone would do, isn't it?' Seeing Brunetti's surprise, he quickly added, 'If they wanted to hurt him, that is.'

'Quite possibly,' Brunetti answered, not sounding at all convinced. Then, almost absently, he said, 'You were talking about her car.'

'Ah, yes, I was, wasn't I?' Veltrini asked. 'About a week after his death, I had dinner with a friend and his wife. While we were eating, she asked me if I knew the woman with the cane who worked in Human Resources. It turns out that, a year ago, this woman had applied for a job and was interviewed by the Dottoressa, but she was offered a better job even before Spattuto made up its mind, so she took that.

'She still remembered the Dottoressa and

414

the cane and said she seemed like an intelligent person.' Veltrini paused to give a prim nod and went on. 'But then she surprised me by laughing and saying that didn't stop her from being a terrible driver. When I asked why she thought such a thing, she explained that she had been behind the Dottoressa on the exit ramp of an underground parking garage about a week before. When the Dottoressa's car got near the top, where the cars have to turn into the street, she turned too sharply to the right and ran the front side of her car along the wall of the garage. My friend's wife said it was terrible to see her do it, then try to correct it by going backwards; only she turned the wheel the wrong way and ran the car back along the wall again. When she was finally loose, she drove away and didn't bother to stop to see how badly the car was damaged.'

Veltrini paused, like a practised speaker who knew when to pause and when to keep going, the better to sharpen the interest of his listeners.

Brunetti obliged. ' "Along the wall again"?'

'That's what she said,' Veltrini answered.

'Where was this?' Brunetti asked, trying to make it sound like an idle question.

Veltrini gave him a large smile and shook

415

his head. 'As I said before, Commissario, first we need to make an agreement.' He waited a moment, and when Brunetti said nothing, he added, 'About our exchange.' Still Brunetti remained silent.

'Her car's been repaired, Commissario,' Veltrini said. 'I can spare you the trouble of finding it and examining it. Looks brand new: probably sanded down to the original metal and repainted. Wouldn't be anything left of what was there before.'

When Brunetti still did not speak, Veltrini went on. 'You can send your colleague out to the parking lot to check if you please: it's a grey Toyota in parking space 12.'

Brunetti heard how much delight this situation was providing Veltrini and how great a sense of power. 'We can do that when you leave, Commissario, if you like,' he added. Brunetti saw him struggle with the urge to laugh, and win.

'Am I correct that the location of the parking garage and the name of your friend's wife are part of what you're offering me?'

'I'd say they are the essential part of what I'm offering you, Commissario.'

'But you don't know for certain that there will be traces of paint from Fadalto's motorcycle on the wall.'

'No, I don't. But I know Dottoressa

Ricciardi.'

'What does that mean?'

'Like all women, she's intimidated by authority. All you have to do is present her with the information you have, and she'll panic and try to explain her way out of it, say it was an accident.' Veltrini stopped and Brunetti watched him continue his analysis of Dottoressa Ricciardi's probable response. 'She'll say something about how she didn't want to be judged as a cripple who shouldn't be driving. Well, she'll drag her leg into it: you can be sure of that.'

'And if I don't speak to her?'

'Then you have no choice but to arrest me for crimes against the common good, wait a few years until there is a trial and then a few more years for the appeal I'll make; a few years until the next trial, and the next appeal. And all this time, you and the local police, if they're interested, can be taking samples of any grey paint scratched on to the wall of any parking garage within a radius of . . . how many kilometres do you think would be best, Commissario?' Veltrini stopped, as if to permit Brunetti the opportunity to respond.

When he did not, Veltrini continued. 'You read *Il Gazzettino,* don't you, Commissario?'

Brunetti nodded.

417

'Then you must have read the article last week about the discovery of PFAS in the Veneto.' Seeing Brunetti's confusion, Veltrini said, 'Oh, sorry. I must speak as a chemist. I mean poly-fluoroalkyl.' His voice had deepened as he found himself on familiar territory.

'I did read it,' Brunetti said, sure of where Veltrini planned to take this information.

'Then you know that the level of contamination in those towns near Vicenza is now estimated to be two thousand times more than normal?' When Brunetti still did not speak, Veltrini asked, sounding indignant, 'What is it, fifteen years, and still no trial?'

'I've read that,' Brunetti conceded.

'So, compared to that level of contamination, what my clients have been doing is insignificant.'

That Veltrini called them 'clients' finally drove Brunetti to rise to the bait. 'That it's less isn't the point, is it?' he asked. 'It's there, and it kills. Eventually.' Then, at a loss as to how to deal with this man, he did not stop himself from saying, 'I still don't understand how a scientist can be part of this. You know what the results are. You're not a street thug, stealing a car one day, mugging an old lady the next. You know the consequence of what you do . . .' Abruptly

418

he shut himself down, numb with futility.

Veltrini's expression softened and he raised a hand in Brunetti's direction. 'It's strange, and you won't believe me, Commissario, but I do admire your skill in argumentation.' He looked to see how Brunetti would respond to this, and when he did not — not in the least — Veltrini nevertheless continued.

'You're right: I do know the consequences. But I also know how little what we do amounts to when one considers how much is being dumped into the rivers.' Before Brunetti could remind him of his promise, he said, 'I'll do as I said, Commissario: I'll stop.' Then, speaking what Brunetti thought was the truth, 'Once I'm retired, you won't have to worry. My assistant, Dottoressa Guttardi, will replace me,' he said, and then added, 'She's clean.'

Veltrini removed his glasses and used his handkerchief to wipe at his left eye. He looked across at Brunetti, who saw that his gaze was entirely blank, as though he were blind without his glasses. He replaced them and his handkerchief and said, 'So is Spattuto. Clean, that is. Two brothers own it, and they say things about the need to think of the future, and their children.' He smiled again, though not necessarily at Brunetti, and said, 'They're young.' Then, as though it were the obvious following remark, he added, 'Just as well they aren't involved in this. I've always preferred to work freelance.'

Brunetti glanced away, seeking something that would distract him from having to look at this man capable of describing what he did as 'freelance'. It was not his responsibility to make judgements about the people who committed crimes; indeed, that often complicated things. His duty was to arrest them and leave justice to other forces of the law.

He locked the fingers of his two hands together and put them between his knees, leaned forward and stared at the floor.

He heard the other man's chair scrape as Veltrini got to his feet. 'I'm going to go for a coffee,' he said. 'I'll give you some time to think about this.' Brunetti heard the door open and close, then Veltrini's footsteps disappeared down the hall.

Well, there he went, free to go and get a coffee, free to circulate, just like the substances that had been dumped into the river. The method was precise; Veltrini received a phone call and did what he was told to do and made sure the sensors showed no sign of what had passed through them. Ask no questions, tell no lies, and never have to give a thought to what was dissolved in the flooding waters rushing towards the Adriatic. The mercury slithered into the water and the tiny fish tried to eat it, and then the middle-sized fish ate the small ones, and then the big fish ate the others, concentrating the mercury in their own bodies. That is, until they were caught and, in their turn, transferred it to the body of the person who ate them. Pregnant women were warned not to eat tuna: Minamata had taught the world at least that.

It was all a crap shoot, really. You'd eat the right fish or you'd eat the wrong fish, or maybe you didn't like fish and would never have to confront this problem. Curious, Brunetti had read a bit about mercury's half-life in the brain and found differences of opinion; there was less dispute about its effects.

The people of Minamata, he told himself, had been poisoned for years, as had the shellfish which made up not only their livelihood but much of their diet. The photo of the Japanese Pietà flashed into his memory: he pushed it away.

Dottoressa Ricciardi had been unlucky with her health, as well. He thought of her cane, remembered her limp, recalled her lack of humour, her seriousness, the intensity and quiet desperation of her manner. Fadalto, perhaps seeing those same qualities, had rejected her affections, or so Veltrini had told him. But why believe a man like Veltrini?

Strangely enough, Brunetti did believe him. Because of that, he believed that the wall of that underground garage, wherever it turned out to be, would show traces of the paint of her car and the paint of some other vehicle, surely identifiable.

Veltrini was probably right, as well, that she'd crumble at the first question, would admit to having gone after Fadalto, first with her words and then with her car.

Fadalto was dead. His widow was dead. The orphans had been taken in by their aunt. If Brunetti accepted Veltrini's offer, he'd have to get the sensor and the report back from them for Veltrini to destroy. No one seemed much interested in the money, so it could stay where it was and do some good.

If he arrested Veltrini, the story of Fadalto's attempted blackmail would emerge, as would Brunetti's delay in turning over evidence of a crime. And in the end, he knew, Veltrini's scenario would play out, disguised as the slow process of the law, leading to nothing.

To arrest Dottoressa Ricciardi would send a criminal to trial, perhaps to prison. The girls would know what had happened to their father. And Veltrini would retire.

His thoughts turned to the *Eumenides* and the characters' desperate search for an understanding of justice based on something other than vengeance. The Furies defended their lust for vengeance: 'We are fierce and cannot be deviated by man.' They punished, always 'mindful of the evil done', and threatened that forgiveness 'will trap mankind in moral chaos'.

Even though the gods chose different sides, the evidence in the trial of Orestes was heard and weighed as the poet and his listeners sought to make sense of justice. Two thousand years, and still there was no answer.

Brunetti was both accuser and accused. He had to decide which crime to punish, which to ignore, and choose the greater criminal. Or the better odds. It came to him then to consider the world in which he lived: who would be punished and to what degree? He closed his eyes and let that beast, justice, run free in his mind.

He thought of going into the corridor to find Griffoni, but he remained in his chair. More time passed, and Brunetti finally got to his feet, suddenly tired by and tired of all of this. He left Veltrini's office and looked up and down the corridor. No one was there.

Remembering the way from the last time they were there, he walked towards the front of the building until he came to Dottoressa Ricciardi's office. He knocked, and he heard a voice from within.

Inside, he saw her at her desk, looking at him, afraid to see him there and not wanting to show that she was. 'Yes, Commissario?' she asked, one hand flat on her desk, the other clenched in a tight fist.

'Dottoressa,' he said, 'I've come to arrest you for the death of Vittorio Fadalto.'

She seemed to shrink, like someone in a science fiction movie. Both hands scuttled to her lap, her mouth and eyes tightened, somehow diminishing her face, and she sank lower against the back of her chair.

She nodded a few times, lips still pulled tight. 'How did you find out?' she asked.

She'd learn it sooner or later, so there was no sense in trying to delay it. 'Dottor Veltrini,' he said.

'Ah.' The noise was as much surprise as it was relief. 'He'd do that, wouldn't he?'

ABOUT THE AUTHOR

Donna Leon is the author of the highly acclaimed, internationally bestselling Commissario Guido Brunetti mystery series. The winner of the CWA Macallan Silver Dagger for Fiction, among other awards, Donna Leon lived in Venice for many years and now divides her time between Venice and Switzerland.